Born in the US, **Stuart Blackburn** gained a doctorate in South Asian Studies and Folklore at the University of California, Berkeley. He taught at several universities in the US and Europe and then for many years at the University of London. During a long academic career, he published more than fifteen books on Indian culture and Tamil storytelling traditions, two of which won awards. Beginning in 2010, he started to write fiction, publishing his first novel in 2014. His second novel, *Into the Hidden Valley* (2016), won the MM Bennetts Prize for Historical Fiction. He lives in Brighton with his wife, and their cats.

ALSO BY STUART BLACKBURN

Murder in Melur (2014)
Into the Hidden Valley: A Novel (2015)
The History Wars (2019)

THE BOY FROM SHENKOTTAI

STUART BLACKBURN

SPEAKING TIGER

SPEAKING TIGER BOOKS LLP
125A, Ground Floor, Shahpur Jat, near Asiad Village,
New Delhi 110049

Published by Speaking Tiger Books 2021

ISBN: 978-93-5447-045-5
eISBN: 978-93-5447-046-2

10 9 8 7 6 5 4 3 2 1

Typeset in Electra LT Std by SÜRYA, New Delhi
Printed at Shree Maitrey Printech Pvt. Ltd., Noida

Contents

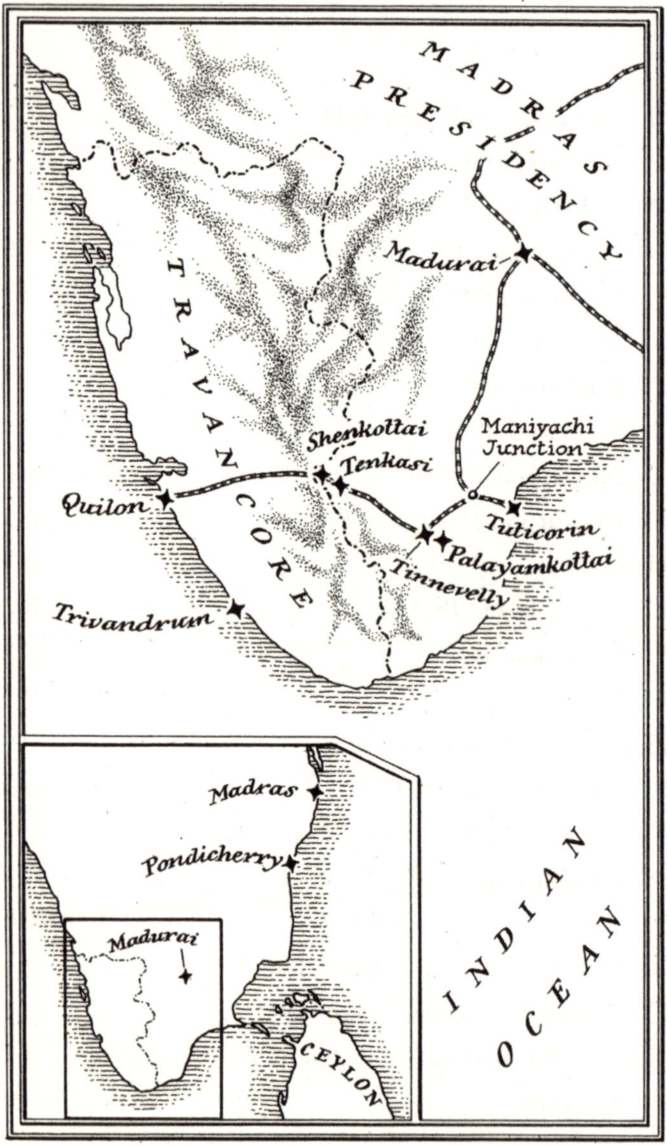

MADRAS PRESIDENCY
Madurai
TRAVANCORE
Shenkottai
Maniyachi Junction
Tenkasi
Quilon
Tuticorin
Palayamkottai
Tinnevelly
Trivandrum
Madras
Pondicherry
Madurai
CEYLON
INDIAN OCEAN

1

Palayamkottai, 17 June 1911

Vanchi awoke early that morning knowing it would be his last. He didn't want to die, but neither was he afraid. His fear was that he would fail and that everything would be in vain.

Lying on his back, he listened hard for something that would break through the void. A sound that would become a line, and generate more lines. Lines that would link together, form a pattern and create boundaries.

He strained every part of him but heard nothing, only Madasami snoring on another mat in the corner. Then came the groan of wooden wheels. A bullock cart. He listened again. The rumbling was not going towards the mountains, but in the other direction, east towards the sea and the ships that sail away.

Lighter wheels trundled by. A horse neighed. A man shouted and a sweeper warned of his approach, even though few people were about at that early hour. Vanchi got up and stood at the small window, his nose pressed between the vertical iron bars. He heard more noises from the market area. The gateway of a temple, with its high flat tower, rose up on his right. To his left, across the river, he could make out the outline of the railway station. Clear boundaries and hard lines. He relaxed and knew it would be all right.

He crept down the wooden stairs and went past the kitchen to the little bathing area outside, where he could hear voices and cooking sounds. He bathed with buckets of cold water. The bar of Pears soap that he had brought from Pondicherry was now just a sliver and slipped out of his hand. He left it on the stone floor.

Going back through the courtyard on his way upstairs, he saw the young girl who had opened the door for him three days earlier. She was dressed in a blue and grey school uniform, her black hair braided in back. She smiled at him and he bit his lip to stop it from trembling.

After Madasami went down to bathe, Vanchi was alone in the room. He placed a thumb-mark of ash on his forehead and adjusted his sacred thread, lifting it off his right shoulder and sliding it back and forth across his thin chest. Sitting down, he closed his eyes and chanted the oath one last time. Kali appeared with her weapons and necklace of skulls. He continued to chant until the stone man emerged from her blue-black body and stood with his raised sword.

Madasami returned and they dressed. Vanchi put on a clean white *veshti* and a dark green tunic, which he buttoned up to its short collar. He checked that his hair tuft hung free at the back of his neck and sat down on the mat.

Aiyar had told him to write what he wanted, but he knew what Aiyar wanted the world to read. Like the blood oath, he'd repeated it in his head so many times that it had become a prayer. He had thought about writing another letter, to his grandfather, but he couldn't get beyond the first words of apology.

Madasami's uncle had provided him with a thin wooden pen and a small bottle of ink. He wrote quickly, not making a single error in the formal Tamil, then took a deep breath and read the last sentence: 'It is what every Indian should consider their duty.'

He folded the letter and pushed it deep into the right-hand pocket of his tunic. Picking up the box containing the pistol, he held it under his arm. A little too prominent, he thought, but Madasami had disagreed. In the end, they had compromised. He would carry the box to Maniyachi Junction, where he would take out the pistol and hide it in his pocket. Madasami would take the box and dispose of it later.

Sitting cross-legged on low, wooden stools in a side room off the kitchen, they had their breakfast. 'Eat well that morning,' Aiyar had told him. 'Double your normal amount.' Aiyar had faith in him, even if others didn't. He had chosen him, and he would not betray his trust. He would not fail. But he ate only two idlis, while Madasami ate half a dozen of the moist little rice cakes. He was offered more but waved them away and waited for the chicory coffee. Everything should be normal. Like every other day.

The woman who served them seemed to come from nowhere and didn't speak. From her white sari, he assumed she was a widow and wondered about her husband's death. He tried to find her eyes as she bent down, but she used the corner of her sari to shield her face.

Back in their room, Madasami loaded the pistol, put it in the box and recited the plan. They would get to the station a little after 9:00. They would buy the tickets and travel in a second-class carriage, while the collector would be in a first-class compartment. The train would depart at 9:30 and reach Maniyachi Junction at 10:35, where the collector would wait for the Boat Mail to arrive from Tuticorin. An interval of twelve or fifteen minutes, during which Vanchi would kill him.

Keep calm, Aiyar had told him. In Pondicherry, he had been taught how to regulate his breathing and slow down his pulse, to take things one step at a time. That way, he would not make a mistake. If he followed instructions, he would not be a failure.

Again, he looked out through the bars. Clouds had gathered with a hint of rain. He wondered why the collector was going to the hills now instead of the month before, at the height of the hot season, when most of the foreigners left the plains. His children were already there, in the hills, so they wouldn't be with him. That was a relief, though he didn't want to admit it.

'Ten more minutes,' Madasami said. Vanchi looked at him closely, as if for the first time. They were supposed to be brothers on a train journey, but they didn't look like brothers or even cousins. He wondered what Madasami would do when it was over. No one had mentioned that part.

Time to go. He picked up the box and followed Madasami down the stairs. The box felt awkward, held in one arm like a piece of firewood. Madasami carried a cloth bundle, as if he were travelling a long distance.

Madasami's uncle put his head around the door of a ground-floor room. 'See you when you come back.'

'Yes, see you later,' Madasami answered.

Outside, he told Vanchi to hurry. They were three minutes behind schedule. Although some shops were not yet open, the market area was beginning to fill up, creating crowds and potential delays. Madasami led Vanchi through the throng, dodging around people with baskets on their heads and stepping aside to avoid rumbling bullock carts.

Gripping the box, Vanchi nearly tripped on the hem of his *veshti* and had to stop for a moment to secure it around his waist. Madasami turned and glared at the box sitting on the ground. They made up time after they cleared the market and reached the bridge. Madasami looked at his watch again. It was 9:02.

'*Kunjam methua*,' he said. A little slower.

They bought their tickets, two returns to Maniyachi Junction. That, too, was Aiyar's idea. A one-way for Vanchi might look suspicious.

They found space in a second-class carriage. Vanchi placed the box across his knees and fixed his eyes in a stare at nothing. Madasami put his bundle down next to Vanchi, got out and walked up the platform. He was hoping to see the collector already settled in the first-class carriage.

Vanchi folded his hands on top of the box and let the voices lap around him.

'Monsoon's weak again.'

'Umm, the river's low and the new irrigation canal hasn't got built.'

'Oh, I forgot to bring sweets.'

'Don't worry; we'll get them at Maniyachi.'

'What time do we get there?'

'No idea.'

The words flowed through him like water, emptying his mind and leaving him clear-headed. He didn't need to think because the boundaries had already been drawn. The chaos eliminated.

He wore a bleak smile when Madasami came back and indicated, without speaking, that the collector had not yet appeared. Madasami sat down beside him and checked his watch. It was 9:21. Nine minutes to go. Maybe he'd changed his plans. But surely Das would have told him.

A mechanical clatter rose above the hum of human voices outside. Madasami craned his neck and looked back down the long platform. The collector and his wife were hurrying along, arm in arm, followed by Das, his head clerk. Behind them came the collector's bearer and the rattling trolley piled high with luggage.

Madasami swore under his breath and pulled his head back inside. He hadn't counted on Das, who would recognize him.

'What's the matter?' Vanchi asked with his first words since leaving the house.

'Nothing. He's come, that's all.' He didn't mention his wife.

After the collector's party had passed, Madasami stepped out onto the platform and followed at a safe distance. Through the billowing smoke and hissing steam, he watched as they were escorted into a compartment at the front of the train. Scurrying back to the second-class carriage, he sat down just as the final whistle shrieked.

'First-class is five carriages ahead, closest to the engine,' he whispered to Vanchi. 'He's in the second compartment. The second one.'

Vanchi acknowledged that vital information with a slight tilt of his head. The morning would soon come to an end. The man deserved to die. And he could not allow himself to live, to survive and reveal secrets.

He closed his eyes and repeated the blood oath for the last time.

2

Shenkottai, 1898

Vanchi stared at the lines drawn by his mother. When he was small, his grandfather used to chide him for day-dreaming, but the old man had given up long ago. 'What's the point? It's the curse of an only child,' he had muttered to his mother, who wouldn't hear of anything wrong about her son and resented the reference to her failure to produce more children, after the second one had died at birth. She defended Vanchi against everyone, even her husband.

Sitting on the veranda, the young boy watched her prepare to draw another *kolam* in front of the house. She'd washed the hard-packed ground with a mixture of water and cow dung, and tied her long hair into a messy bun. Now, while she squatted with her sari rucked up to her bony knees and studied the smooth surface, he tried to see what she saw. After a long minute, she dipped her hand into a coconut half-shell and lifted a pinch of rice powder. Her hand hovered in mid-air before dropping down to deposit a small white dot on the ground. More dots followed, nine of them, evenly spaced in a line. On either side of that line, she made two more lines of seven dots each. Then two lines of five dots, followed by two lines of three dots and, finally, two single dots. She rocked back on her heels and examined the grid pattern while sucking in air through gaps in her teeth.

'Star,' he cried from the veranda.

'A star? That's for your grandfather to tell you about, not me.'

She pinched a little more powder and drew the first section of a curving line, took another pinch and extended the curve into a circle that looped around one of the dots. Soon she hit her stride, lifting and releasing the white powder in a series of quick movements that created a single continuous line, looping around all the dots and ending up where she had begun. It was beautiful and dangerous, he thought, like a snake curled around its prey.

She made the *kolam* drawings first thing in the morning, even before she served him and his grandfather breakfast. All the women on the street drew similar patterns, but hers were special. There were no gaps in the white lines and their width was uniform. He hated it when the ground underneath showed through because the power wasn't spread thickly enough.

His mother told him that the drawings were something to protect the house and prevent misfortune to the family. Any evil spirit would get trapped in the maze, she said, and never get out. When he was young, he thought that was why his father hardly ever came home. It kept him away. The designs were also an escape. Inside them, he was safe. The boundaries were firm and the dots were all connected.

His mother straightened up and surveyed her work with a smile that revealed her missing teeth but also emphasized her strong, square face. Her skin shone charcoal-blue in the early morning light, and Vanchi thought she was beautiful.

When she went inside, he remained on the veranda. Wrapping one of his thin arms around a wooden pillar, he stuck out his leg and swung it like a dancer. He saw an older boy come out of the house opposite and ducked back into the shadows. He was short for his age and avoided playing games with the other boys in the street. Hitting a piece of wood around with a stick didn't interest him. He liked goats-and-tigers but wasn't brave enough to ask anyone to play with him.

Instead, he marked out the grid with his mother's rice powder, drawing a large triangle crossed with a rectangle, and moved the stones around by himself. Whenever a goat was trapped by a tiger, he worked hard for its release.

'Vanchi, come and eat,' his mother called.

He stepped over the high threshold of the open door and onto the pounded earth floor. The room was small and dark, with light coming in through two unglazed windows in the front wall. The smell of burnt lamp oil hung in the air, a rickety table stood against one side wall, and reed mats were rolled up and stacked against the other side wall. There were no chairs. Clothes were kept in an old sari, which hung like a hammock from the rafters. A doorway in the back wall led into the only other room, which served as a kitchen and storage space. The three of them slept on the veranda, unless it was too wet or cold, forcing them inside.

Thatha sat in the smoky kitchen on a wooden plank, sipping his coffee. It was his only concession to the changing times, which he funded through the modest proceeds of his herbal preparations. He had first tasted it when he'd bumped into a small group of foreigners while they were trekking in the hills behind Shenkottai. They appeared lost and he guided them to the trail that took them back to the falls, their starting point. They gestured for him to sit down with them and offered a mug of black liquid. He'd heard of *kappi*—it was served in one or two stalls in the nearby town of Tenkasi and at the railway station—but he'd never tasted it. Even without milk and sugar, he found it delicious and broke into a broad smile when he handed the enamel mug back to the white people. Looking around quickly, he plucked a leaf, ground it in his hands and found a broader leaf in which to wrap it.

'*Ithu yedunga*,' he said. Take this. He wanted to tell them that it would soothe headaches and started to mime this information, but they only laughed. One of the women smiled and took the leaf, but he saw her discard it after she thought they were out of sight, some distance down the trail. The taste stayed with him, though, and now he started each day with a bowl of milky coffee, often laced with brown jaggery sugar.

'Hungry?' Thatha asked his grandson, as he savoured another sip.

'Umm.'

'Eat up. We're going into the hills.'

Vanchi gobbled up his cold rice and swallowed his buttermilk before his mother could scold him for eating too fast and leaving a mess. During the holidays there was nothing better than going with his grandfather on his treks.

Standing in front of the house, Thatha strapped on a thick leather belt and checked the blade of his knife. Then he led Vanchi down the narrow strip between the two rows of houses, about thirty in all, which comprised the Brahmin street, or agraharam. Balancing a wicker basket on his head with one hand and holding two jute sacks with the other, the boy struggled to keep up.

Each house on the street had a front veranda, where men sat and gossiped, said prayers and performed daily rituals. Off to one side stood the menstruation house, a small enclosure with a low door, where women spent days during their periods. While there was little vegetation in front of the houses, the back gardens flourished with coconut trees, banana trees and betel leaf vines trained onto wooden stakes.

The two ends of the street were clearly marked. An open-air brick building with a thatched roof stood at the top, where the street joined a dirt road that led to the main road. Men gathered there for special occasions, such as the thread-changing ceremony every August. Behind that square structure lay the cremation ground. The other end of the street, which trailed off into the jungle, was demarcated by a small Shiva temple.

Thatha stood in front of the temple and waited for Vanchi to join him. Ducking his head and stepping inside, he placed two bananas and a red hibiscus flower at the base of the black granite image. Palms pressed together, he said a brief prayer and backed out, keeping his face towards the god. Vanchi entered the confined space, smelling of bat droppings, and chanted the same Sanskrit verse. 'May Shiva liberate me from death, may He lead me to immortality.' When he finished, he shivered a little and readjusted the thread on his shoulder.

He followed his grandfather along the footpath that ran behind the temple and into the forest. After a few minutes, they came out of the dense growth and walked on top of the narrow mud bunds that separated the paddy fields. It was April, the beginning of the hot season, but in Shenkottai, at the base of the mountains, the air was still fresh.

Ahead of him, through the swaying coconut trees, Vanchi saw the two steep hills that formed a V-shape in the mountain range. That was the valley, Thatha had told him, through which an ancient sage had entered the mountains, climbed to the highest peak, sat down and compiled the first Tamil grammar. Thatha had also taken him to the foot of that mountain and pointed out the places where rare plants grew. Vanchi had stared at the sheer rock face, rising hundreds of feet above him, and wondered if he could see the rivers from the top.

Now, leaving the paddy fields, they wound up through the foothills, following a narrowing path that took them into deep forest. From time to time, they emerged from the tree cover and crossed patches of scrub grass with rocky outcrops. After an hour and a half, Thatha sat on a flat stone and beckoned Vanchi to sit beside him.

'We'll start here,' he said in his pinched voice. 'With this patch of kacholam.' The fragrant ginger plant was his staple, used to treat all kinds of skin ailments, wounds and bruises.

Thatha unsheathed his small knife and sharpened its curved blade on a stone, which he carried in a pouch tucked into the folds of his *veshti*. Crouching low, he grabbed clumps of the wide, round leaves, sliced them free of the ground and tossed them into the basket. Vanchi collected any cuttings that landed outside the basket, something which he noticed was occurring with increasing frequency during the past few months.

Grunting and wheezing, his grandfather moved on to a tall, iris-like plant. The old man carefully parted the long, straight leaves to reveal spiky outgrowths about the size of his forefinger and covered with tiny yellow-green flowers. Those, too, went into the basket, though Vanchi had to be careful to lay them gently on top of the ginger plants in order to prevent the delicate flowers from falling off on the trek back home.

When the basket was full, his grandfather moved into a still darker part of the forest, where he usually found the glistening green patchouli leaves. Both of them used their hands to uproot the tall plants, twist off their thin roots and lay them in one of the jute bags. Vanchi had been taught to avoid the plants already in flower and look for those in the deepest shade.

'You can identify them easily,' Thatha had said. 'They always smell sweet. Those are the ones that people like.'

When the two jute bags were full, they walked back to a sunny spot, where Thatha sat down again and prepared betel nut for himself. Smearing a dab of lime paste on a leaf, he added a few shavings of the nut, folded the leaf and popped into his mouth. While he sat and chewed, Vanchi wandered out to the edge of an escarpment and let his eyes wander.

The green carpet of paddy fields was dotted with coconut and areca nut trees. He could see the tower of the temple in Tenkasi. He knew it was tall, but it looked strangely stunted and cut off from the market town. Where is the bridge over the river? he wondered. He walked over that old bridge every day on his way to school, and he'd once seen chained elephants being led across its wobbly planks. The huge animals had been trapped in the hills and taken to the plains. He hated to think of them, dragging timber or boulders in the unfamiliar hot sun.

He found the Chittar River and tried to follow it beyond Tenkasi, but it was lost in the blur of tree tops and streaky sky.

Somewhere in that haze, Vanchi knew, the Chittar joined the larger Tambraparni, which ran all the way to the twin towns of Tinnevelly and Palayamkottai. The ever-widening river then meandered, formed a delta and flowed into the Bay of Bengal near the port of Tuticorin. He had never been farther than Tenkasi, but he knew that the river flowed from the mountains to the sea. He knew because he had followed his grandfather's finger as it traced the course of the Chittar. The rest he had seen on Dr Raghavan's map.

Squinting into the distance, he saw with his inner eye what he knew was true: the small river merged with the bigger one and all the water ended up in the sea. But the unbounded sea was too much and he had to open his eyes.

Hearing a whistle, he walked back to his grandfather and sat beside him. Thatha issued another long, piercing sound, followed by two chirpy ones that jumped up and down.

'That's the thrush,' Thatha said when he'd stopped and heard a bird singing in reply.

'What's it saying?'

Thatha looked at his grandson with watery eyes. 'I don't know for sure,' he said. 'But it sounds like he's hungry.'

'And what were you saying, before?'

'Nothing. Just saying hello.'

Vanchi screwed up his face and looked away. He didn't always believe his grandfather. Not that he lied exactly, more that he hid things.

'C'mon, my boy. Time to go home.'

Halfway down the hilly path, his grandfather uttered a cry and darted into the forest like a young deer. Vanchi put down his basket and bags and followed. There it was, a modest-sized tree with stick-like tendrils shooting out from the trunk at odd angles and covered with little magenta flowers. His grandfather called it the 'caterpillar' because it was slender and sectioned. Powdered and mixed with wild garlic, it was his best remedy for colds and coughs, a bit expensive but popular.

During the rest of the trek down the hill and across the paddy fields, grandfather and grandson remained silent. It was only when they reached the Brahmin street and the small Shiva temple that Vanchi spoke.

'When was it built, Thatha?'

'This? A long time ago.'

'Before the white people came?'

'Yes, long before that,' he said with a chuckle.

'When, though?'

Thatha sat on the low stone wall that defined the courtyard in front of the temple.

'Hundreds of years ago, a Pandyan king extended his rule into this southern area. He built temples everywhere. The big one at Tenkasi and this one, which is linked to it.'

'When did we…I mean, who lived here then?'

'The king needed Brahmins, so he gave land to our ancestors to settle here. To be priests and scholars and poets.'

Vanchi frowned again. His father was none of those things. He was some kind of clerk, though he liked to call himself an 'official employed by the Maharaja of Travancore'. It was true that he worked for a department of the princely state with its headquarters in the royal palace in Trivandrum, but Vanchi knew it was a minor post.

'What happened when the white people came?'

'There was a lot of fighting, not here in Shenkottai, but all around. The soldiers came, British and Indian soldiers, and defeated the local rajas in this area. There's a big fort in Palayamkottai, which they turned into a prison and kept people there.'

'They built temples, too, didn't they?'

'What?'

'That big, white building in Tenkasi, where they pray. Didn't they build that?'

'The church? Yes, they built that. But that's different.'

In the late afternoon, after his grandfather's nap, they sat together on the veranda. Thatha pounded with a heavy brass pestle, and Vanchi fed him more leaves and bark to crush in the mortar. As they worked, a flock of black goats ambled by with wooden triangles around their heads to prevent them from getting through fences and eating crops. An old man also appeared, dragging palmyra fronds, which trailed over his shoulder and clawed grooves in the dirt. Wide and stiff, the fronds were the kind that would last through years and years of sun and rain. Vanchi was about to say something when his grandfather cut him off.

'It's all right,' he said, still pounding away. 'That's Muttu. He's bringing them to repair Ramamurthy's cowshed.'

His grandfather began to whistle again, and that's when Vanchi remembered. The Kanikkar tribe, who lived in the hills, spoke to birds in their own language. Thatha said he had learned from them and had tried to teach Vanchi. But when the young boy shaped his lips and blew, no sound was heard. He wasn't good at anything, a failure in his father's eyes.

*

The following morning, Vanchi sat among a dozen other young and bare-chested boys on a deep veranda. It was hot with flies buzzing around. Each boy held a tattered schoolbook or a bundle of palm leaves inscribed with spidery letters. A slightly older boy stood on the ground in front of them, his *veshti* folded up to his knees, and led them in reciting verses. That boy chanted from memory while the others, heads bowed, repeated his words. Their uneven chorus was too much for Dr Raghavan, who rose from a lounge chair and scowled beneath his white turban. Tapping his pointer stick against the side of his leg, he surveyed his charges with the disdain of a drill sergeant.

'No, no, boys. Do not recite like screeching monkeys, please! The poet, who lived not far from here, on that mountain peak, might think he was hearing washerwomen chattering by the river.'

Hired by a temple charity to instruct Brahmin boys in Sanskrit and Tamil, Dr Raghavan had come to Tenkasi with a BA from Madras University. He was provided with a two-storey house, a servant, a cook and a modest annual income of 125 rupees. Local gossip maintained that his leather shoes were the first to protect the feet of an Indian from the dust and dung of that southern market town. Their smooth brown covering only reminded the boys of the legs of an animal used to transport laundry, and he soon acquired the affectionate nickname of 'the Donkey'. Some of the boys also made jokes about an unseen 'Mrs Donkey'.

Still tapping his pointer, the teacher ordered the boys to try again and this time to think of a mouthful of sweet honey when they recited the ancient aphorisms. Sitting in the second row, Vanchi ducked his head even lower and barely managed to open his mouth. His obligation to help his grandfather collect herbs in the hills meant that he was often late to the teacher's house in Tenkasi, which was half an hour away from his own house in Shenkottai. To assuage Dr Raghavan, he ran errands for him after the lessons, usually going to the market to buy kerosene oil or fresh fruit.

That afternoon, Vanchi was sent to fetch Raghavan's newspaper. The Tamil daily was published in Madras and brought south by train, reaching Tinnevelly the same evening and Tenkasi the next day. Bearing a note from his teacher, Vanchi went to the local government office, the tahsildar's office, where he was entrusted with the six foolscap pages folded and bound with string. A newspaper was something he had never before held in his hands.

As he walked back to Raghavan's house, he had time to look at the front page. Under advertisements for a sewing machine and hand soap, he read the headline in Tamil: 'Indian National Congress Session: Self-rule Gains Support'. He also noticed that the paper itself was called *Swadesamitran*, 'Friend of Swadeshi'. He knew that the word swadeshi meant 'own country', but he wasn't sure what that was.

He stopped and began to read more when he was distracted by a troupe of street entertainers in the market. Decked out in faded circus costumes, they leaped and lunged, swinging long poles in a mock battle. Vanchi watched, fascinated by their athletic skill and lack of inhibition in public. Of course, they were like that, the lower castes, he thought, but still the choreography of the gyrating bodies had a symmetry that attracted him. Only when a hand missed and a pole hit the ground, did he regain his sense of time. Fearing the Donkey's wrath, he folded up the paper, retied it with the string and hurried on.

It was dusk when he reached the rusty gate that led into the compound. With a furious flapping of wings, a flock of crows emerged from the coconut trees and circled overhead, squawking like seagulls above a fishing boat. The sun had sunk behind the mountains in the west, and the coconut fronds groaned in the wind. Holding the newspaper close to his chest, he felt the ground grow cold.

'Bring it here, boy! What are you waiting for?'

His teacher's command made him quiver, but he advanced to the high veranda and begged forgiveness as he offered up the paper. Raghavan snatched and unfurled it in a single jerk of his hand. Unobserved in the dusk, Vanchi watched him stoop beside the lantern on a table and read the front page.

'Madness,' he heard him mutter. 'Utter madness.'

The crows were still cawing as Vanchi passed out through the gate on his way home. What did he mean by that? he wondered.

3

Berhampore, 1898

Robert Ashe blinked as he emerged into the dazzling sunlight. With Mary on his arm, he smiled at the guests lined up to shower them with confetti and congratulations. He led her down three shallow stone steps and onto the ground, parched and cracked in the April heat. Behind them, the church tower rose in the sky.

This is when the bells should be ringing, Robert thought and tried to hide his disappointment. He had wanted it to be a proper wedding, even in the heat and dust of India. 'No, there's no bell in the bell tower,' the minister had informed him with a pinched smile when he'd made the arrangements several weeks ago. He cast a glance at Mary, who didn't seem to have registered the absence.

Beneath her white veil, lifted up and fastened to her high-pinned hair, Mary's eyes shone with wariness rather than merriment. Her rose-embroidered wedding dress fell to her shoes, a line broken only by the garland of flowers held at her waist. She stooped slightly so as to minimize her height and kept bobbing her head to acknowledge the men and women who scrutinized her as they bestowed their warm wishes. She had arrived in India only days before and knew no one. She hardly knew Robert, if she were honest, though he had wooed her for seven long years.

*

It had all started when his father had been viciously killed by an inmate in the psychiatric hospital in Dublin where Mr Ashe senior worked as a doctor. Mary Patterson was the nurse who found his father's body, riddled with knife wounds, on the ward floor and made a special point of conveying condolences to the widow at the funeral. Not for a moment did she think that she would become another Mrs Ashe, though she did catch the eye of the son.

Young Robert, then a student at Trinity College in Dublin, noticed the attractive nurse who spoke kindly to his mother and later introduced himself. The shared trauma of the terrible death, which fractured their fragile faith in the world, brought student and nurse together. They were both nineteen years old.

Trinity College was close to the Patterson home, a handsome Georgian building with two drawing rooms, linked by folding doors. It was in the 'green drawing room', so called because it led out to the garden, that Robert first sat alone with Mary. Mrs Patterson, knitting quietly in the other drawing room, rocked back and forth and nodded her head from time to time.

After months of supervised tête-à-têtes, Robert proposed an escalation, but Mrs Patterson did not think that Mary should be permitted to take tea alone with a young man on the high street. Her objections—'It's not respectable. She must have a chaperone'—were overruled by her husband, a wealthy civil engineer, who was keen that his daughter should be a new woman.

When the day came, Robert dabbed lavender water on his clean-shaven cheeks and brushed his hair so hard that his scalp hurt. Having borrowed ten shillings from his mother, he called at the house and waited in the hallway while Mary prepared herself. Staring at the grandfather clock in the hallway, he counted the minutes—all twelve of them—before she appeared in a high-collared mauve blouse tucked in at the waist of an ankle-length skirt. He stifled a cry of delight at her impressive stature and straightened himself up an inch or two.

Walking together on the high street for the first time, Robert got in a muddle about who should be on which side. Without a word, Mary manoeuvred herself onto his left, as she had been taught, and smiled sweetly. Two minutes passed before he spoke, blurting out a much-rehearsed sentence.

'You look smashing,' he said, not looking at her.

'Thank you. That is ever so kind,' she said, and blushed.

She wished she'd brought a parasol but made the most of the situation by taking his arm. When Robert seemed unsure what to do with this entanglement, she again soothed his anxiety with a quick smile and a little tug on his arm. No matter how intently the dog-walkers, pram-pushers and bicyclists stared at them, Mary did not loosen her grip.

Brennan's Tea Shop was always crowded in the afternoon, which was why Robert had chosen it. The bustle of waiters and the chatter of other conversations would, he hoped, fill any silences in theirs. This was his first liaison with a young lady, and he had no one to turn to for guidance, though he had memorized several poems, just in case.

Light poured through the high-arched windows, bathing the scene with a softness that lay on the tablecloths and muffled the scrapping of the dark brown chairs. Everything gleamed—the mirrors, the tea service, the copper pots with ferns, even the starched white uniforms of the waitresses. The motes floating in the air reminded him of the snow that drifted down when he turned over his glass-domed paperweight.

Robert had selected a corner table, where he was straining to catch every word that Mary spoke, though just watching her lips move was pleasure enough. She was talking about a concert her parents had taken her to, describing its stirring music and the young foreign conductor. He listened, spellbound by her flushed cheeks and flashing eyes.

'Tea for two, sir?' the waitress asked, for the second time, and tapped on her notebook with a sharpened pencil.

Robert merely nodded and stuck a forefinger under his collar to loosen the tight band. Then came the dreaded silence.

He fidgeted in his chair, while Mary used the huge mirror on the back wall to inspect the other women in the room. Too young to wear their wide-brimmed, cock-feathered hats, she touched the brooch at her neck for self-assurance.

Robert began to talk about poetry. Yeats and Rossetti were his favourites. Encouraged by what he thought was a smile, he launched into a description of his own verse until a three-tiered stand of cakes and sweets landed on the table between him and his listener.

That tea-room tryst was followed by others in the National Museum, the Botanic Gardens and various concert halls. But the highlight of those Dublin years was a trip to the Gaiety Theatre, where Robert and Mary tingled with excitement at the deep emotions displayed on stage. Mary replayed those stories in her head while working on the hospital ward, and Robert ploughed them into his poems of forlorn love. He was particularly proud of one that he sent to Mary after he had attempted a kiss under an elm tree in Phoenix Park. The first verse read:

Oh, bee that hovers o'er the blossoms
And knows not the nectar at thy feet,
Oh, bird that tweets not knowing
Where to find its sweet mate.

Mary laughed when she read the full poem but never mentioned that to the author.

*

Following four years of courtship, Robert's decision to join the Indian Civil Service was only taken after long discussions with both Mary and her father. 'It's a good life, out there, I hear,' Mr Patterson said when Robert first broached the issue. 'And twenty years of service earns you a handsome pension back home in retirement.' Mrs Patterson had not been so fulsome in her expectations.

They all knew that Robert, now a graduate with a widowed mother, had poor prospects for salaried employment in Ireland. Not a good basis for a happy marriage, they had to admit, and Robert was too proud to depend on money from a future father-in-law.

'Let me see what it's like out there,' Robert said to Mary one evening in the green drawing room. 'And if it's any kind of life for us, I'll come back and we'll get married.'

Mr Patterson thought this was a 'sensible plan' and, having secured his wife's acquiescence, gave his blessings to the engagement. Mary was both anxious and thrilled at the idea of going 'out east', while Robert was merely terrified of the entrance examinations.

Held every summer in London, which was almost foreign territory for him, the exams attracted fierce competition. The written tests and extensive interviews took place over several days, conducted by old India hands keen to find anything that might disqualify a candidate. Knowing that he was at a disadvantage compared to candidates from Oxford and Cambridge, Robert spent months revising his Greek and Latin, yet still scored low in languages. Only decent marks in law and history saved him from disqualification.

The personal interview was not a success, either. It got off to a bad start when Robert reached into his jacket pocket and pulled out a pipe, which he had purchased only the day before. Having inserted it between his lips, he sucked noisily and furrowed his brow. His impersonation of a serious scholar would have been more convincing if he had remembered to bring some tobacco. Again, he scraped through, this time on the basis of his perceived sincerity and commitment.

Still more hurdles remained. He passed his medical but failed the riding test and had to retake it. That was followed by a full year's probation, during which he studied the law, history and languages of India. He did miserably in Sanskrit and Persian, as well as Telugu, a regional language, but just well enough in the other subjects to pass.

Given his low score, Robert was not surprised to find himself assigned to Madras Presidency, considered the Indian equivalent of being 'sent to Coventry'. Besides being extremely hot and far from the cosmopolitan centres of Calcutta and Bombay, it was hidebound and out of step with changes taking place elsewhere in the subcontinent.

'Guess what, Mary?' he said to her one afternoon while walking in the garden of her parents' house. 'I'm going to Mull.'

'Mull?'

'Mulligatawny. You know, the soup. It's popular in Madras.'

*

In December 1895, Robert Ashe was shipped out to join a thousand other British men who ruled India. At twenty-three years old, with his administrative experience limited to serving on the college poetry prize committee, he became second-in-command of an area with nearly one hundred thousand people. Ganjam District was located on the east coast, hundreds of miles north of Madras, with poor rail and road links, a high incidence of malaria and numerous tribal groups, who had no interest in being governed by Her Majesty or anyone else. It was not a plummy post.

'You'll like it there,' he was told upon arrival by a functionary in the governor's office in Madras. 'What most people don't appreciate is the autonomy you'll have. You see, down here in the south, we weren't affected by the Mutiny. Things haven't changed much in the past forty years. None of those silly reforms in Calcutta and Bombay. You can run your own little patch, like a proper raja.'

As assistant collector, Robert Ashe kept his head down, followed procedure, drank whisky with his colleagues in the local club and fought off despair with feigned confidence. It wasn't just the loneliness and disorientation—he was completely baffled by the languages he was supposed to learn—

it was the unnerving realization that he wasn't really in control of anything. He read files, signed documents and checked accounts, but the 'paper Raj', he discovered, was wafer-thin. At any moment, the fiction that sustained the Empire might be exposed, local people would storm into his office and...well, it didn't bear thinking about.

He entertained himself in the long, hot evenings by reading poetry and rereading Mary's letters. The distance stimulated his imagination when savouring her expressions of affection, such as 'my wondrous Mr Walrus' and 'your devoted Pussycat'. When a new letter arrived, he read it every night until the next one was delivered three weeks later.

Robert proposed to Mary while back home on his first long furlough, after more than two years in India. But he waited until the night before his return journey, which meant that they had to be married in India and that she would travel out alone. During her three weeks at sea, Mary was chaperoned by a number of English women, principally the wife of the chief medical officer in Simla. When she docked at Bombay, she was met by the older sister of one of Robert's colleagues, who then accompanied her on the next leg of her journey, a forty-two-hour train ride across the subcontinent.

They got on well, the spinster sister believing that the bride-to-be was absorbing all the valuable information she imparted to her concerning the role of a memsaab, while Mary was content to knit and listen with half an ear. Alone in her bunk, she avidly read the book her father had given her on the eve of her departure. *The Complete Indian Housekeeper and Cook* was detailed and engrossing. Dedicated to 'English girls to whom fate may assign the task of being house-mothers in our eastern Empire', it declared that the first duty of a woman in India was to give clear instructions to servants, which required that she learn the local language. Mary took note.

*

Robert now stood beside his wife outside the church in Berhampore. He looked down with satisfaction at his white trousers tucked into high black boots. He'd polished the boots earlier that morning, removing any hint of a scuff mark with a long horsehair brush. His slight frame barely filled the dark frock coat set off by a purple cravat. With thinning brown hair and hunched shoulders, he looked out on the world with apprehension. He had never really recovered from his father's horrific death, and three years in India had fortified him with only a thin layer of confidence that he was in charge. That morning, though, he felt supported by his bride, a woman his equal in age, as in most things.

After the confetti settled, Robert handed Mary into a two-wheeled cart yoked to a pair of bullocks decorated with bright ribbons on their short horns and a faded embroidered cloth on their bony backs. Sitting side by side in the tight space just behind the driver, the newlyweds rode through the market area, past the railway station and out onto the open road. As they bumped along, he explained that the region had been wrested from the French as part of a wider war in the 1750s. He spoke with pride, pointing out the site of the British victory, but chose not to mention the diseases and famine that had plagued the district through much of the nineteenth century.

When the cart turned off the road and continued down a dirt track, Robert pointed to their right.

'It's just there,' he said.

Mary craned her neck and saw a clump of trees in the middle of the otherwise deserted countryside. Getting down, she faltered on the low metal step and Robert used both hands to guide her to the ground. Flushed, with her hair unpinned in places, she looked at her marital home. It was a one-storey, white-washed building with a low-sloping thatched roof supported by stout wooden pillars.

The most impressive feature was the veranda, which was raised high off the ground.

'To protect against flooding,' Robert said, noticing her creased brow.

'Yes, of course. Flooding.'

'Not from a river,' he added. 'The danger comes from the Bay of Bengal. Cyclones.'

The brief tour revealed three rooms, a sitting-cum-dining area in the centre flanked by a bedroom on either side. There was also a kitchen in the back, but no inside bathroom.

'Not much, I'm afraid,' he said, 'but I've tried to make it comfortable.'

'It's fine,' she said, dabbing her hot face with a handkerchief. 'I just need to lie down for a while.'

*

Two hours later, they rattled along another rutted country road to another colonial bungalow. The collector's house, however, was a far more impressive building, and Mary's spirits rose as Robert led her up the steps. Refreshed and determined to make a good show for her husband, she pinned back her veil and smiled through a second set of introductions to the civil and military officers of Ganjam District and their wives, all in formal dress. After the bowing and muttering, the collector's wife took her to the ladies' room for repairs, while Robert enjoyed a lime soda with ice.

The wedding reception dinner was served by the collector's staff, who were more adept at carrying file folders than food platters. The special fare consisted of mulligatawny soup—which made Robert and Mary exchange smiles—grilled fowl, mutton curry and curried vegetables, plus a good claret. During the long meal, Robert kept an eye on Mary, who was seated on the opposite side of the table between the collector, with his pencil moustache, and his wife, with her piercing blue eyes. Noting his superior's authoritative appearance, Robert decided that it was time for him to let some hair grow between his nose and upper lip. Not that little thin line, but something thicker.

When the women moved to a separate room for their coffee, Mary was the centre of attention among the chinking cups and fingered pearls.

'Do keep an eye on your servants, dear,' one of the wives warned. 'Can't trust them, you know.'

'Indeed,' another chimed in, 'especially your maidservants. Don't let them handle your things. You might never see them again.'

'And the ayahs. Of course, you don't have any children now, but when you do, well…'

Mary wanted to protest but was too exhausted to say a word. She had already argued with these opinions while reading the housekeeping guide given to her by her father. 'Every Indian servant,' she had read, 'is a child in everything save age and should be treated as a child.' She had wanted to bring her own housemaid from Dublin, but the ruddy-cheeked Rose had declined the offer to live in 'the back of beyond', as she put it. That's fine, Mary had decided. I will manage, but without being unchristian towards the natives.

'Mrs Ashe, I do hope you will be happy with us here. Robert is such a fine officer. My husband always says so.'

As she spoke, the collector's wife examined the newly arrived Mary with her icy eyes. 'And don't worry about the heat, dear,' she added. 'We'll all be going to Ooty soon.'

'Snooty Ooty! You'll love it!' snorted another woman.

'I really don't know,' Mary said. 'I'm not sure what plans Robert has.'

'Oh, but you must, shall we say, "help" him with his plans, Mrs Ashe.'

Overcome by her long journey, the wedding, the heat and the attentions of strangers, Mary excused herself and sought a couch.

'Poor thing,' the collector's wife murmured to the others. 'But she seems to be a strong girl. She'll pull through. Not like that silly Elisa.'

Heads shook as the ladies recalled the nineteen-year-old who had succumbed to the loneliness of life in a provincial town. With her husband away for weeks on inspection tours, she began talking to herself. Within months, the rambling speech became howling screams, and she was sent back home.

*

At sunset, Robert and Mary escaped from the reception and returned to their bungalow. Funny, Mary thought as she mounted the steps to the high veranda, it already feels familiar. The low ceiling and small rooms made the inside as hot as the outside, but after a hip bath, she changed into a thin house dress and felt cooler.

Robert smoked a pipe while she knitted.

'Well, what do you think?' he asked.

'Mother might have a few suggestions for improvements,' she said with a little laugh. 'And I might want to order new curtains from Arnotts, but I think I'll survive.'

'Good. I hope we can make a good life here, Mary. It is hard at times, but it's a job that has to be done.'

'Don't worry about me. I have the assistant collector of Ganjam District to protect me.'

He smiled, though when he thought about it later, he wasn't sure what had been the target of her sarcasm.

'And we have helpers, too, I notice,' she said.

The servants were huddling by the door that led to the kitchen, eager to inspect their new memsaab.

'What's cook's name, by the way?' she asked, remembering the task she would be expected to perform in the morning.

'Ah, I really don't know.'

'Well, let's find out.'

Robert used poorly pronounced Hindustani to call them all in. Cook, cook's assistant, bearer, sweeper and gardener shuffled forward.

'Name?' Robert commanded, pointing at the man he thought was the cook.

'Ravidas, *saab*,' the bony man replied, and the others struggled to suppress their giggles.

Mary mouthed his name twice and was pleased that it rolled off her tongue.

'All *jao* now,' Robert ordered, using the one native word he was sure he knew.

His imperious tone startled Mary, though she was too tired to comment. Robert, too, had decided to defer any coaching about the delicate task of handling the servants. He was more concerned with other matters on his wedding night.

The bedroom had been scrubbed clean and the bed laid with fresh-smelling linen. After pulling down and arranging the enormous mosquito net, so that the bed became a tent, he said something about extinguishing the candles but realized that Mary had already disappeared behind the rattan screen. He got into bed in his pyjamas and lay on his back, hands behind his head in feigned nonchalance. Many anxious minutes later, Mary emerged in her nightgown, without her hair in a net (as a Dublin friend had advised) and made her way across the coconut-fibre matting that covered the hard earth floor.

Neither spoke as they lay side by side, only inches apart. All of a sudden, a jackal howled in the near distance and she nudged towards him.

'Promise me something, Robert,' she said, without looking at him.

'Of course. What is it, my dear?' he said, as several ideas whizzed through his mind.

'That no matter what,' she said, and drew herself up to face him, 'we will go to Ooty, every year.'

'Yes, that's a splendid idea.'

'And there's something else to say before we…you know. I want more than one child.'

Robert drew her close and said, 'I think that can be arranged.'

4

Trivandrum, 1903

The stone floor was clean but cold, and Vanchi hadn't slept well. He looked around him at the others lying half-asleep and spotted a young Brahmin man about his own age. That had been his method for the past five days—sleep in a travellers' rest-house and find someone to give him information about the next leg of his journey. He followed the man to the common bathing area and then to the room where Brahmins ate, while the others filed into another room. The piping-hot idlis were cooked the way he liked, as a ball of noodles smothered with sambar.

He would reach the city by mid-afternoon, his companion told him. The temple tower would be visible from about noon, and after that, it was easy, a few hours down through the sloping forest and teak plantations. 'They'll feed you at the temple, one hot meal a day, and you can sleep there, too. A lot nicer than this place,' the man said, sweeping his eyes around the damp enclosure.

*

Vanchi's journey had begun three months earlier when his father was home during an infrequent visit.

'Father, I... I...' Vanchi stammered at breakfast.

'C'mon, speak up.'

'I want to study at college when I finish school this summer.'

He was now seventeen and did not want to become a government office worker, as his father expected, or a jobbing priest, as his grandfather suggested.

His father kept his head bent, lifted handfuls of cold rice into his mouth and chewed slowly.

'Father?'

'It's out of the question.'

'But—'

'No. In fact, I've got other plans for you.'

The wedding took place three weeks later. Vanchi's father accepted a long-standing offer from his wife's brother, who had an unmarried daughter. Vanchi could not object and meekly tied a yellow thread on the neck of a fifteen-year-old girl before leading her around a ritual fire.

At the conclusion of the four-day ceremony in his father-in-law's house in Tenkasi, Vanchi went back to Shenkottai. The marriage would not be consummated for at least a year, when his bride, Ponammal, might have matured. An unforeseen and fortunate consequence of the marriage, however, was that Vanchi became friends with Ponammal's older brother, Shankara.

'I know you want to go to college,' Shankara said to Vanchi one afternoon as they sat outside the house in Tenkasi. 'But don't go to that Christian place in Palayamkottai, they'll tell you lies. The best place is Maharaja's College in Trivandrum. You can study Sanskrit and Tamil there.'

Vanchi made up his mind when he found out that the Travancore government would pay his fees because he lived within the borders of the princely state. The only problem was that he had to produce a document proving his residence in Shenkottai and he couldn't ask his father to help. A school report would have sufficed, except that he attended a secondary school in Tenkasi, which was across the border in Tinnevelly District. Shankara convinced him to approach his old teacher.

Dr Raghavan was wrapped in a dark shawl and absorbed in

a book when Vanchi crept once again through the rusty gate. A chill wind blew down from the mountains and threatened more rain. It was January, during the Tamil New Year festival, which heralded the warming of the earth and the paddy harvest. On the steps up to the veranda, he noticed two clay pots painted with geometric patterns and necklaced with marigold garlands. That's a good sign, he thought, though he regretted not having brought a gift. He could turn around, go to the market, and get some fruit and betel nut.

'Ah, it's you!' Raghavan cried, looking up from his book and removing his spectacles. 'What brings you here on this auspicious but horrible day?'

Vanchi remained rooted and speechless, still several paces from the veranda.

'Come on, my boy. You've not come all the way from Shenkottai just to gape at your old teacher, have you?'

'No, sir. I… I have a request.'

Vanchi had practised his speech with Shankara.

'Yes. What is it?'

'A letter, sir. You see, I want to go to Trivandrum to study at Maharaja's College, and I need a letter.'

'Trivandrum, eh? And what does your father say?'

That, too, had been anticipated by Shankara.

'My father is away at present'—which was true—'and so I have come to you.'

'I see.' Raghavan laid his book down and interlaced his fingers, wiggling them a little.

'Yes, sir. I will not have to pay fees because I live in Shenkottai.'

'That's right. A very enlightened policy, too. A letter, you say?'

Half an hour later, Raghavan handed Vanchi the signed statement verifying his residence in Travancore.

'And what will you study there?' he asked.

'Sanskrit, sir.'

'Good. But you must also study Tamil. Study it and you will learn that we are a very old race, thousands of years living in this land. Study our ancient literature and learn the value of tradition. Dharma is our strength. And it's even more important in these turbulent times.'

Raghavan often spoke like this, expressing ideas that Vanchi didn't fully comprehend. Sometimes, if he remembered the words, he would ask his grandfather, who would answer using an analogy with a tree or plant in the forest. He would have told his grandfather about his Trivandrum plan, but Shankara warned him against it. 'Who knows?' he said. 'He might want to stop you.' Vanchi wanted to say that Thatha would understand, but he wasn't sure of that anymore.

Shankara arranged everything. Vanchi would leave the house one morning as if he were going to school in Tenkasi, even carrying his book bag.

'Just like a normal day,' Shankara said. 'Don't worry about anything. I'll tell your mother in the evening, when you're miles away.'

'Make sure you speak to Thatha, too,' Vanchi said. 'Tell him that I will make him proud.'

He wondered if Shankara would say anything to his sister—Vanchi didn't yet think of Ponammal as his 'wife'—but he didn't ask.

When he left the house, Vanchi had seen his mother bent over in the pale light. She was drawing her *kolam* outside the front door with the rice powder. Having acknowledged him with a little wag of the head, she concentrated on the task in front of her. He had opened his mouth to say some words of goodbye but went past her without speaking.

The winding route through the mountains to Trivandrum was well known to traders and travellers. The initial steep climb was rewarded by dropping down into a long valley, which ended in a track that snaked through high-forested hills and narrowed to a gap just wide enough for a bullock cart. A second climb, halfway through the trek, was more difficult, but it led down to a river, which flowed through the forests and fields, all the way to Trivandrum on the shore of the Arabian Sea.

*

Having left the travellers' rest-house in the morning, Vanchi climbed into a bullock cart loaded with teak logs. Although that was no faster than walking, the soles of his feet had cracked and his legs ached. Soon, the chilly forest gave way to warm rice fields, and, for the first time in six days, he let himself go slack with relief. He slept the rest of the way to Trivandrum.

Walking through an arch in the city's walls, he saw the eastern tower of the temple rise in front of him. Nearly as wide as it was tall, and covered with carved images, the tower resembled the one in Tenkasi. The people around him were also dressed in familiar clothes and spoke a language close to Tamil. Yet everything seemed different. For a moment, he had no idea why he had come so far, hiding everything from Thatha and his mother.

A wide approach road led up to the tower and the entrance underneath. To his right, he saw an oblong bathing pool and, on his left, a long veranda of carved stone pillars. He stood for several minutes and watched groups of people disappear into the temple.

'Hey, kid. Move!'

A man trudged past him, pulling a cart piled high with lengths of sugarcane, their long, greenish purple stalks flopping behind. Vanchi turned and saw a caravan of more than a dozen carts bringing the sweet cane to the temple. Decoration for a god, he imagined, and looked forward to entering the temple.

He washed his clothes and laid them out to dry in the sun while he bathed in the shallow pool. Through the splashing, he tried to follow the talk of the men bathing near him. It seemed that they had come from a nearby town to see a celebration that would take place the following day. Curious, he worked up the courage to ask what it was, but more bodies plunged into the water and drowned out his words, which were barely audible in any case.

Having wrapped a towel around his waist, he sat down in one of the small, open-air stone pavilions by the side of the pool. Passers-by would not have looked twice at the thin, young man who was saying prayers. They would only have registered that he wore his hair cropped close to his head, with a little tuft at the back, the *kudumi*, which identified him as a Tamil Brahmin. Had they looked more closely, they might have remarked that he was handsome, with a perfectly formed oval face and dark brown eyes.

He opened his eyes when he heard a voice.

'Just arrived?'

Vanchi tilted his head in affirmation.

'If you're hungry, a meal will be served soon. The big hall, inside the compound.'

Vanchi put on his damp clothes and followed several paces behind the older man, past the pillared veranda and under the tall tower.

The temple was at least a thousand years old, but the kingdom of Travancore had been established only in the mid-eighteenth century. Having defeated the Dutch in a naval war, which ended European control of the spice trade on the west coast, the maharajas played a clever game of pitting the British against rival Indian powers. Later, Travancore expanded its territory and became a model princely state. And by the early twentieth century, the capital Trivandrum was a modern city with universities, art galleries, scientific institutions, libraries, hospitals and a legislative council. The heart of the city, though, remained the old temple dedicated to Vishnu, who was the tutelary deity of the kingdom. The maharaja was his servant.

Shoes in hand, Vanchi stepped over the stone threshold and into the large compound, where he washed his feet in a small pool and walked clockwise around the main shrine. As he stood in front of the wooden structure with its red-tiled and sloping roof, he screwed up his face, searching for something he could recognize. He relaxed only when he realized how proud his grandfather would be to see him about to view the famous image of Vishnu.

Constructed from brightly painted plasterwork, and seen through a row of wooden screens, the sculpture was both monumental and serene. Sri Padmanabhaswamy rested on the coils of a snake sleeping on the surface of the ocean. The god's right hand lay on a small Shiva lingam, and the snake's five heads were raised above the god like a protective shield.

'Hurry along, son,' the uniformed attendant said. 'Your two minutes are up.'

Outside the main shrine, but still within the temple precincts, he found his way to the Brahmin feeding hall. Vanchi was just in time to join a hundred other men sitting on the floor in two rows, with their backs to the wood-panelled walls and facing each other. A young man passed down the long gallery, between the rows, slapping down banana leaves, one by one. A succession of older servers carrying large buckets ladled out steaming rice, vegetable dishes and a thick curry sauce. The young man then reappeared and dropped a papadum on top of each rice mound.

After a meal eaten in near-total silence, the men began to talk as they filed out of the hall. From their voices, Vanchi understood that they came from various parts of both Travancore and the Tamil country. They talked about home, the weather and the important event to take place the following day. Vanchi followed a group to a pilgrims' rest-house not far from the temple. Although the sky was darkening, the air was still warm and muggy, and he remembered the cool evenings in Shenkottai.

The rest-house was a large, open-air structure with stone pillars supporting a high roof. Vanchi was directed to the sleeping area and issued a pillow and blanket. A wooden sign attached to a pillar announced 'No Spitting', in both Malayalam and English.

*

Later, whenever he described it to Shankara or Thatha, he tended to emphasize the elephants. They were familiar, even if their numbers were not. What he could not express was his thrill at seeing the maharaja in person.

After a breakfast of cooked rice and vegetable curry, Vanchi followed the others and found himself pushed up against the shuttered shop windows on a narrow road. Policemen and soldiers controlled the crowd with thick sticks, while people watched from roofs and windows on both sides of the street.

The blaring music and loud cheering came first. Then he saw a procession of royal elephants and a carriage drawn by white horses, their dark plumes waving in the air. The four-wheeled carriage, which resembled a miniature temple, was escorted by palace servants in white uniforms and red sashes, followed by bare-chested priests in white *veshtis* and pink hats. Behind them came ranks of cavalry and scores of foot soldiers with curved swords and round shields. A marching brass band blared, and men on horseback banged kettle drums.

Squirming his way to the front, Vanchi followed the cavalcade as it turned a corner and came to a halt in the approach road to the temple. Soldiers restrained the boisterous crowd, while the servants and priests lined up on either side of the carriage to form a passage to the pillared palace.

Vanchi had thought that this was a procession of the temple deity and that the carriage contained an image of Vishnu. So, he watched in awe as a short, stocky man emerged and attendants arranged a golden robe around his shoulders. He wore a blue sash across his chest and a helmet-like crown with a white plume on his head. When the cheering subsided, everyone put their palms together and held them high until the maharaja had disappeared inside the palace. Half an hour later, even after the crowd had dispersed, Vanchi remained. He had never before seen a maharaja. A Hindu ruler of a Hindu kingdom.

*

'You've got to come,' Ramakrishna said, cocking his head and angling his eyes so that Vanchi could not avoid them. 'A man from Nasik will be speaking. Vinayak Savarkar. You've heard of him, I'm sure.'

They were sitting on the grass in front of Maharaja's College. Set on a rise about a mile from the temple, the college was part of the city's red-brick modernity. The three-storey building was massive yet elegant, fronted by a long and deep veranda supported by a series of slender, white wooden arches. The college was encircled by spacious grounds entered through wrought-iron gates.

Although it had been established in the 1830s by a ruler impressed with Christian missionary schools, and although its first principal had been an Englishman, Maharaja's College had a reputation for excellence in classical Indian languages, as well as English literature. Ramakrishna was studying English and History, while Vanchi had chosen Tamil and Sanskrit.

'You must come,' Ramakrishna continued when Vanchi said nothing. 'You see, he's started an organization to fight against British rule.'

'Then why's he coming here?' Vanchi asked. 'The British don't rule Travancore.'

'I'm afraid they do. The governor in Madras is in charge, even in the palace.'

'But I just saw the maharaja, last week.'

'Yes, he wears a crown. They let him have that, but they kept the real power for themselves.'

After listening to Ramakrishna explain the provisions of a treaty under which the British stationed troops in Travancore and retained control over finances and external affairs, Vanchi was still perplexed.

'So, what I saw last week—the maharaja and his procession—it's a fraud?'

'Correct. It's an illusion. Maya.'

Vanchi sighed and fell silent. He had begun his study with high hopes. After all, he had a solid foundation from Dr Raghavan in Tenkasi. But he soon found himself floundering with the classical texts he was expected to read. He could follow the words but often had no idea what they meant. What was worse, he discovered that he couldn't pronounce them properly. When he was called on to explicate a passage, his accent stood out as the mongrelized speech of the border. He lived on the wrong side of the mountains, he discovered, too close to the plains of Tinnevelly. Stung with humiliation, he kept to himself during breaks between lectures.

Ramakrishna, who was a few years older, took the wounded Vanchi under his wing. As the informal leader of a small radical group at the college, he kept a sharp eye out for potential supporters and informers.

'Please, Vanchi. Come to the meeting,' he said again. 'You'll learn something.'

Vanchi had paid little attention to politics. Overwhelmed by his new situation and struggling with his studies, he had not found time to read newspapers in the library. Although he had heard other students talk about swadeshi and the recent coronation of King Edward, he was more interested in the new railway line that would run through the mountains and connect Quilon with Shenkottai. But he was curious.

*

At dusk, he walked the short distance from the college to a roundabout in the centre of the city. On the way, he watched lamp lighters prop their bamboo ladders up against a metal post and secure them on a purpose-built horizontal bar. Having climbed the ladder, the men lit the kerosene lamps on top using a slow-burning rope that hung from their waist. By the time Vanchi reached the meeting, the city was bathed in a hazy blue light.

In the middle of the road, a temporary stage had been erected with wooden planks laid on a bamboo frame. The gathering was not as large as Ramakrishna had predicted, only fifty or sixty people, mostly students and other young men. Vanchi listened with half an ear to those who addressed the crowd in advance of the main speaker.

Speaking in an educated form of Malayalam, which he could just about follow, they accused the maharaja and his counsellors of injustices. The palace, they said, favoured candidates from outside the kingdom when making appointments to high positions. In addition, some castes were denied entry to temples. And, finally, the maharaja kowtowed to the governor in Madras by preventing Indian judges from presiding over trials with European defendants.

All that struck Vanchi as wrong, but he wasn't moved by any of it. He let his eye roam over the crowd and noticed a group of uniformed men standing at the back.

'Police,' Ramakrishna whispered to him. 'They watch these events. All of us, the speakers and the audience.'

The main speaker was introduced as 'the leader of the nationalist youth'. He was only twenty, three years older than Vanchi. Wearing round spectacles, a thin black tie and black coat, the young Savarkar began by apologising for speaking in Hindi instead of the local language and waited for an assistant to translate his apology into English. His speech started with a prayer.

'Let us pray to Lord Rama, who is our true ruler. Let us ask for the liberation of our motherland!'

His attention grabbed by those words, Vanchi began to listen closely as Savarkar offered another quick-fire round of criticisms, this time focusing on the colonial government. Then he urged his listeners to study history.

'Italy was under colonialism until it was liberated by Mazzini,' he shouted. 'America was an English colony until it fought a war of independence. We also fought a war of independence in 1857. And we will fight for our freedom again.'

The crowd rippled with excitement and shouted slogans advocating swadeshi.

'I urge you, here in Travancore, not to worship your ruler as a god. He is a man, not a deity. Do you know why he is happy today? Not because your land taxes have been reduced. And not because more low-caste children are in school. No, he is happy because he has been granted an extra two-gun salute when he visits the governor in Madras.'

Loud cheers drew the police closer to the stage.

'Finally, I urge you to begin a newspaper. Let it be handwritten, let it be a monthly, but let it show the country that we will not be slaves. We will rule ourselves!'

The audience burst out into coordinated shouts of 'Burn foreign cloth!' and 'Defend Hindu India!' In an instant, the police moved in, brandishing long cane sticks, and dispersed the crowd. There was no violence, and no one was injured, but the show of force left Vanchi shaking. He was about to walk away, when Ramakrishna put an arm around his shoulder.

'We can talk about this tomorrow,' he said.

Vanchi turned down the sloping road that took him back to the rest-house.

*

Vanchi didn't see Ramakrishna the following day or any other day for more than a year. When he learned that his friend had been expelled from college and left town, he withdrew further into himself. Although he went to college regularly, he made no new friends and discovered that he was the only student living at the temple rest-house. Other students lodged in rented rooms, sat in coffee houses, strolled around the public park, went to the zoo and visited the art museum. They went home on holidays.

Vanchi had no pocket money and spent his time in the public library, where he struggled with classical Sanskrit and Tamil literature. His only letter was written a month after his arrival:

> Dear Grandfather,
>
> As you know, I am studying here in Trivandrum. It is a good city. I will receive my degree in two years and return home. Then I will find employment and earn the money to support myself and a family. Please tell mother not to worry. I hope that Shankara is well.
>
> Vanchi

*

Although Ramakrishna disappeared, he had left his mark on Vanchi. When he was tired of trying to penetrate an ancient poem, Vanchi now read newspapers in the public library. There were more than a dozen dailies and weeklies, mostly in English and Tamil. He was flipping through a weekly paper in Malayalam, which he could now read, when he saw Ramakrishna's name listed as the editor. *Swadeshabhimani* (*The Patriot*) was published in a small town on the coast, north of Trivandrum. From that day forward, he read every article in every edition of the paper, absorbing the ideas that his friend had once shared with him in person.

In the end, he wrote him a letter, saying that he admired his paper and hoped that he was doing well. A few days later, his old friend appeared before him in the library, though Vanchi hardly recognized him. The editor dressed differently to the student. He wore a white collar, dark tie and frock coat, like an Englishman, despite his virulent anti-colonial editorials. His short, dark hair was brushed aggressively to one side.

'Still studying those dusty old texts,' he said to the astonished Vanchi.

Ramakrishna led him outside to a wooden bench placed on the lawn in front of the red-brick library. They sat down and looked at the clouds massing overhead. It was mid-September, the interval between the two monsoons known locally as the 'interregnum'. It was warm, but not hot, with streaky sunshine and the promise of more rain. Onam, the annual festival, was only days away.

'I'm glad you wrote,' Ramakrishna began, 'because I always knew that you were a patriot, deep down.'

Being thrown out of college, he said, was the best thing that could have happened to him. It made him free to act, just as the country should be free.

'Remember what Savarkar said at that rally?' Ramakrishna asked. 'About the importance of a newspaper? Well, I persuaded one of my uncles to import a printing press from England. He's got lots of money, exports spices.'

While waiting for the machine, Ramakrishna had begun to learn the print trade by apprenticing himself to another paper. When the old Stanhope press arrived, he hired two men with experience and *The Patriot* published its first issue.

Vanchi could not help but smile. The energy and ambition were impressive.

'I know what you're thinking,' his friend said.

'No, you don't know,' Vanchi blurted out. 'I just want to finish my studies and get a degree. Besides, I'm married.'

'Right, that's fine. We need people like you. Just remember that education is a tool, not an end. And the end is freedom from British rule.'

'That's why I'm here, in Trivandrum,' Vanchi said, anxious to shift the conversation.

'You might think you're in Hindu India, but you're not. Look up there,' Ramakrishna said, pointing to the high-arched entrance to the library, which bore the inscription: 'Victoria Diamond Jubilee, 1897'. He smiled and said, 'This so-called princely kingdom is nothing more than a vassal state of the British Empire.'

'So, why have you come here?'

'I'll tell you. You read the paper. You admire it, you said. Well, it might not last much longer. The government is cracking down on all swadeshi papers.'

He paused, but Vanchi said nothing.

'That's why I've come. We're holding a rally tomorrow afternoon, to protest against the new legislation. It gives the British Resident the power to arrest and deport anyone merely suspected of printing "seditious" ideas.'

Again, Vanchi remained silent.

'I know you don't like political activism. But I also know you share our beliefs. At least, the right to express them in print. Join us at the Residency at four o'clock.'

*

Built in 1815, the Residency was the home of the British official who represented the governor in distant Madras. It was a sprawling structure, combining local and European features designed to enable a British family to live in the tropical humidity of Trivandrum. Its three storeys were topped by a steep roof that ensured maximum circulation inside. Outside, a pillared portico led to a large semi-circular veranda. When the bamboo blinds were lowered, the veranda became an interior room without walls, where the Resident and his wife entertained their guests. The spacious veranda was replicated above on the first floor, which also contained a dozen bedrooms with punkhas, high windows and more bamboo blinds.

When Vanchi arrived at the Residency, twenty or thirty men had already gathered in front of its heavy iron gates. Vanchi recognized no one among the mixture of students, clerks, shopkeepers and merchants. Most wore the traditional *veshti*, others a suit and tie. Ramakrishna gave him a wave of acknowledgement but was locked in discussion with others, so Vanchi looked through the gates and admired the landscaped gardens surrounding the mansion.

'Just like a royal palace, eh?' one of the protestors whispered, sidling up to him.

The rally began with chanting, led by Ramakrishna. There was no stage, temporary or otherwise, no introductions and no speeches. Only voices of dissent.

'Repeal the law! The press must be free!'

At first, everything seemed under control. The shouting was loud but orchestrated. Hands were raised high in the air, though no one moved towards the gates. Ten minutes into the protest, uniformed police appeared and stood just beyond the edge of the gathering. They were dressed in a khaki shirt and knee-length shorts, knee-high socks and heavy boots. Thick sticks dangled by their side.

Everyone continued to chant. Everyone except Vanchi. He opened his mouth, but no words came out. He caught Ramakrishna's eye and raised his hand halfway into the air and tried again. Still nothing.

Ramakrishna edged up beside him and whispered the slogans into his ear. Vanchi found his voice and started to chant in unison with his friend and the others. As wave after wave of energy surged through him, he began to shout and hold his hand higher and higher.

A carriage rolled up towards the gates, and the police rushed in. Although they didn't use violence, they firmly pushed the crowd to one side. The carriage moved through the gates, the people closed in and the shouting became louder. Vanchi became hoarse and had to stop for a moment. Looking at the upper floor of the Residency, he saw lights appear and silhouetted servants moving behind the blinds.

Suddenly, the shouting became more raucous, and a radical chant was heard: 'Self-rule now! End British rule!' Ramakrishna looked about, anxiously trying to identify its source, but he was too late.

The police charged with raised sticks and swung them as they sliced through the crowd. Vanchi turned and tried to run, but he was struck from behind, a heavy blow that knocked him to the ground. On all fours, he looked up and saw that the man was about to strike again.

'Don't!' he whimpered.

The policeman looked down at Vanchi, cringing like a frightened animal, and dropped his arm. Vanchi crawled away on his hands and knees, over the ground where others lay with blood streaming from their heads.

Reaching a line of trees, he stood up and looked back. In the fading light, as Ramakrishna was marched away by two constables, he heard a rumbling over the mountains in the distance. It built up and burst into a crackle of thunder. Lightning flashed through the clouds and sheets of rain fell. Vanchi started to call out, to say something to his friend, but fear swallowed his words.

He never saw Ramakrishna again, though he read about him in the newspapers that he combed through every day in the library. From a Tamil daily, he learned that Ramakrishna was convicted of sedition and transported to the Andaman Islands to serve a sentence of three years. The same paper also had an article about plans to build a swadeshi textile factory in Madras. Foreign textiles—cloth manufactured in England from cotton grown in India—would be boycotted. The new factory would make prices cheaper, create jobs and keep profits inside the country. Vanchi made a note of the two men behind the scheme: Chidambaram Pillai and VVS Aiyar.

5

Shenkottai, 1906

Vanchi looked at Ponammal in the low light of the kitchen. Even squatting down to stir a pot on the clay hearth, she seemed off balance. Maybe one leg was slightly shorter than the other, he wasn't sure. But he remembered when he first saw her, at his uncle's house in Tenkasi.

She was a gangly girl, tall for her age and bony. She and her younger sister were playing a board game on the raised bank of hardened earth that was the front veranda. Between the girls lay a wooden board carved in the shape of a fish, with two rows of shallow depressions, containing different amounts of black tamarind seeds. Hiding behind a wooden pillar, he watched as she calculated how many seeds to move to which hole in order to capture her sister's seeds.

Halfway through the game, Ponammal became aware of his attention, raised her face and swept back her lank hair. She had large, unguarded eyes that knew she was not pretty. And it was made worse when she smiled, which was often, by exposing a thick wadge of gum between her lifted lip and upper row of teeth. Still, she had been a good child, not easily flustered or distracted. Shankara said that she had never cried.

He watched her straighten up in the kitchen, move about with ungainly steps and crouch down again. She had come to live with them a few months earlier, after he'd returned from Trivandrum. He hadn't heard her complain or seen her cry, but he knew she was unhappy.

Vanchi was employed as a guard with the Travancore Forest Department, his reward for coming home with a college degree. He hated to admit it, but his father, who held a middle-level position in another government department, had helped him secure the position so close to home. Every day, Vanchi sat on a bench at the border crossing just outside Shenkottai, while Thatha roamed in the hills. Sometimes, when his morning shift ended in the early afternoon, he left the checkpoint and went up into high forests. It was different, being by himself, but then everything was different.

Even his mother looked older. At first, she'd welcomed Ponammal as a daughter, taught her things, let her comb her hair and pick out the lice. The household had a good balance—his mother and Ponammal, he and Thatha. Until his mother's expectations and Ponammal's desire for a child fed on failure and became an obsession.

He was on the afternoon shift and lingered in the kitchen that morning to savour a second cup of chicory coffee. His grandfather had already left to gather leaves and bark in the hills, and Vanchi wished he could have gone with him, but those days were gone. Thatha said he should spend more time working and try to save money.

Vanchi's mother entered the kitchen and glared at Ponammal.

'No,' she barked. 'Not like that. How many times do I have to tell you? Don't stir the sambar too much. Let it thicken.'

Startled, Ponammal jerked and dropped the ladle. His mother was about to yell at her again when she saw Vanchi's face and only sucked in air through her clenched teeth.

'Right,' she said. 'Go grind the turmeric. And collect some more cow dung.'

When her daughter-in-law had retreated to the veranda with the grating knife, she bent down and ladled more sambar on to Vanchi's idlis.

'Clumsy, that girl. She must have been born funny.'

'Give her time. Her house, her family. They're different.'

'I can be patient, but there's that other thing.'

Vanchi lowered his eyes.

*

His mother had let them sleep together in the kitchen, and their confused fumblings had led to a consummation of sorts. Intimacy without intercourse. For months, his mother was disappointed when she looked for the blood-stained petticoat in the morning. Shankara had 'instructed' him, and Ponammal was willing, but Vanchi couldn't bring himself to perform the act. His erection was fine to begin with, but by the time he had found the right place, it had gone limp. Ponammal would sigh and whisper, 'Next time.'

I must lack something, he thought, some essential quality of a man. He had the desire, but maybe not the need. Or, perhaps, he was just not normal. He didn't know how to explain it. Thatha probably had a remedy, though he was too embarrassed to ask. He considered and rejected the idea of consulting Shankara, but he did speak to a sannyasi.

Everyone had heard of Ram Baba, who lived in the precincts of the large temple in Tenkasi. He had travelled to the high Himalayas, they said, bathed in the headwaters of the Ganges and spent years on the burning ghats of Varanasi.

Clean-shaven and barrel-chested, more a wrestler than an ascetic, Ram Baba was not what Vanchi had expected. He found him in a small office inside the temple compound, sitting in a chair and reading a newspaper. The office walls were covered with astrological charts, Tamil and western calendars, and one large photograph of a saint whom Vanchi did not recognize.

'The seed of Shiva is potent,' Ram Baba said after hearing Vanchi's garbled explanation. 'Pray to the Shiva lingam inside this temple, twice a day.'

Although the temple was five miles from home, Vanchi managed the required number of visits for several weeks. He said nothing of these trips to anyone at home and no one asked, though they all understood why he undertook them.

It happened only when he had given up hope. She did it for him, took him and guided him. After his mother saw the blood, her half-toothed grin remained unchanged for days.

But Ponammal continued to go into the menstruation hut each month, and Vanchi's mother sulked and moaned as if someone had died. She started taking her to a small temple beyond the Brahmin street. Every Tuesday, the day for the goddess Mariamman, she led Ponammal to the shrine under a tamarind tree where women from all castes gathered. The small white-washed structure contained a stone image of the goddess, but the ritual took place outside, in the shade of the tree. Some of the women smeared their shaved heads with turmeric paste, many wore mustard-yellow saris and all carried clay pots decorated with shiny leaves.

After she and Ponammal offered milk and prayed for fertility, they watched as the other women let down their long hair and began to sway at the waist. Possessed by the goddess and driven by the rapid beat of small hourglass-shaped drums, their movements became a frenzy of whirling and jerking. The low-caste temple priest approached them, one by one, daubed their cheeks with holy ash and pushed a tiny barbed spear through the soft skin. When the slender piece of metal emerged on the other side of the woman's mouth, the priest stuck a lemon on its sharp point. Ponammal winced with each piercing, while her mother-in-law shouted blessings to the goddess.

Vanchi's mother also hung a miniature wooden cradle on the tamarind tree beside the goddess temple, where it joined a dozen similar cradles hung there by women who feared they were barren or who had been told they were. A woman without a child, the saying went, is like a cart without wheels. 'Doesn't fancy you, does he?' other women would say. 'Lost his thing in the forest?' Even a woman with a single child was mocked as incomplete.

Ponammal had not been subjected to this abuse, not as far as Vanchi knew. At least, she hadn't said anything to him. But then, she never complained about anything. When he suggested that she go see a doctor in Tenkasi, she said it was too expensive. 'God will help us,' she said. 'Mariamman will give us a child.'

Thatha had also searched for a remedy. 'There's a special kind of sago palm,' he'd said, 'but it doesn't grow in these hills.' Pressed by Vanchi's mother, he agreed to undertake the long journey to a mountain in the north. Ten days later, he returned, accompanied by another man, who carried a load of the palm fronds on his back. When laid down, the thick green spines stretched from one end of the veranda to the other. Thatha got to work, stripping off their glossy leaflets and pounding them in his brass mortar. Ponammal drank the sticky, bitter potion every morning.

Their love-making became a joyless task, performed at night in the sooty kitchen. Vanchi grunted and Ponammal groaned; they rolled apart and went to sleep, without exchanging a word. Sometimes he did feel a flicker of desire when she lifted her sari, but it died by the time he was inside her. One night, hearing a dog bark in syncopation with his thrusts, he smirked in disgust.

Ponammal answered her mother-in-law's questions about their coupling without mentioning the pain. The older woman examined her physically every now and then, commenting on her bony flanks and flat chest. Ponammal kept quiet but wept when she was alone, fearing that she might be forced to undergo the cheek-piercing at the goddess temple under the tamarind tree.

Vanchi watched her drink Thatha's potion for two months. 'That's it,' he said one morning when there had been no change. 'I don't want to talk about it anymore. Or hear about your period or anything.'

He stormed out of the house and cooled down only when

he reached the forest checkpoint, half a mile outside Shenkottai on the main road to Tenkasi. It was a busy border crossing, with four full-time guards, including Vanchi, plus a peon, a sweeper, a night watchman and a clerk. The clerk, a grizzled old man, sat in a makeshift shack without windows and smoked beedis. Their boss, Mr Rama Rao, turned up from time to time in a starched uniform and pith helmet. He was conducting a survey of forest birds, he claimed, and ordered them all to take notes for him. The guards were officially known as 'watchers', though the only thing they watched was the white-painted horizontal pole that blocked the road.

In addition to the checkpoint, a depot had been built to store timber and other produce awaiting transport across the border into Tinnevelly District. Travancore State ran a regime of permits that allowed contractors to fell a certain number of trees and store them at Shenkottai. Those permits had to be checked to ensure that they were fully paid, up to date and issued to the person who was exporting the goods. The crusty old clerk entered those details in a thick ledger, which was kept under lock and key; Mr Rama Rao signed each page at the bottom to ensure no figures were fiddled. Nevertheless, a little money passed in private often hastened the cumbersome process or removed what at first had seemed to be a problem with a permit.

For those wishing to avoid the time-consuming paperwork, the largely unguarded border offered other possibilities. The difficulty of transporting timber through the high hills meant that smuggling was dominated by charcoal, which fetched a high price in Tinnevelly District due to its lack of forests. After negotiations with the British authorities, Travancore had prohibited the export of charcoal and hired more border guards, but large quantities continued to cross over the mountains every day. And if the smugglers were caught by the understaffed police, the bribes were pitched at a lower level than at the official crossing outside Shenkottai.

Vanchi had no involvement with any paperwork and spent most of his six-hour shift sitting on a wooden bench. When a bullock cart appeared, he unhooked one end of the long pole and let it rise, while the other end sunk under the weight of an attached stone. After the cart trundled through, he pulled the pole back down and secured it again to a wooden post.

Although he didn't mind sitting down all day, he'd rather be reading newspapers than staring at a pole. On his day off, he sometimes went to Dr Raghavan's house and borrowed old papers, but more often he talked to Shankara, who worked part-time, helping his father manage their paddy fields. Whenever his brother-in-law showed up at work or the house in Shenkottai, the two of them talked politics, which meant that Shankara summarized for Vanchi what he'd read in the papers in the Tenkasi library. That's what Vanchi missed about Trivandrum, the newspapers in the public library.

Vanchi never grumbled about his job to anyone, and certainly not to Thatha or his mother. Six hours, six days a week, with ten days' paid leave and ten days' sick leave, not to mention government holidays, earned him eight rupees a month. Not much, but it enabled him to contribute to household expenses and earn a measure of respect from Thatha.

'You'll be due for a raise before too long, I suppose,' his grandfather had said to him. 'That'll help when the child comes.'

*

On that morning when his mother scolded Ponammal about cooking the sambar, Vanchi left the kitchen and went out to the veranda. Dozing off, he heard a dog bark, sat up and rubbed his eyes. Shankara was coming down the street, not shuffling as usual, but striding with his head up and arms swinging.

'Guess what?' he said as he plopped down beside Vanchi.

'There's going to be another meeting in Palayamkottai, next week. The one in Tinnevelly didn't support the demand for self-rule, so the radicals are organising another one. A "Swadeshi Congress", they're calling it. Subramania Aiyar will be the main speaker. And Chidambaram Pillai, too.'

Vanchi didn't reply and Shankara persisted.

'Chidambaram Pillai. You know, the one who's been speaking out for the nationalist cause.'

'So, you're going?'

'Yes, and I'm taking you!'

'But I can't just—'

'Of course you can. You've got extra days, I'm sure. Listen, this is more important than sitting on a bench and counting logs.'

'Maybe. But what is swadeshi, anyway? It'll never work.'

'Yes, it will. Because it's sound economics. Buying shirts woven in Manchester out of cotton grown in Tinnevelly is crazy. We need to stand up on our own two feet. You want us to be independent, don't you?'

'Maybe, but what can we do?'

'We'll go to Palayamkottai and find out.'

*

After Shankara left, Vanchi went to bathe in his usual place. Reaching the main road, he walked west, through the Shenkottai market and towards the mountains. Half a mile outside the town, he turned off the road and crossed the rice fields by picking his way along the narrow bunds. The mud walls, two or three feet high, had been built up and smoothed by hand to create boundaries in order to control the flow of water into and out of the fields. By taking advantage of the slight slope of the land, and by cutting holes through the bunds, the farmers could flood or drain a field as they saw fit. It was an irrigation system developed over hundreds of years, though the farmers relied on both the winter monsoon and the government, who maintained a series of canals that directed water to the fields.

Vanchi was still thinking of what Shankara had said when he climbed out of the fields and walked along a dirt path through the forest. Sunlight shone through the translucent leaves, illuminating their vein-striated undersides like a pale green X-ray. A moment later, the leaves hung dark green. A sudden shift of light changed everything.

He felt that Shankara was right, but it all seemed so remote. Reading newspapers and talking about politics was one thing; doing something about it was another. Why did he always depend on others to tell him what to do? Dr Raghavan, Shankara, Ramakrishna. Sometimes, he wished he could go back to roaming the hills with his grandfather.

Muttering to himself, he nearly collided with a man carrying a bundle of freshly cut bamboo poles on his head. The man uttered a curse and Vanchi stopped to watch him disappear among the trees. Turning back around, he saw that he was close to the banyan tree.

It stood tall and spread wide in all directions. He always thought of it as his tree. Not many people came on that path leading to the bathing pool, which was reserved for the few Brahmin families in the area. If he did see someone on the path, he wouldn't stop at the tree. He'd come back later and slip between its aerial roots, into a space where he would be alone.

He didn't go inside this time but continued along the path to the bathing pool. As usual, he saw no one and enjoyed lathering himself with the bar of soap he had brought with him. Pinching his nose and dunking three times under the water, he shook himself, duck-like, and climbed out. As he dried himself with a thin towel, he heard the birds speaking of things that he wished he could understand.

He wrung out his wet loin-cloth as best he could, put it back on, and dressed in his *veshti* and tunic. Refreshed and still with plenty of time before work, he followed the path that climbed into the high hills. As the tree cover thinned out, he saw the stone and realized why he had decided to come that way.

It stood upright, like a headstone, about three feet high, a little way off the path, in the middle of a clearing. Its grey pitted surface had been carved to show a man in relief. Vanchi stared at the stick figure striding forward with a raised sword.

Thatha had told him the story. He'd heard it from his own grandfather, who lived about a hundred years back, during the fight against the British. There were no armies to speak of, Thatha said, only local rajas with a few dozen soldiers inside forts built of wood and sun-dried mud. Some of the soldiers had rifles, most had swords and there were no cannons, at least not on the side of the rajas. In an attack near Shenkottai, one of those small forts was destroyed but not before a man had cut off the head of the foreign commander. Later, after that man was himself killed in another battle, he was commemorated by the carved stone.

Local people prayed to him and repeated his story. The dead hero became a god, the stone was carved and a ballad was composed about his life. Later, a proper temple was erected in a village near Shenkottai and a larger image of the warrior installed. Every year, during a festival at that temple, the story was sung. And when the singers described the warrior's death, and the drumbeats grew insistent, worshippers became possessed by his spirit. They danced in ecstasy and relived his act of bravery. Thatha, like other Brahmins, did not go to that temple, but he liked to tell the story. And Vanchi always stopped to look at the raised sword.

Resuming his walk, Vanchi crested a high hill and saw a second range of hills above a long valley. He scanned the far hills, saw nothing and was about to turn away when his eye snagged on a movement below. As his sight adjusted to the distance, he saw a block of grey slide past the rocky hill behind it. The colour then took shape as a bull elephant leading two females and three or four babies. They plodded forward on pillar-like feet, heads swaying from side to side. Silent, distant and reassuring.

He monitored their progress until the small ones passed out of sight and the valley was motionless again. He looked hard for something else to measure himself by. A hawk sailed above the valley, back and forth, cutting the view into pieces that did not fit together again. He became dizzy and hurried back down the hilly path. It was a steep incline, made slippery by a light drizzle.

Running through a patch of forest, he stumbled against a jutting rock and fell. Instead of getting up, he rested on the soft ground and watched the sunlight gather strength. It shone between the tree trunks at different angles, like the criss-crossing beams of a search party. The light was so intense that if he tilted his head, just a little, he was able to count the white flowers on a teak tree branch.

The sunlight shifted again, and the trees no longer stood straight. He cocked his head to the other side, trying to get the angle right between the vertical trees and the sloping hill, but that only increased the misalignment. Still lying on his back, he repositioned his body so that his head pointed directly uphill. He listened again for the birds, but they had gone silent. The whistling wind began to blow in powerful gusts, and a far-off rumble came closer.

Vanchi gripped the earth and shut his eyes tight. He was certain he would be crushed. The crooked trees, loosened and uprooted, would fall on him. Another peal of thunder gathered force and exploded, nearer this time. He opened his eyes and saw a bolt of lightning shoot straight down through the forest.

Scrambling to his feet, he crashed down the hill, scraping his hands on the tree trunks as he tried to cushion his descent. By the time he reached the bottom, the rain was falling hard and steam rose from the warm earth. He slipped off a mud bund and sloshed his way through the paddy fields.

When he reached the main road, he slowed to a walk. He would be late at the checkpoint, but he didn't care. He would go to that Palayamkottai meeting with Shankara. He would go because he trusted him. And because he was no longer a young boy or a college student.

More than an hour late at the checkpoint, he expected angry words from his boss, and prepared himself to tough it out and say nothing. But he didn't get the chance. As soon as he arrived, he was sent home.

'Your grandfather left word,' one of the guards told him. 'Go home immediately.'

'What is it?' Vanchi asked.

'He didn't say.'

The sun was still high when he rushed down the street to the house. Thatha was working on the veranda and looked up when he heard him approach.

'No blood for more than a month now,' he said with a smile. 'Your mother just checked her. She's with child.'

6

Tuticorin, 1908

Vanchi sat on the quayside and looked out to sea. It was like a train on water, just as they had said. Smoke rose from a black stack but without the sound of grinding steel and shrieking whistles.

The steamer was larger than he had imagined, much larger. With its bow thrust upward and its white hull slung low, the ship glided into harbour. Vanchi watched it all the way and could make out figures on the main deck. He kept thinking that the steamship had stopped, but it continued to slide towards him. He raised his sight, beyond the ship, and traced the horizon from right to left. The thin line that should hold everything in place seemed fragile.

'Magnificent, isn't it?' Shankara said to Vanchi.

Vanchi murmured in agreement, and together they watched the passengers disembark. The steamer had anchored offshore and ropes were lowered over one side. Having sailed for sixteen hours across the straits from Colombo, the passengers now had to climb down the rope and leap into pilot boats that would ferry them to the pier. As the women and elderly men were winched down in a chair, one rotund gentleman fell through the arms of those below and ended up in the water.

'He'll never make it to shore,' Shankara with a chuckle. 'But maybe Pillai planned it that way. Might be one of his enemies.'

Shankara and Vanchi were sitting on a wooden crate with a third man, named Madasami. He was short, even shorter than Vanchi. Also darker, with a stocky build and tense eyes. Born in a village near Tuticorin, Madasami had brought them to the harbour to see the SS *Galia*, one of two vessels owned by Chidambaram Pillai and his Swadeshi Steam Navigation Company.

The three young men were killing time before going to a political rally at sunset. Bales of cleaned and pressed cotton stood in front of them in deep rows. Off to one side, gunny sacks of paddy were stacked so high they cut off their view of the sea. The other side of the quay was covered with sacks of senna leaves, the medicinal plant introduced to Tinnevelly District in the last century. More sacks and bales were being unloaded from bullock carts, handcarts and pony carts. All of it would soon be ferried to the anchored ship for its return voyage to Colombo en route to ports in Asia and Europe.

As more and more passengers reached dry land, the harbour area became a noisy marketplace of porters, agents and coolies competing for business. The first group of passengers who walked down the pier to the quayside were businessmen and planters dressed in linen suits, ties and leather shoes. One could usually tell the Europeans from the Indians by their headgear—the pith helmet versus the turban, though some European newcomers wore a straw hat. Only a dozen European women, and even fewer Indian women, were among these first-class passengers.

Most of them boarded a special train that took them from the quayside to the railway station in town, while others were escorted into private carriages and driven to the station. There, in the first-class waiting room, they would be served an excellent tea and provided with newspapers while they waited for the arrival of the Boat Mail from Madras, which would turn around and take them on a twenty-two-hour journey back to that metropolis.

Next came the second-class passengers, mainly Indian shopkeepers, clerks, traders and merchants, who would travel onward by train or carriage or cart. They were followed by Tamil labourers, primarily tea plantation coolies crossing the sea in order to visit their families in their home village or town. When all the passengers had reached dry land, sacks of tea leaves, coconuts and cinnamon bark from Ceylon were offloaded from the little boats, piled into carts and stored in warehouses before travelling to markets throughout the country.

*

The port town of Tuticorin was always busy, but not always as tense as on that day in early March. A year ago, the young Chidambaram Pillai had decided to challenge the monopoly of the British-owned steamships on the profitable route between Colombo and Tuticorin. The son of a prominent lawyer, Pillai had worked in a sub-magistrate's court before moving to Tuticorin, where he set up a legal practice. After the division of Bengal in 1905, he joined the nationalist movement, as many others did, and soon became the leading spokesman of the swadeshi movement in south India.

In print and in person, Chidambaram Pillai argued that the land of one's birth is 'like one's mother', to be loved and respected. He urged people to boycott British goods and services, which was the inspiration behind his steamship company. As soon as his two ships began sailing, however, the rival British companies slashed fares and offered free umbrellas to first- and second-class passengers. Local British officials also unleashed a campaign of harassment against Pillai's fledgling company. Instead of backing down, Pillai upped the ante by supporting striking workers in a local cotton mill.

The cotton industry in Tuticorin had its roots in the American Civil War. When cotton exports to England were strangled by the North's naval blockade of the South's ports,

Britain turned to India, and in particular to the Tinnevelly region, where cotton thrived in its black soil. The local variety became so popular that it was known as 'tinnies', an affectionate abbreviation of the district's name. The cotton boom culminated in the British-owned Coral Mills in the port area of Tuticorin. Powered by new machinery, the factory turned out 750 pounds of cleaned and pressed cotton every day, not least because the workers started work at five in the morning and left at seven in the evening.

In March 1908, low wages and dangerous working conditions led to a walkout. When the strike was teetering on the brink of collapse, Chidambaram Pillai stepped in with legal and financial assistance. He urged the workers to continue the fight while he raised money to compensate for their lost wages.

As usual, it was Shankara who had convinced Vanchi that they should travel to Tuticorin to support Pillai. Both of them had followed the story of his shipping company in the newspapers and had heard him speak at the meeting in Palayamkottai two years earlier, where they also met Madasami. But the strike in Tuticorin was different.

'It's happening right now,' Shankara said. 'A fight we can be part of.'

'But what can we do there?' Vanchi said. 'Listen to speeches and cheer?'

'We've got to support our leaders, to be united.'

Worn down by Shankara's arguments, Vanchi took two days' leave and prepared for the journey, telling his family that he was visiting a friend in Tuticorin. Hearing the famous swadeshi leader speak was not, however, his only motivation for leaving home. He also wanted to escape from his father's mockery. Home on one of his rare stays in Shenkottai, he had needled his son from the first moment. 'Just sitting on your backside, then?' he said. 'No idea how to get a promotion, I suppose. Especially with those friends of yours. Call themselves patriots, do they? More like petty criminals.'

Vanchi had also faced quiet but firm resistance from Ponammal. She had given birth to a baby girl, Vanni, who had been ill with diarrhoea. Ponammal made it clear during their night-time whispering that she did not want to be left alone with her in-laws.

'They won't look after Vanni,' she said. 'They wanted a son. Even Thatha, though he doesn't show it.'

Vanchi assured that her that he would return soon and asked his grandfather to keep an eye on the baby's health.

The next morning, he and Shankara had travelled by train from Shenkottai to Tinnevelly and by pony cart to Tuticorin, where they met Madasami. The little dark man was an ardent supporter of Chidambaram Pillai. They both came from the same small town near Tuticorin, and Pillai had once defended Madasami in a legal case brought against him by his own father.

*

Relaxing on the wooden crate in the harbour, the three men spoke with admiration about Pillai's achievements and wondered what would happen next.

'Last month,' Madasami said, 'we were told that someone had planted a bomb in the hold of his ship. I was the one who found it, under the cotton bales. Sticks of dynamite!'

Vanchi regarded him with questioning eyes.

'They call us violent,' Madasami added, 'but they're the ones with the bombs and guns.'

Having watched the passengers disperse from the harbour area, they walked away along the Beach Road. As Shankara and Madasami discussed the rally that would start at sunset, Vanchi stopped and stared out at Pillai's steamship anchored in the harbour. It looks solid, he thought, unlike the wavering line on the horizon behind it.

Shankara sensed an absence, turned around and saw his brother-in-law standing stock still, a slight smile playing on his lips. While Madasami waited, he went back a dozen paces and took Vanchi by the hand.

'All right?' he asked.

'Yes, it's just that the sea changes so quickly. It looks calm, but it's so big and might not hold.'

Shankara decided not to ask him to explain and brought him back to Madasami, who led them away from the seafront and towards the centre of town.

'You know, the English will not last,' Madasami commented as they passed a cathedral with a tall spire. 'This thing was built by the Portuguese in 1610. And then they left.'

'But we didn't make them leave, did we?' said Shankara.

'No. Because they, and then the Dutch, didn't try to conquer us and destroy our culture. Only the English have tried to do that. And for that, we will drive them out.'

'It's not that easy,' Shankara said sharply.

'Oh, yes, it is. The English will leave. In fact, we will make them use their own ships to take them back to England.'

Vanchi snickered, but not Shankara.

'This isn't a joke, you know,' he said, and grabbed Madasami by the arm. 'They have a large army, in case you haven't noticed.'

'No, I haven't. Most of them are Indians, anyway,' snapped Madasami.

The two men stood face to face in the middle of the street, with bullock carts and people passing by on both sides.

'You're right. We do not have an army,' Madasami admitted, 'but we have brave warriors.'

As they continued to walk to the market area, where the rally would shortly begin, Vanchi wanted to ask who those warriors were and what they would do.

'Is Pillai the main speaker tonight?' he asked instead.

'No, that's Subramania Aiyar, editor of *Swadesamitran* in Madras,' Madasami said. 'But Pillai will introduce him. Then you'll hear something to remember.'

7

Tuticorin, 1908

That prospect troubled Robert Ashe as he ate breakfast earlier that same day in his bungalow. After a six-month furlough in Ireland, he had been sent back to Tinnevelly District as sub-collector with an office in Tuticorin. Forking down his eggs, he recalled the warning he'd received when he'd taken up his new post the previous month.

'Glad you're with us, Ashe,' Collector Wynch had said, welcoming him to his bungalow in Palayamkottai. Noticing his guest's admiring glance at the deep verandas and high peaked roof, he swung out an arm. 'Built in the days of old Lushington,' he said. 'They knew how to build these things then. Ventilation was everything.'

'It's a fine building, sir,' Ashe said. He'd lived in much worse accommodation during previous postings all over the Madras Presidency, including a brief stint in Tinnevelly before the long furlough.

The collector gestured for his guest to sit down and offered him a cigar. Ashe declined and took out his pipe. One snipped while the other tamped, and when the ritual fires were lit, they settled back, puffing and sucking with gratification.

'Yes, Tinnevelly is a wonderful district,' the older man said. 'Not appreciated by most, but it's got the mountains to the west, the sea to the east and the rivers between. The finest cotton in the world, new water-power plants and—'

'Yes, sir, wonderful. I served here in 1907. I was wondering about the current political situation.'

'Yes, all right. I was coming to that.'

The collector put down his cigar and leaned forward in his chair.

'Listen, Ashe. It's only fair to tell you that things are heating up here. Have been all over the country, of course, ever since that idiotic partition a few years back. But down here, the resentment is stronger than ever. We know all about the radicals in Calcutta and Madras. Well, we've got them here, too. Pamphlets everywhere, supporting this boycott business. "Swasdish" or something.'

Ashe restrained himself and said, 'I see. What about Tuticorin itself? I heard it's a relatively peaceful place.'

'So it was, my dear chap. So, it was. Important but quiet little town. Has been ever since the Portuguese arrived in 15…'

'Thirty-two.'

'What's that?'

'In 1532, I believe, sir.'

'Just so. But there was trade before then, too, you know. The Romans were there, or near there. God knows we could use a few of their legionaries now.'

'Quite,' Ashe replied, turning down the corners of his mouth.

'And now we've got this Pillai fellow causing trouble. But more about that later. Let me hear about England. Ireland, I mean.'

The bell rang for dinner and the two men, in formal dress, led their wives into a dining room blazing with candles.

*

The idea of returning to India had tormented Mary Ashe. She was convinced that one of her four children would not survive another long stay in a backwater post like Tuticorin. Ranging in age from three to nine, they had all been born in south India and spent years in small towns there. But she had a premonition that one of them would die if they went back.

Thanks to God, she said to herself, Molly, Arthur and Sheila had not contracted any disease, but little Herbert was less robust. When he came down with a terrible rash and ran a high fever, Mary took him back to Dublin, where the whole family later joined them for Robert's long furlough.

During the six months in Dublin, Mary noticed how thin they had all become, how scabby their skin and frequent their coughs. Walking down a busy street in the centre of town, she felt they looked like immigrants. At the end of their stay, the children had regained missing weight and the colour had returned to Mary's cheeks. But her fear remained. She liked to think that she had to make an awful choice: let Robert return alone while she raised the children in Ireland, or gamble with their lives in India.

'You could stay here with us, dear,' her mother had said. 'At least for a while. I'm sure Robert would understand.'

The dilemma, which Mary rolled around and around in her mind, injected drama into the humdrum pattern of her life back home. The predictable meals, stale conversations and obligatory visits to aunts and uncles made her restless. Even her old friends, now married to solicitors and accountants, seemed small-minded. The children kept her occupied during the day, but when she went to bed alone, her thoughts turned to India.

Despite the debilitating climate and lack of hygiene, something in her had responded to the challenge of living in a country where she never knew what might happen next and where she had no real control. It was also where she had experienced the mystery of a human bond without words. That's how she described her friendship with Selva.

Her full name was Selva Mary, and she had charmed her way into Mary Ashe's heart on the first day of her employment. She and Robert had had other ayahs, but Selva was different. Plump, black as night and always wearing a bright red sari, she radiated a defiant joy. Where did she get that cherubic face? Mary wondered. So round and full. And how did that smile glow in the withering heat? Her husband, by the name of Easter, was hopeless, given to self-pity and drink, and her wages hardly allowed her to provide her family with a good diet. Yet, all her children seemed well-nourished, unlike most of the families Mary saw around her.

When Mary enquired about their shared name and was told that *selva* meant 'wealth', she smiled. How true, she thought and wondered about the cold grey of her own married name.

Early one morning, Mary opened the front door of their bungalow and was told by Selva's husband that she had died in the night. Something she ate. She had been taken to the hospital, but the doctors could do nothing. Mary paid for the funeral and made monthly payments to the husband, hoping he would use it for the children, though she dared not check up on him. Once, she saw Selva's oldest daughter in the market, and wanted to say something, but the girl was gone before Mary had been able to arrange the Tamil words in her head.

Over the years, a string of cheerful young women took Selva's place, but none could dislodge her in Mary's mind. Sometimes, on a winter evening, when the temperature might drop to twenty degrees Celsius, and the rose-ringed parrots flocked around the trees in their garden, Mary thought about her dead friend and tears came to her eyes.

By the time her two oldest children began to go to school in Kodaikanal, Mary decided to dispense with ayahs altogether. 'They just get under my feet,' she said to Robert when he'd asked about finding a new maid after the last one left. But the truth was she couldn't find it in her heart to see someone else in Selva's place.

As their long stay in Ireland drew to a close and preparations for departure began, Mary sighed with resignation and admitted to herself that her 'terrible dilemma' was not really a choice at all. She would not desert Robert, not when he clearly needed her. He would never admit it, but she knew that he didn't always like his work, that it exasperated him and that he was not as efficient as he liked to pretend. And there was the occasional controversy, such as that business about the bathing pools during his earlier posting in the district.

Robert had told her that Brahmins had exclusive rights to the best spots at the Courtallam waterfalls close to Shenkottai. Exercising his power as a magistrate, he had issued an order that abolished all caste-based restrictions. 'After all,' he'd said in a smug voice that she disliked, 'water is nature's gift to everyone.'

When Mary mentioned his little triumph to Mrs Wynch, the collector's wife had smiled indulgently.

'Of course, what he did was right,' she said.

They were sitting in wicker chairs under a tent, while dozens of European and Indian guests nibbled cucumber sandwiches and sipped warm tea in the dry back garden of the collector's bungalow. Beneath her straw hat, Mary's light brown hair was pinned up in a roll just above the ear. She wore a string of pearls and a muslin dress of pale purple that hung straight from the shoulders to mid-calf.

'Yes,' Mary replied, 'he seems very pleased with the result.'

'But, you know, my dear,' Mrs Wynch said, lowering her voice, 'they really just push papers around, hoping that something will stick.'

A few days later, an Indian Christian woman sought her out after church and told her that her husband had done the right thing 'to stand up to the Brahmins'. She was a Nadar, traditional toddy-tappers and the most populous caste in the district. Ever since Protestant missionaries had begun to work in Tinnevelly District, more than a hundred years earlier, Nadars had converted in large numbers.

'Yes,' the woman said, her grey hair in a tight bun and a Bible in the crook of her arm. 'Your husband has earned the respect of us all.'

Later, however, Mary heard a different story from an Englishman, a judge and avid game hunter, whom Robert invited to dinner one evening.

'Shooting's been wonderful this year,' the judge said as they sipped their coffee in the sitting room. 'And you know why, Mrs Ashe? Because your man here told those Hindus they can't use the bathing pools until after ten in the morning. They're all reserved for us. Jolly right, too.'

'Oh, yes,' Mary had replied, dipping her eyes towards her coffee cup to avoid looking at her husband. Afterwards, she had decided not to ask Robert about the bathing pools or anything else connected to his work.

*

It was now early March, a month after their return from Ireland, and the heat was already building up in Tuticorin. The milk had gone off again that morning and there was none for Robert's breakfast tea. He ate his watery scrambled eggs with a scowl.

'That damn Pillai is stirring up trouble again,' he fumed, sitting with Mary at the square table that didn't quite fit into the corner of their front room. 'He's organized another meeting to support the strikers at the mill. More than that, he's got people to donate to the strike fund. He's a clever devil, that one, but he'll pay for this. Rest assured, he will pay for it.'

Mary nodded, put down a piece of toast and paused a moment before speaking.

'I'm sure you're right,' she said. 'But, you know, Robert, we need to make arrangements for Kodai.'

As a hill station, Kodaikanal was newer, more American and less fashionable than Ootacamund. Ooty was where most of the British sent their children to school, especially if they couldn't afford to send them to Britain, and where they themselves spent the hot summer months. Kodaikanal, however, was cheaper and closer to Tinnevelly. Besides, Mary had made friends with an American missionary who had started a school there. It wasn't a proper school with a building and classrooms, though the teachers were excellent.

That was the pronouncement of Molly and Arthur, the two older children. From March to November, they attended that school in Kodaikanal, boarding with the Wilkinsons, a retired couple whom Robert knew from his time in Madras. When Robert and Mary went up to the mountains for the annual six-week summer holiday, they took the younger children, Sheila and Herbert, with them. The whole family were also together for three winter months, when Molly and Arthur came down to live with them in Tuticorin.

'I've already booked that cottage starting 15 June,' Robert said.

'I know, but I'm worried about Herbert. He's showing rashes again.'

'All right, all right. I'll send a message to Palayamkottai and ask that doctor—what's his name? Rama something—to come out here.'

'And if he doesn't improve?'

'I don't know. I—'

'We'll have to take him up there early, won't we?'

'I guess so. Look, I've got to get to the office now.'

'Please, Robert. Can we get train tickets at short notice if we need to?'

'Yes, yes. Das can do that.'

Mary gave him his coat, brushed dandruff from the shoulders and indicated the bits of egg sticking to his moustache. He looked in the mirror and struck at the yellow flakes with such ferocity that his hand banged against the wall. Cursing under his breath, he left without the usual kiss on the cheek.

Robert Ashe walked to his office dressed in a single-buttoned beige coat, matching trousers and black boots. When he'd arrived in Tuticorin a few weeks earlier, his head clerk, Das, had asked him what kind of horse he preferred as transport.

Ashe mumbled something about 'exercise', confident that his head clerk, or anyone else in the district, for that matter, would not have access to the personnel file in Madras that contained an unflattering assessment of his equestrian skills.

During the fifteen-minute morning constitutional, he was accompanied by his personal servant, or bearer, who carried a stack of files. The man was silent as a wall and kept his distance, which Ashe appreciated, though sometimes he did wish he could confide in someone. Given time, that person might be Das, he thought. He certainly needed to talk to someone about Chidambaram Pillai.

He had already clashed with the man over his steamer company, threatening him and his directors with accusations of fraud. It's outrageous, he told himself, that anyone should call his company 'swadeshi', a direct challenge to the government. Urged on by Collector Wynch, and the handful of British businessmen who controlled the port of Tuticorin, Ashe had attempted to intimidate Pillai. Accompanied by two policemen and a sub-magistrate, he had barged into the steamship company offices late one afternoon and demanded to see the accounts. When the startled clerks produced the ledgers, Ashe sat down and pretended to scrutinize them. He was good at that, appearing to read documents without actually taking in their contents. Half an hour later, he had slammed shut the last account book, stood up and told the sub-magistrate, a Tamil gentleman, to explain that he had found several discrepancies and that further investigations would follow.

'Damned if I'm going to let him get away with this meeting,' Ashe now muttered as he mounted the steps to his own office. With an arched portico, faded yellow walls and peaked roof, it looked more like a Catholic shrine than a government building, and Ashe often thought he could use a little divine intervention. After his bearer stacked the files on his desk and left, Ashe filled his pipe and tamped it down with more force than was necessary.

By noon, the heat was stifling, and the punkhas swaying above him only seemed to create waves of hot air. He pushed the papers to one side. A resolution to the dispute between Muslims and Christians over their funeral procession routes would have to wait. He also decided to cancel a trip into the countryside to inspect a new masonry irrigation channel.

'Das,' he cried, summoning his clerk from a tiny outer office.

The dapper little man hurried inside and stood before the sub-collector's desk, arms at his side. He had short-cropped greying hair and wore spectacles. Could be thirty, or could be fifty, Ashe thought.

'Yes, sir,' Das said in a clipped tone. His grammatically impeccable English was spoken with the rapidity of his native Tamil, and Ashe was often forced to ask him to repeat himself.

'There's that meeting this evening—Pillai again—and we need information. Understand?'

'Yes, sir.'

Das understood. He would arrange for two men to join the crowd and later write down notes from memory of what was said, with special attention to anti-government sentiments. Das would translate and expand those notes into a handwritten report that would land on Ashe's desk by the time he arrived at ten o'clock the following morning.

They can shout 'Hail to Mother India' all they want, Ashe said to himself after Das left. But anything that hints at violence or suggests sedition, and they'll end up in prison. He was still grinding his teeth when a peon brought in his lunch of fish cutlets and a boiled egg.

*

As the sun faded that evening, more than a thousand people gathered in the market area. Men of all ages and walks of life, plus a smattering of women from low castes, faced a man standing on a wooden box. Wearing a dark blue turban,

Chidambaram Pillai spoke with passion but in an even tone, building up a legal case against the mill owners, citing example after example of their failure to comply with legislation concerning hours, overtime pay and factory conditions.

Standing near the back of the crowd, Vanchi was a little disappointed with Pillai's courtroom oratory and found Subramania Aiyar more engaging. The editor from Madras, who was considerably older and more experienced than Pillai, urged direct action to support the strike, now in its fifth day. He gained the sympathy of the audience by giving vivid details of other cases of the 'lawful withdrawal of labour' taking place around the country.

The word 'swadeshi', which Vanchi had been listening out for, had not been uttered once. Both speakers had been careful to aim their criticism at the private owners of Coral Mills and not the government because the new sedition law applied to the spoken as well as the printed word. Only when Pillai again took to the stage at the end of the two hours was anything controversial said.

'Next week,' he announced, 'we will show everyone the power we hold. Next week, we will celebrate the release of a great patriot. Next week, when Bipan Chandra Pal is freed from prison, we will honour him here in Tuticorin. Next week, we will show the country that Tuticorin is the capital of swadeshi in south India!'

The clamour from the crowd was hushed when Pillai raised his hands in prayer. Then, in the eerie pin-drop silence, he began to chant, 'God is one. God is one.'

Vanchi now knew what Madasami had meant by 'brave warriors'. He had just heard one speak. His only regret was that he could not return to Tuticorin for the celebration announced by Pillai.

*

Ashe read Das's report the next morning and sent a note by special messenger to Collector Wynch in Tinnevelly. 'We cannot allow a public meeting that will honour a traitor,' he wrote. 'With your permission, I will issue an order prohibiting the congregation of twenty or more persons within the harbour and market areas.' Ashe received permission and issued the restrictive order. Handwritten and signed copies were posted in the market, quayside and other key places in Tuticorin.

Then Ashe summoned Chidambaram Pillai to a meeting. After being made to wait for a full hour, the tall Tamil walked into the sub-collector's office wearing a white *veshti*, a white turban and a dark tunic buttoned up to the neck. A small red dot glistened in the middle of his forehead. He looked around for somewhere to sit and realized that the chairs had been pushed back against the wall.

Ashe savoured the man's discomfort for a moment, cleared his throat and laid his forearms on his desk, fingers interlaced.

'Now, listen to me, Mr Pillai,' he said, having rehearsed his speech. 'You are prohibited forthwith, under threat of arrest, from holding any meeting of twenty or more persons. Nor may you meet privately with four or more persons. Lastly, you will not make any speeches or issue any written communications that advocate, or suggest in any way, the overthrow of His Majesty's government.'

Although Pillai said nothing, Ashe thought he detected a slight upward tug on the corners of his mouth.

'Yes,' he continued, pulling himself up in his chair, 'you are being watched, you see, and will be arrested and charged with sedition if you breach these regulations. Is that clear?'

'It is clear,' the erect Pillai said with a visible smirk. 'However, I am constrained to enquire whether any spontaneous gatherings of three or fewer persons might also be sufficiently dangerous to warrant the exercise of your considerable powers.'

Cheeky bastard, Ashe thought, probably studied law in London, like the rest of them.

'You will see what powers we have if you ignore this order. That is all. You may go.'

'Vande Mataram,' Pillai said in a calm voice. Hail Mother India. 'We will not be enslaved by you for much longer. Good day to you, sir.'

Worried that Pillai would not abide by his restrictive order, Ashe prevailed upon Wynch to intervene. The day before the banned celebration, Pillai and two associates were summoned to the collector's office in Tinnevelly.

'You have stirred up trouble and incited violence,' Wynch told them. 'You have disgraced your race by your criminal intentions.'

'Is it a crime to love one's country?' Pillai replied. 'Is it wrong to seek freedom from poverty, from your plundering of our land? Will the God Almighty permit this?'

The accusations and denials dragged on for hours, in part because of Pillai's legal acumen. Word had spread quickly that the 'swadeshi man' was being interrogated, and by mid-afternoon, a large crowd had gathered outside the collector's office. Chanting 'Vande Mataram' and 'Freedom for Pillai', they waited anxiously for the conclusion of the proceedings.

At five o'clock, after Pillai had repeatedly argued against the allegations of treason, he and his two associates were arrested and remanded in custody.

That was the spark that lit the fire. The crowd had not been optimistic that the men would be exonerated. Although they did not anticipate leniency for those who challenged British rule, neither did they expect to see their leaders sent to prison. At first, they watched in stunned silence as the accused men were bundled into three separate jutkas. But when the carts began to roll away, they rushed forward and were only prevented from freeing the prisoners by fixed bayonets.

After the carriages disappeared, the mood turned ugly and the crowd became a mob. The district police station, its entrance neatly lined by little, white-painted stones, was set on fire. The post office and municipal storehouse were also torched, while British-owned shops were attacked and looted.

The protest intensified after dark and lasted for two days. Wynch dispatched a hundred reserve police, including a section armed with rifles. Calls to disperse went unheeded, confusion reigned and the police opened fire. Four Indians were shot dead.

When news of the rioting and fatalities in Tinnevelly reached Ashe in Tuticorin, he took immediate precautionary measures. In the course of one day, he secured his office and bungalow with extra police sent from Tinnevelly; he persuaded Wynch to dispatch an additional three hundred constables; and he arranged for British and other European residents to be evacuated to ships anchored in the harbour.

He also sent Mary, the two children and the servants to a church in a nearby town. Not wanting to alarm her, he played down the threat, which meant that she could not understand the need to leave. She agreed to go away only when he promised that they would finalize the plans for Kodaikanal as soon as she returned.

*

The following morning in Tuticorin began like any other weekday. At nine o'clock, ranks of students in blue and white starched uniforms stood in the hot sun and listened to headteachers. In the market area, traders hawked their wares, and a new stall boasting 'English clocks' drew unusually large crowds. Bony dogs lazed in the sun on the quayside, and thin-chested porters waited in the tea stalls, smoking beedis. The steamer from Colombo had come and gone.

The first brick was thrown at two-thirty in the afternoon. It crashed through the front window of A & F Harvey, agents for both the cotton mill and the steamer company competing with Pillai's ships. Shops near the harbour yanked down their shutters, and agitated crowds roamed the streets in the centre of town.

Barricaded inside his office, Ashe received reports every

half hour. The assistant superintendent of police, a Tamil man, stood by his side, his dark brown eyes darting from side to side as he assured Ashe that his men were ready. The young man's three-week training had consisted of sitting in the offices of various police inspectors and observing them transact daily business. It had not included the suppression of a public riot.

Ashe acknowledged the man's assurance, though he knew that more men were needed. He checked his pistol. Firearms was another area of the examinations that he had nearly failed in London, and he had not held a gun in his hand since visiting the firing range at the army barracks in that city many years ago.

At four-thirty, he was informed that the police station had been set alight. He could also see flames shooting up in the air from the municipal oil storage tank. At five o'clock, when he was told that a crowd had massed in the market area, he decided he could not wait for Wynch's reinforcements.

Ashe and the assistant superintendent stepped in front of two rows of mounted police. Behind them, many more police stood to attention, many of them with rifles.

'You men are here to protect civilians, their property and their lives,' Ashe barked. 'Do not use force unless and until I give the order. Remember, you are representatives of the governor-general.'

When the assistant superintendent gave a rough approximation of these words in Tamil, the police on horseback gripped their long cane sticks and those on foot clutched their rifles close to their chest. Ashe mounted his horse, held his hand high and waved them forward.

The people in the market area were listening to speeches and shouting slogans. They were an angry but not a riotous crowd. They had not burned any shops in the area because they were all Indian-owned. Bursts of laughter rang through the air.

Ashe blinked in the sunlight as he scanned the scene from

a hundred yards. He felt the eyes of the men behind him as he waited for someone to throw a stone or shout abuse. Anything to relieve him of the burden of responsibility. But the gathering had not yet heard the boots and hooves. Telling himself not to panic, he brought his men closer.

Suddenly, heads turned. Fearing an attack, Ashe ordered the mounted police to advance and the constables to rush in with fixed bayonets. A stone struck Ashe's horse, and he gave the order for live ammunition to be fired above the heads of the crowd. His command for the crowd to disperse went unheard, leading to a furious charge by his men. They burst forward, cracking heads with rifle butts, smashing shoulders with cane sticks and knocking bodies to the ground. The market area was soon emptied, the ground stained with blood and a squadron of black crows squawking overhead.

Of the thirty-six people arrested that day, thirty-two were charged and convicted of disturbing the peace. Several of those arrested, including Madasami, were admitted to the local hospital with serious injuries. Unlike in Tinnevelly, no one had been killed, but the newspapers portrayed Ashe as the personification of the evil inherent in British rule. One editor claimed that he was the new Hiranyan, the blood-thirsty demon of Hindu myth.

Two days later, the sub-collector read those editorial comments in Das's carefully worded report. He told himself that they were the ravings of extremists and did not reflect public opinion. The great majority of natives, ordinary people like Das and others he met in his office and at church, were decent and kind. Let the extremists rant and pay the price.

He couldn't suppress a chuckle, though, when he saw a political cartoon clipped from a paper and included in the report. Standing next to a pile of dynamite labelled 'agitation of the people', Wynch was about to ignite it with a cigar of 'injustice'.

Pushing the report to one side, Ashe reflected that he

had done his duty. He'd quelled public disorder, prevented criminal acts and protected lives, not least those of his family. No, he said to himself as he slapped his desk hard with an open hand, it was the editors of those newspapers who should be fearful. Aurobindo and Bharati. He knew their names, and they had come close to crossing the line. They might be sincere in their cause, but that was no excuse for seditious activity. In fact, their passion is just what will put them in prison.

He leaned back and laced his hands behind his head. It was at times like this that he wished he smoked cigars. Mary had disapproved—put her foot down, in fact. He got out his pipe, the new one she'd kindly brought back from Ireland, lit it and savoured the aroma.

He'd been almost fifteen years in India now. Made a few mistakes, got the wrong man at times and hadn't always known or followed correct procedure. On the whole, though, he thought he'd been a good, or at least a fair, administrator. If he had any regret, it was tinged with pride.

He reckoned that a few misguided newspaper editorials weren't going to ruin his career or topple the British Empire. If anything, the ferocity of the attacks against him only demonstrated that he was doing the right thing. And, in the end, those revolutionary ideas would probably discredit the nationalist movement and rally the country to the King. Drawing heavily and exhaling, he smiled to himself. He was playing a part—only a small one, mind you—but a part nonetheless in the course of history.

'First-class report, Das,' he said to his head clerk.

'Thank you, sir. I'll continue to monitor the press, if you wish.'

'Good idea. No, on second thought, we have more important tasks ahead of us.'

*

Before Das left for home that evening, he fidgeted with his black tie to ensure that it was tucked inside the top button of his white coat. Skipping down the steps, he allowed himself the indulgence of feeling optimistic about his overdue promotion. He started to count the extra rupees while watching the paan-seller prepare his usual mixture under the tree opposite the office. When he'd popped it into his mouth and was chewing with satisfaction, he made a sudden decision. A clean shave and an ear-cleaning would be noticed by his wife with approval.

'The usual,' he said to the barber as he took off his glasses and sat down in the comfortable chair. He relaxed when the man began to lather his face with warm soap. Enquiries about each other's health and families and comments on the weather gave way to talk about the recent riots in the market area.

'Good thing they stopped the mob,' Das said while the barber was sharpening his razor on the worn leather strap. 'Can't have violence on the streets.'

The barber dropped the strap and told Das to leave, forcing him to appear in public with a face covered in white foamy soap. Das hid his humiliation as best he could until he ducked into a dry goods shop and was given a towel. Can't be sure of anyone these days, the head clerk reflected as he made his way home.

8

Shenkottai, 1908

'Ashe?' Vanchi asked.

'Yes, the sub-collector in Tuticorin,' Shankara answered. 'The papers are full of him.'

'But why him? You said the deaths were in Tinnevelly.'

'That's right, but Ashe fought Pillai from the beginning. He's the one who humiliated him. They're saying it wasn't the magistrate who sentenced Pillai. It was Ashe.'

'Forty years hard labour—that's cruel. We may never see him again.'

'And the police are looking for anyone connected with him.'

'What do you mean?'

'I mean we have to be careful. Madasami was arrested a few days ago.'

*

News of the killings and rioting had spread across the district and over the border to Shenkottai. Equally newsworthy was the arrest and subsequent trial of Chidambaram Pillai, which ended a few months later with a sentence of two terms of transportation for life, each for twenty years. As a result, Vanchi found himself the centre of attention at work. He had actually seen and heard Chidambaram Pillai speak. Days at the checkpoint suddenly became more exciting.

They called him *thambi*, little brother, not just because of his size and age but also his shyness. He had worked at the checkpoint for three years and still had not made friends with any of the other guards or the old bookkeeper. They were all friendly towards the quiet Brahmin, though they scarcely noticed him. And he paid little attention to them, and none to the peon or sweeper.

It was their mid-morning tea break, a time period with no fixed duration. The guards kept an eye on the road, and now and then someone would have to stroll out to check a bullock cart. Empty carts were let through without delay, but if one were loaded with teak logs or sacks of charcoal, the driver was told that he'd have to wait. Usually, the man joined them on the benches around the back of the makeshift wooden structure that functioned as the office.

The guards were nursing their cup of tea while also drawing on beedis. The peon and the sweeper crouched on the ground and sipped their tea from shallow terracotta bowls, which would be thrown away afterwards. The surly accountant had perched himself on the only chair and was preparing a wadge of betel nut. Having chosen the best leaf from a slender tin box, he smoothed it out on his thigh with the heel of his hand and spread a layer of lime paste that he had dug out with his fingernail from the same box. Using a special knife, he cut shavings from an areca nut, making sure they fell onto the leaf. Then he folded the leaf and placed it in a corner of his mouth, where it would remain until lunch.

All of them were focused on Vanchi, sitting at the end of a bench, his empty hands folded in his lap. His legs barely touched the ground, so he pulled them up underneath and sat cross-legged. They wanted to know about the rally in Tuticorin that had led to the riots there.

'How many people?'

'What about the police? Were they all Indians? Or English, too?'

Little by little, they pulled out the details from him, some of which Vanchi only half-remembered. Whenever he felt at a loss, he reverted back to the steamer in the harbour, the swadeshi steamer, with its black smokestack and layered decks.

His audience also wanted to hear about Chidambaram Pillai, whose name was now on everyone's lips. Borrowing phrases from the newspapers, Vanchi told them he was a 'great patriot' and the 'victim of injustice'.

'But what does he look like?' asked the old bookkeeper.

No one there had ever seen the man in person, and photographs in newspapers were worse than smudged.

'He wears a dark turban, with thick folds,' Vanchi said after thinking for a moment. 'There's a little moustache. And his eyes are black.'

'Like a maharaja,' one of the guards suggested.

'Yes, like that,' Vanchi said. 'And when he speaks, it's like a tiger roaring in the forest.'

At home, Vanchi faced a different set of questions. His daughter had recovered from her diarrhoea, but Ponammal was furious that he had gone to Tuticorin at a critical time. Fortunately, his father had been away auditing the financial accounts of another temple, but both his mother and grandfather were angry with him for lying about his trip and getting involved in things 'over there'.

'Let the people in Tinnevelly deal with the British,' his grandfather advised him. 'Let us enjoy a peaceful life here, in Travancore.'

Vanchi nodded but was not convinced. That was the lasting effect of his time in Tuticorin. Things were connected, they did not stop at borders. Not even at the edge of the sea. The ideas that Pillai had spoken about—freedom and self-reliance—were not confined to the workers in a cotton mill. Like the steamers that criss-crossed the ocean, they were part of a larger world, a world he had seen on a map but in which he could not place himself. Until now.

He remembered what Pillai had said about rallies and demonstrations in other cities. In his mind's eye, he traced the new railway line that went west through the mountains and ended up at Quilon on the Arabian Sea. Other lines, he knew, went north to Madras and beyond, to Calcutta and Bombay. That's what Pillai meant when he said that swadeshi was a national movement. Self-rule was not just for the towns of Tinnevelly and Tuticorin. It was for the whole country. And that made him recall what Ramakrishna had said to him years before. Travancore might be a princely state, not ruled directly by the British, but it was still part of the Empire, its maharaja a pensioned-off puppet.

*

The next morning, Vanchi looked down at the *kolam* his mother had drawn with rice powder. It was different to the ones she usually made, more intricate with dozens of small circles and squares. Some circles had a dot in the centre and some were left empty. He got lost when he tried to find the starting point. Again and again, it eluded him.

'Quit day-dreaming,' his mother called, having stuck her head outside to see him lounging on the veranda. 'I know it's your day off, but go out and find Ponammal. I need her in the kitchen.'

His wife was out collecting cow dung, and their daughter, Vanni, was sleeping in a cradle made by tying the ends of a sari to pillars on the veranda.

'All right, all right,' he said, and slid off the veranda of hard-packed earth. 'But first, I'm going to take a bath.'

He smiled, thinking that his mother and Ponammal were on better terms lately. It seemed to have started about the time of Vanni's illness, when he'd gone to the rally in Tuticorin. Although his mother still hoped for a grandson, she was not about to lose a granddaughter through neglect. During his absence, Ponammal told him, his mother had kept a constant vigil over the sick child, pestered his grandfather to collect special leaves from the forest and even begun to sing lullabies to her.

Since his return from Tuticorin, he had heard the two of them, mother-in-law and daughter-in-law, singing softly in the night. One would begin, and the other would join in halfway through a line.

> Vine by vine, my child,
>   the creeper crawls over the hill.
> On the crest of the hill, my child,
>   a tree sparkles with jewels.
> You are the beautiful one,
>   oh, little thing, you'll marry a king.

They sang in low voices, piling up images of abundance, though the slow tone was more mournful than joyous.

'She thinks she's teaching me,' Ponammal whispered to him one night as they lay side by side in the kitchen. 'But it's the other way around.'

'Like a lot of things,' he had said.

'What?'

'Oh, nothing. You wouldn't understand.'

*

He was about to leave for his bath when he realized that something was bothering him. It was Shankara. He hadn't seen him for weeks, not since he had come to Shenkottai and told him about the riots, Ashe's actions and Pillai's imprisonment. When he failed to show up at his parents' home in Tenkasi, they thought he might be staying in Shenkottai. Messages went back and forth between the two houses, but no one had seen him.

Worried, Vanchi had decided to go to Tenkasi himself.

'It was Tuesday, I remember because I went to temple,' Shankara's mother told him. 'A man came and asked for him.'

'What man?' Vanchi asked.

'He didn't say. But he wore a uniform.'

'Police?'

'More like government.'

Vanchi suspected it was CID.

'Anyway, I told him to try you in Shenkottai. And I mentioned it to Shankara when he came back that evening. Next morning, he was gone and hasn't been back since.'

'Don't worry,' Vanchi said with feigned confidence. 'He's probably gone to Tinnevelly. You know we have friends there.'

The ordinary police are bad enough, Vanchi said to himself as he walked back home. But the CID will go anywhere, cross the border into Travancore and chase him. Madasami had already been caught, and Shankara could be next. Of course, he and Shankara hadn't been involved in the riots, hadn't even been in Tuticorin that day, but people were being arrested for 'aiding and abetting'. Someone might have told the police that Shankara and Madasami were friends. Maybe someone in the Tenkasi library had noticed Shankara's keen interest in 'seditious' publications and reported him. People certainly knew that Shankara often came to see his brother-in-law in Shenkottai. Vanchi had tried to reassure himself that he was safe.

*

Still mulling over these thoughts, he went out for his late bath. At the end of the Brahmin street, he turned right and right again onto the main road, which he followed straight through Shenkottai and headed towards the mountains. The paddy fields on both sides of the road had been ploughed and manured, in preparation for the coming rains.

He cut through the fields and found the footpath that took him into the forest. Passing the banyan tree, he reached the bathing pool but didn't stop as he had intended. Instead, he continued down the path until he faced the carved stone half-hidden in the undergrowth. Who was he really, that man with the sword? And who was the man he had killed? Thatha had not told him everything he wanted to know.

Back at the bathing pool, he was alone, as usual. Only Brahmins could use it, and most of the families in Shenkottai didn't even know where it was. The clear, cool water was shoulder height, just the right depth for Vanchi to immerse himself and scrub the dirt from his body.

Stripping off his clothes, he heard a voice behind him.

'Vanchi, over here.'

Startled, he turned, wearing only his loin-cloth, and saw Shankara, standing behind a leafy mango tree. He dressed quickly and stepped into the undergrowth, where Shankara grasped his hand and led them farther into the forest. Who are we hiding from? Vanchi wondered.

'Where've you been all this time?' Vanchi asked when they had found a place to sit. 'Your mother's worried sick.'

'I've been staying in various places. Making new contacts.'

'Contacts?'

'You don't know this, but I spent a lot of time with Madasami before we went to Tuticorin. Planning rallies and distributing leaflets.'

Vanchi frowned. 'But what are you doing now?'

'After Pillai was arrested, I was contacted by a man called Nilakanta, from Madras. He's organizing groups here, in the southern districts.'

'What happened to Madasami?'

'He escaped from jail and went to Pondicherry. That's where he met Nilakanta and told him about me. The police can't touch him there.'

'And what about you?'

'I'll be fine. They won't look for me in Shenkottai. I'll stay with you for a while, then move to Punalur.'

Vanchi stared at his brother-in-law. He was on the run from the police. And involved in a secret organization.

'Vanchi, I need your help. We need information, from the newspapers, but I can't go to the library in Tenkasi.'

*

The next day Vanchi was on the early shift, so he left the checkpoint at one o'clock in the afternoon. He had to hope that Dr Raghavan would be at home and that he would agree to his request. But what should he say? He hadn't been to his old teacher's house for years.

Rather than walk the six miles, as he usually did, he decided to board a train at Shenkottai station. He would look better, cleaner and less flustered, when he arrived at Raghavan's house, which was only a short distance from Tenkasi station.

He wore his leather shoes and put on an ironed white tunic, brushed his short hair, and told his wife and mother that he had an appointment at the Forest Department regional office in Punalur. They didn't press him for details and wouldn't know that he took a train in the opposite direction. Halfway down the Brahmin street, he realized he had forgotten his old book satchel and went back to fetch it.

He bought a return ticket for Tenkasi and wandered out onto the platform. He was peering down the line, wondering if the train from Quilon would be on time, when the door of the first-class waiting room opened. An Englishman in a Panama hat and crumpled cotton suit gestured towards him.

'Hey!' he boomed. 'I need a porter.'

Vanchi, who understood only the last word, looked down at the platform and didn't move.

'C'mon, hop it! Bags are in here.'

As soon as the man disappeared inside the waiting room, Vanchi slunk away down the platform and out of the station. His body was still trembling when he stopped and sat on a tea stall bench. He kept going over the scene in his mind. He wasn't dressed like a porter or a coolie. But maybe the man couldn't see his leather satchel slung over his shoulder. To be fair, he had been standing with his back to him, alone on the platform, idle and slouching.

Vanchi heard grunting and looked up. A man, wearing only a loin-cloth and a checked towel wrapped around his head, was pushing a cart piled high with bamboo poles. The cut bamboo had been dried in the sun to make it lighter, but the man still struggled, pushing the cart with his arms extended and his body nearly horizontal to the ground. Like an animal, he thought. Exhausted, the man stopped opposite the tea stall and looked at Vanchi for a moment. He had a bright red flower tucked behind his ear and gave Vanchi a toothless smile.

He arrived in Tenkasi by a later train and walked to Dr Raghavan's house. The rusty gates were as creaky as ever, but weeds now covered the usually bare patch that led to the veranda. Everything was strangely silent. No students, no dogs and no crows. The terracotta pots, neatly placed on both sides of each step, held leafless brown stalks. The veranda itself was empty except for a kerosene lantern hanging underneath the eaves.

He wanted to turn around and go back, away from this silly plan, this subterfuge. What did Shankara mean by 'organizing groups'? He was hiding from the police. Might be arrested and thrown in jail. He should just go back home, to his job at the checkpoint. To the forest and the hills.

'Oh, it's you!' Raghavan's voice boomed out from the doorway. 'Come in.'

Inside the dimly lit interior, Vanchi saw the lounge chair that used to be on the veranda. Arranged round it, like a campfire, was everything that his old teacher might need. A table with books, newspapers, an ink bottle and loose sheets of paper. On a shorter, table, he saw a thin glass vial, some brass tumblers and another lantern.

No Mrs Donkey, then, Vanchi thought as he watched his teacher shuffle over to the chair and crank himself down in incremental movements.

'The doctors don't know what it is,' Raghavan said when he'd settled. 'Can't walk very well now. But I can still read, and that's God's blessing.'

'Ah…'

'Now, what about you, my boy? How is your education coming along? Trivandrum, was it?'

'Yes, sir. I received my degree and now I'm in employment.'

'Excellent, excellent. I heard you got married.'

'Yes, sir. And a little daughter, too.'

'Well, well. Let's see, now. You haven't come here to enquire about a difficult verse in the *Kamba Ramayana*, have you?'

'No, sir.' Vanchi had inched forward and stood only a few feet from the reclining figure.

Jerked forward by a hacking cough, Raghavan gripped the broad arms of the lounge chair and grimaced. Then he fell back, heavily.

'Bring me that bottle and a tumbler,' he said. 'Don't worry. It's only a tonic.' After swallowing the medicine, he readjusted his glasses. 'All right, out with it. Why are you here, young man?'

Vanchi left with a satchel crammed full of newspapers. Mostly old issues of *India*, *The Madras Standard* and *The Hindu*, but also one he'd never seen before. *Vande Mataram* was an English-language weekly from Calcutta, printed on light green foolscap. On the train back to Shenkottai, he read several issues, mainly editorials by Aurobindo Ghose, who called for immediate and complete freedom from British rule.

More recent papers reported on a failed assassination attempt. A bomb had been tossed into a carriage in Muzaffarpur, in north India. The target was an English official who had handed out harsh sentences to several Bengali revolutionaries the year before. Unfortunately, the assassins chose the wrong carriage and killed two Englishwomen by mistake. Ghose and several others were arrested on a charge of 'waging war against the King'. The trial, officially called 'Emperor vs Aurobindo Ghose and Others', had just begun.

Vanchi squeezed his eyes looking at a grainy photograph of Ghose, taken on the day of his arrest. Lanky, unkept hair, bushy moustache and scraggly beard, he didn't look anything like Chidambaram Pillai. But his message was the same.

'If it is a crime to desire freedom for my country, then I am guilty,' Ghose had reportedly said at his trial. 'Convict me, chain me, imprison me. You will never make me renounce that goal.' Vanchi also noticed that Ghose spoke of freedom by referring to Hindu tradition, quoting ancient texts and invoking gods and goddesses. Vanchi folded the paper neatly and stored it in his satchel. Shankara and this Nilakanta, whoever he was, would want to read every word.

*

It was the middle of May, the heat was extreme and thick clouds clung to the mountain slopes. The brothers-in-law met at various places, mostly in Shenkottai and Punalur, which was the next station on the rail line west through the mountains. Vanchi provided Shankara with a regular supply of Raghavan's newspapers, as well as messages from his family in Tenkasi. When the family learned that he was safe and well, they didn't enquire further about his whereabouts. Vanchi never mentioned Shankara to anyone at home and invented excuses for their clandestine meetings.

After two months had passed without incident, they relaxed their guard and Shankara came out of hiding. On his way home, he stopped in Shenkottai and visited the house in the Brahmin street.

'You're looking thinner and thinner every time I see you,' Ponammal said to her brother.

Shankara, Vanchi and Thatha were sitting cross-legged on the bare kitchen floor with expectant faces as she laid a banana leaf down in front of each. Vanchi's mother followed behind, scooping a large portion of steamed rice from a brass pot and piling it on the glossy leaf. Ponammal added a thick brinjal curry over the rice and set a papadum on the side. After more rice and curry, the three men were served a tumbler of milky curd. Everything was eaten in near silence.

When the leaves were picked up and thrown outside for the cow, Thatha prepared his special mixture of betel nut for each of them. To the usual ingredients, he added crushed wild cardamom and a local variety of lemongrass. Masticating with pleasure, the men leaned back against the dry mud wall and began to talk. Thatha said that he knew Shankara's father was ill and promised to get a remedy, but it was difficult to climb up into the hills with the monsoon rains. Vanchi spoke with uncharacteristic levity about a recent case of attempted smuggling at the checkpoint. Men had come in the middle of the night, drugged the watchman and slipped through. No one mentioned Shankara's long absence.

'Now listen,' Vanchi's mother said to the two young men when Shankara was about to leave. 'We're planning a trip to Courtallam, when the rains stop. You're both coming, too.'

The new moon in the Tamil month of Adi was celebrated with a festival at the Courtallam Waterfalls, only a few miles distant. It was a time of swelling rivers and flooding fields, when women prayed for a child and for the health of their new-borns. Anyone who bathed under the falls and in the pools forgot the months of scorching sun and cracked earth when many people ate a single meal of cold rice and went to bed hungry.

As the day of their expedition approached, Vanchi's mother and Ponammal prepared vegetable dishes and special pickles. They forced Thatha to surrender eight annas from Vanchi's pay in order to purchase a new sari and glass bangles for Ponammal, as well as a pink dress for little Vanni. Everyone, even the withdrawn Vanchi, was excited when they awoke on the morning of their departure.

The prepared food was packed into a jutka, along with

cooking utensils and pots, a lantern, sleeping mats, a small bag of paddy and a change of clothes for each of them. Vanchi's mother and Thatha squeezed in under the curved hood, leaving just enough space for Ponammal to dangle her legs out the back, while holding her daughter in her lap. Vanchi and Shankara followed on foot, keeping a good distance behind the creaking wheels of the pony cart.

The dirt road led out of Shenkottai, bent south and ran straight towards the mountains. Tall tamarind trees rose up on both sides and touched in the middle, forming a high canopy.

'I met Nilakanta in Punalur a few days ago,' Shankara said as he walked with Vanchi. 'He told me something we won't read in the papers.'

Vanchi waited.

'Chidambaram Pillai's been yoked to an oil press, like a bullock, and made to pull the thing in the sun.'

Vanchi saw it in his head. A man trudging around and around in a circle, pulling a heavy wooden beam connected to a pestle that rotated inside a stone mortar, crushing seeds to make oil.

'That can't be true.'

'But it is. He wrote about it to his wife and she told a reporter.'

'That's cruel.'

'It's inhumane. And they will pay for it.'

The two of them discussed other recent news as they walked. The man who had thrown the bomb into the wrong carriage in Muzaffarpur had been sentenced to death. Aurobindo Ghosh had been held in prison in Calcutta. In Bombay, the arrest and trial of a swadeshi leader had sparked rioting. And the government had introduced more legislation to control the press.

'That's why Nilakanta has come down here, to organize a group,' Shankara said.

'But what does that mean, "a group"?'

'He'll tell us, when we meet him. We have to be patient.'

After passing through the tamarind tree-tunnel, the road wound around a teak plantation, rising all the way towards the mountains. Beyond the teak trees, the dirt road flattened out and zigzagged through paddy fields. The ground had been ploughed once, the seeds sown and the soil turned once again. Now, the muddy earth was being smoothed down by thick wooden planks pulled by bullocks. Water would soon be released from the rivers into the irrigation channels and the planting season would begin.

When the jutka came within sight of the falls, Ponammal, who was facing backwards, could not see the white ribbons streaming down the rock face. But she could hear the roar.

'Listen, my sweet,' she whispered to her child. 'That's the sound of the gods dancing.' She jingled the new bangles on her arms. 'Listen, and they will keep you safe.'

The cart halted near the bathing pools and they all tumbled out. Ponammal looked up at the dark clouds cloaking the mountain tops and counted the waterfalls against the background of green foliage flecked with brown. They were all there, all nine of them, just as Thatha had said. A wide one in the middle and thinner ones on both sides.

'What's keeping them?' Vanchi's mother cried as she peered back down the dirt road. 'We need to set up a fire now, before the good spots are all taken.'

Thatha thought he knew but said nothing as he unloaded the provisions and arranged them on the ground. Ponammal set her daughter down on a mat and played with her.

'Well, I'm not waiting for those boys,' Vanchi's mother announced and began to scout around for a flat patch of land.

She continued to mutter, but no one heard her words. Or Vanni's little cries of delight. No one heard anything except the water thundering down the mountain. Even standing at some distance, Thatha felt the spray.

When Vanchi and Shankara did appear, a few minutes

later, they offered no excuse for their delay and forestalled any questions by going out to collect firewood. By late afternoon, when they had set up their cooking site, the Adi festival was well underway.

The path to the shrine was lit by hundreds of little flames. Two rows of women sat facing one another, each with a small brass lamp and a banana leaf, on which she had arranged several glass bangles and a clay pot of milk. Their soft voices carried in the night air but only as far as the next woman.

Dressed in a new red sari, Ponammal shielded her flame as she waited her turn to approach the temple. She counted the bangles on her leaf. Five red and five green. Odd numbers, just as it should be. Vanni was once again in good health, but Ponammal was still worried. The little child was frail, she coughed a lot and her bowel movements were often loose. She would pray for her, but she also wanted a second child. If she had only Vanni, other women would sneer and call her 'a one-r'. She cupped her hand once more around the flickering flame and nearly burned her fingers.

In the darkness, the lamps formed a bridge of light towards the goddess waiting in her temple, an unremarkable, squat structure with a stunted tower. Behind it, the water roared down from a height of several hundred feet. On the slopes, deer strained to hear the crackle of twigs warning of a predator. An eagle swooped overhead, attracted by the yellow dots dancing in the dark below.

Women had been approaching the temple in small numbers since dusk, and Ponammal's turn came just after midnight. She poured milk over Parvati, wife of Shiva, and placed the bangles at her feet. From the pile of bangles offered by other women, she chose ten, five gold and five green. Hurrying back to show Vanchi, to make him believe that she would have another child, she found him fast asleep, rolled up in a blanket near the dying fire.

*

At sunrise, the family went to bathe, the men to a large pool near the main falls, and the women to a smaller pool a short walk away. A thin towel wrapped around their waist and yesterday's *veshti* in their hands, Vanchi, Shankara and Thatha picked their way barefoot over the sharp-edged rocks. The spray-drenched path was dangerous in the poor light, and Thatha fell but escaped with a scraped palm.

'No change, then,' Shankara said as they reached the bathing spot and noticed only other Brahmins. It seemed that the recent government order had been ignored.

'It's still early,' Vanchi said, as he slipped off his towel and lowered himself into the pool. After Shankara helped Thatha enter the cool water, the three of them shared a bar of soap to wash themselves and their clothes. Climbing out, they wrapped their towels around their waist again and laid out their clothes to dry in the strengthening sunlight.

'Now, for the falls,' Shankara said.

'You go on. I'll stay and look after our things,' Thatha said and sat down on a flat rock.

The two young men made their way to the main falls, over the slippery rocks and through the shallow pools. Even on the path, the boulders were bunched so close together that it was difficult to put a foot down. The final approach was a steep but mostly dry path, which led up to a narrow rock ledge under the falls.

Vanchi and Shankara climbed up and stood with their backs against the rock face, as the water streamed down in front of them. This was the most popular place in all the nine waterfalls, crowded with men and boys, all castes and all ages, half-delighted and half-terrified by the curtain of water only a foot away. Ignoring the posted warnings in both Tamil and English, some bathers stood directly under the powerful downpour, and every year a few slipped, fell onto the rocks below and sustained serious injuries or died.

Vanchi stood stock still. Bodies jostled on both sides, edged past him and stepped on his toes. He steadied himself with a hand pressed to the overhang and pushed his back hard against the rough rock wall. He couldn't see out beyond the roaring water. The sound was deafening, and he closed his eyes.

Shankara looked for Vanchi among those huddling under the overhang. They had become separated, and it was difficult to identify anyone who wasn't standing next to you. Shankara called out loudly, but his words were lost amid the shouting and the drumming cascade. He inched his way along the ledge until he reached the end and stepped free of the waterfall.

'Vanchi!' he cried again and again, spinning around in all directions.

He forced himself to look below, at the jagged rocks in the rapids. Huge boulders blocked his sight, and the undergrowth was thick enough to conceal a body. He scrambled down the ravine, found a spot to stand in and pivoted from left to right.

'There you are, you idiot!' he cried.

Crouched down behind two boulders, Vanchi was blue-lipped and shivering with cold. Shankara whipped off his towel, wrapped it around Vanchi's bony shoulders and began to rub his back.

'What happened?' he asked.

'I got cold and left. That's all.'

He had been watching the water froth in the deep pools, the water that flowed into the streams that fed the rivers that ran all the way to the Bay of Bengal. From the mountains to the sea. A beginning, but no real ending, not even at the horizon. It should have an end, he thought.

*

Having put on their other set of clothes, and saying nothing to Thatha, Shankara and Vanchi returned to the fire site. Vanchi's mother and Ponammal were squatting down close to the flames and stirring pots while, at the same time, flicking out their hair in an attempt to dry it. Little Vanni, also washed and dressed in her new frock, was skipping around and falling down.

Vanchi looked at his daughter. Had he ever been that happy as a child? Not when his father was in the house. He remembered his mother crying a lot and wondered if that was why she didn't have another child. He knew that Ponammal wanted a second one, but he didn't like the grappling around on the floor. It was undignified. Like animals. It reminded him of the wild dancing he'd seen at the Sudalai Madan temple in Shenkottai. Low-caste men and women flinging themselves around with abandon. People said they were possessed by the god, but it looked more like the devil.

The smell of frying spices drew the men close to the fire. Mustard seeds, curry leaves, cumin, ginger and onions. They rested on their haunches in a tight circle, folding up their damp bodies and relishing the tingle of heat from the blazing fire. Thatha pulled the thin towel around his bare shoulders and spat into the flames.

'A little red chilli wouldn't go amiss, you know,' he said.

'Stick to your potions, you quack, and let us do the cooking,' Vanchi's mother said, and Ponammal let out a loud laugh.

Vanchi and Shankara smiled at each other, while Thatha rubbed his wrists and coughed. They all stared at the shallow brass pot sizzling away in front of them. Vanchi's mother nodded to Ponammal, who dropped in several handfuls of lentils and fried them with the spices. Shielding her face from the spitting flames, Vanchi's mother added cooked rice and stirred everything with a long wooden spoon. That was the signal for the men to move back and sit cross-legged. Ponammal laid down the banana leaves, and Vanchi's mother filled them with the fragrant mixture of rice and lentils.

Bending over, Thatha guided a warm handful into his mouth and chewed noisily. Reaching out for another portion, his hand stopped in mid-air.

'Look!' he spluttered and pointed.

Vanni had wandered off and was heading towards a deep bathing pool. Leaping up, Ponammal scrambled over the rocks to her.

'You were supposed to watch her,' Vanchi's mother screamed at him. 'We can't cook and look after her at the same time. Sometimes I wonder if you…'

Vanchi and Shankara watched wide-mouthed as Ponammal scooped up the child at the edge of the pool. When she came back, the little girl was gurgling with joy at being carried by her mother. Ponammal put her on the mat and held her hands, letting her do a little dance. No one said anything until Vanchi's mother issued an order.

'Sit down, your food is getting cold.'

She gave them all a second helping and carried a leaf over to Ponammal, too. They ate but without enjoyment. She was about to sit down and eat herself when she noticed a group of people coming towards them.

'Vanga, vanga,' she shouted. Come, come.

'I thought it was you,' said an older man as he got closer. 'You said you'd be here again this year. And so are we.'

'Come and eat. We have plenty.' She had never liked her uncle, but his arrival had relieved the tension.

Vanchi had just finished washing his hands when he saw them, a set of relatives who lived in a small market town not far from Shenkottai. The head of the family was some kind of uncle, he wasn't sure, but he knew they were richer than his family. They owned land, acres of sugarcane and paddy.

His mother and Ponammal, assisted by two daughters-in-law, worked up another batch of upma, while a teenage girl looked after Vanni, and the older children splashed around in the pools. Thatha talked weather and medicine with the uncle, while Shankara entertained two male cousins by describing what he and Vanchi had witnessed at the rally in Tuticorin earlier that year.

'Isn't that so?' Shankara said and looked at Vanchi.

Staring over their heads at the waterfalls, Vanchi didn't respond. Shankara repeated his question, a little louder this time, and Vanchi lowered his eyes, tilted his head and muttered something.

'What's that?' one of the cousins asked.

'Yes,' Vanchi said more clearly. 'I saw what he saw. The same thing. Exactly the same.'

Shankara resumed his story, and two minutes later Vanchi wandered off, saying he needed to urinate. He returned an hour later, with no explanation.

It was late afternoon when they returned to Shenkottai. Everyone was exhausted but also exhilarated, spilling over with stories about the festival, the lights and the bathing. When they retold those stories to their neighbours that evening, the crowd became bigger, the lights brighter and the falls higher. Vanchi sat with them on the veranda, half-listening, the water still roaring in his head.

*

After his early-morning shift the following day, Vanchi came home and heard voices in the house.

'Where is she?' Ponammal screamed at her mother-in-law.

'I don't know,' Vanchi's mother yelled back. 'She was on the veranda when I went to grind spices.'

'Well, she's not there now, is she?'

'Don't talk like that to me, you little fool!'

Vanni had been missing since mid-morning. She was last seen when Ponammal went for her bath and Vanchi's mother was in the kitchen. That was five hours ago. Since then, the two women had looked everywhere, they told Vanchi, but couldn't find her. Thatha had not yet returned from the hills.

It wasn't the first time the three-year-old had disappeared. She liked to explore places on her own, going into neighbours' houses, wandering down the street towards the temple and even ending up in the fields. She was often gone for an hour or more but was easily found because she didn't hide. Ponammal would form a search party of one and discover her playing on her own, happy to see her mother come after her.

Once or twice, she'd been brought back home by an

older child or an adult in the Brahmin street. Ponammal and Vanchi's mother had scolded her, and Thatha had told her frightening stories of lost girls, but nothing seemed to put her off. Vanchi hadn't been much worried, largely because he had not been home during any of her disappearances and merely heard about them later.

This time was different, though. Ponammal and his mother couldn't sit still.

'We've looked everywhere,' his mother said to him. 'Can't find her anywhere!'

'Three times I've gone up and down the street,' Ponammal said, wiping the sweat from her face with the border of her sari. 'What else can we do?'

She looked at her husband for an answer. If only Thatha were here, Vanchi thought.

'All right, let's look again,' his mother said to break the silence. 'This time, I'll go up to the top of the street. Ponammal, you go down to the temple. And son, you check with the neighbours.'

Vanchi went from house to house and asked if anyone had seen Vanni. But he thought he knew the answer. His mind kept returning to the deep well behind the temple at the far end of the street. She would be lying there, under the water, at the bottom. She would have climbed up on the stone wall, looked down, seen something and leaned in to get it.

'Come in, have something to eat,' his neighbour Ramamurthy urged.

'No, I can't.'

'She's probably fine. You'll find her.'

'We've looked everywhere.'

'What about the cowsheds?'

Yes, that's it, Vanchi said to himself. She's curled up in there and gone to sleep. He hurried out around the back of Ramamurthy's house and ducked under the low-thatched roof of the shed. A placid cow stared at him as he scrambled around, digging through the thickly piled straw. He threw fistfuls of it in the air, kicked at it and fell down. Closing his eyes, he again saw his daughter at the bottom of the well.

When he got up and walked back to the house, it was dusk. His mother was bustling around in the kitchen, jumping from one thing to another, without finishing anything. Thatha had returned and was trying to calm Ponammal in the front room. When he heard Vanchi on the veranda, he came out and shook his head.

They ate in silence by the light of a kerosene lamp. Everything was exaggerated. The smell of the cow dung used to clean the earth floor, the sound of lips sucking rice from fingers and the dogs barking in the street.

'We'll look again after we eat,' Thatha suggested.

The women agreed, but Vanchi continued to eat in silence. He knew he would never see her again.

'Never!' he screamed in a voice that startled them all. 'That's it,' he said. 'She's gone. Dead. I'm not looking anymore. It's useless.'

'Vanchi, we have to.'

'No. It's over,' he said and stood up. 'There's no point.'

Grabbing a light shawl to throw around his shoulders, he fled. No more pain, he thought, as he skulked away in the cool night air. It's better this way. Accept that she's gone and won't come back. Better that than hoping without knowing. Better to draw a line and leave it all behind. Better than open-ended, ongoing agony.

He went beyond the Brahmin street, to the main road, through the market area and towards the mountains. Once in the forest, his breathing slowed. Damp, green and dark, there was no pain there. No expectations and no demands. He went as far as the banyan tree, slipped between the aerial roots and lay down on the soft earth. What could he do? He had no purpose, no direction. A forest guard, a man who saw but did not act. A husband in name only. A father who lost his only child.

He crept back at midnight, stiff and cold. As he lay down beside Ponammal in the kitchen, he listened. Her breathing was uneven, her body spent, with no more tears to give. He couldn't sleep and the night sounds grew louder. Her soft panting, his grandfather's cough, his mother snoring.

Then the cry of a jackal. Not far away, and it sounded different. A lonely howl, as if the animal were speaking to someone. He heard it again, louder and closer.

Vanchi slipped out of the house and down the street, pausing every few steps to identify the direction of the sound. He followed it beyond the temple and onto a footpath that skirted a paddy field. There it was beneath a tree, nose pointed up and ears pinned back along the sides of its sleek face. He heard another sound, a whimpering. It came from the tree with its low branches.

'*Appa*! *Appa*!' Father! Father!

He scaled the tree and found his daughter, squeezed into a ball amid the dense foliage. Cradling her in his arms, he ran back home, shouting, 'Got her! Got her!'

He and Ponammal slept that night with their daughter wedged between them on the mat. Ponammal slid off into sleep, while he kept opening his eyes and looking at the curve of his daughter's face. She will marry, he thought, and I'll become a grandfather.

He sat up, lifted the sacred thread from his shoulder and slid it back and forth. Fingering the separate strands, he remembered the little boy who had sat cross-legged on a raised wooden board, his shaven head smeared with turmeric paste. A white cloth was wrapped around his thin waist, looped over his neck and tucked back in at the waist. Facing him, two priests chanted and rang handbells while offering plates of fruits and flowers to a fire burning inside a small brass vessel. As the chanting and ringing grew louder, one of the priests placed a cotton thread over the boy's shoulder and under his arm. Leaning in close, he whispered, 'The three strands represent three obligations. To honour your teachers, your parents and the ancient sages.'

Now, with Ponammal beside him, he counted the strands, one by one. As a husband and father, there were six.

9

Palayamkottai, 1910

The hot season was advancing again. The Tambraparni river, which only three months earlier had been gushing beneath the great bridge beside the railway station, was sluggish. Rocky islands had appeared in the wide riverbed, providing convenient places for the dhobis to dry the piles of washed clothes. So popular was this spot that the neighbourhood on the Palayamkottai side of the river was known as 'Washerman Town'. By late morning on any single day, white stripes and coloured rectangles covered the newly emerged islands, forming a cotton archipelago that stretched from one bank to the other. At dusk, the stiff *veshtis*, tunics and saris would be peeled off the rocks, rolled into bundles and carried on a man's head or a donkey's back.

Robert Ashe paused on the bridge during his late-afternoon walk home from the office. It was out of his way, but he liked to watch the riverbed lose its colours as the clothes were stripped from the rocks. That end-of-the-day task was soothing, the silent movement of the men, the rolled-up bundles and the biblical donkeys. Everything warm and complete, like the setting sun.

He was happy to be back in Tinnevelly District, especially now as collector. The incumbent had been sent back home on sick leave, so, strictly speaking, he was only acting collector, though that distinction didn't seem to be observed by his staff or the local population.

After those 'difficult times' in Tuticorin two years ago, he had been sent to another part of Madras Presidency, an even more isolated district in a Telugu-speaking region. 'Nothing personal, old man,' they'd assured him. 'Just part of the rotation system.' That's how he'd explained it to Mary, and there was some logic to it, he did agree. You don't want to become too involved with the powerful landlords and rich merchants in your district. Those kinds of alliances can evolve into a personal fiefdom, with bribes and unofficial favours. That was the lesson learned from the East India Company's rule in Bengal in the past century. And, after all, Ashe told himself, British India should be a model of good government, not a collection of corrupt rajas.

Having returned to the deep south, he was determined to set his own record straight. He might have acted a little too hastily when dealing with Chidambaram Pillai, he could admit that, but the man was now behind bars. And with any luck, he'd never hear his name again. Having put that unfortunate business behind him, he was excited to start again. He had plans to improve the port at Tuticorin, to dreg the harbour and extend the pier. Also to build new schools and to extend the system of irrigation channels across the entire district. Yes, he was hoping to make a name for himself, something that would lead to a promotion in Madras. Mary would like that. It could take a year or two, he reckoned, but it was a definite possibility. He just had to play it right.

*

'It's good to be back in the south,' Mary had said, as the whole family travelled down from Madras a few weeks earlier.

He had agreed. It all seemed familiar. He didn't know the language spoken in any the places where he'd been posted during the past fifteen years, but the rapid clickety-clack of Tamil was at least recognisable. 'Did you know the trains here actually speak Tamil?' That was his little joke.

Mary smiled but didn't laugh. During their earlier stay in Tuticorin, she had put in an effort to acquire a basic facility with the language. For two hours, three times a week, she had endured Mrs Solomon's pedagogical regime. 'We begin with the script,' the Tamil lady had declared at their first lesson. 'The script is the backbone of the language; without it, you cannot move.' Mary never worked out that anatomical analogy, but she knuckled down and mastered all 247 letters.

'Now, we move to literature,' Mrs Solomon intoned and went straight to the Tamil translation of the New Testament, written with eight-syllable words and vertiginous clauses. 'You must learn pure Tamil,' her teacher insisted. 'Not the vulgar talk in the marketplace.' Which was, of course, exactly what Mary wanted and needed.

Mrs Solomon did eventually compromise and agree to teach her from a book of folk tales rewritten by a Christian missionary. Mary might have recognized a few of Aesop's fables if her teacher hadn't spent so much time trying to explain the difference between the inclusive and exclusive first-person plural pronoun. Not to be deflected from her goal, though, Mary practised her child-like Tamil with the servants, especially the cook. Although the eggs she ordered sometimes became coconuts, and eight annas turned into ten, the mother of invention prevailed in the end. By the time they had left Tuticorin two years ago, Mary was ordering complex meals and issuing instructions to the gardener.

So, it was with some excitement that Mary looked forward to their return to the district. On the long rail journey, she tried out her dormant Tamil on stationmasters, who smiled, embarrassed that they hadn't understood this foreign woman's English, and murmured, 'Yes, madam.'

Frustrated but undeterred, Mary decided she would work harder when they settled into their new bungalow in Palayamkottai. A collector's bungalow, she said to herself, with a proper sitting room, hot water and a large garden. She was also looking forward to meeting new people at the English church.

Even the children were excited. They knew that Tinnevelly was closer to Kodaikanal, where the two oldest went to school and where the other two were taken during the summer. They couldn't get enough of 'Kodai', as they called it, with its lake, cool air and pine forests. Mary was convinced that the months spent in the mountains accounted for her children's continuing good health. Her fears that one of them would contract a fatal disease had nearly kept her in Dublin. But during the two years since their return to India, and despite the outbreak of cholera all around them, the children remained unscathed. Molly kept her pink cheeks, Arthur seemed to grow an inch every month, Sheila played happily with her dolls and little Herbert laughed more than ever.

'What about Das?' Arthur had asked his father on the train. 'Will he be there?'

At the sound of his name, the other children had begun to chant, 'Das, Das, candy floss, what became of your underpants?'

Yes, Mary had thought as she shushed them, India is home.

*

When Robert Ashe left the bridge at sunset and headed towards his bungalow, deep lines creased his face. Try as he would to concentrate on his new plans, he could not forget the warning that lodged in a corner of his mind. Within days of his arrival, the superintendent of police had advised him not to walk around on his own. A district collector had recently been shot dead in western India, and Tinnevelly District, he was told, was still simmering with nationalist activity. Ashe knew only too well the depth of anti-British sentiment in the area, but he remained convinced that such attitudes were not widespread. The Indians he knew were all good people, who might criticize some government policy but never expressed hostility to the idea of British rule. As he kept pointing out to Mary, who had her doubts, 'This country will never have a revolution. Look at the countryside, where ninety per cent of the population live. They don't give a fig about politics. What they care about is food, family and God. In that order.'

Nevertheless, he could not dismiss what Superintendent Hartley had shown him. A recent CID report from Madras had identified the hotspots of revolutionary activity across the whole country, and Tinnevelly District was top of the list. Heeding his advice, Ashe had agreed to be taken to and from the office in a carriage driven by a man recommended by Hartley himself. His only caveat was that he would observe this restriction for five of the six working days each week. On his 'free' day, he would walk the two miles to the office, and the two miles home, on foot and alone. Although frustrated, Hartley had relented. He could hardly order the collector to follow his advice, but he did recommend that he vary his route. That made sense, Ashe admitted to himself. However, there were only so many routes one could take and only so many days in the week. Before long, he had fallen into the habit of Friday and stuck to a single route.

Having left the bridge that afternoon, he followed the main road to Palayamkottai and walked through the busy main market. It was the most direct route, and a crowded one, which enabled Ashe to satisfy himself that he did 'move among the people'. It also allowed the man who followed him to avoid detection.

Towards the end of the line of shops, Ashe turned down a side road that led to the old fort. That was another reason he walked that way. The fort had been partially destroyed when the British conquered the area in the mid-eighteenth century, though it later housed a military barracks and a prison. Further damage was done throughout the nineteenth century when many of its massive blocks had been hauled away to become pillars for the bridge across the river and foundation stones for the public library. It had also been weakened by the sun, the rain and the vegetation growing in cracks. Still, much of the three-hundred-year-old fort remained. As Ashe walked beneath those high, crumbling walls, he wondered about his predecessors, whose names he did not know.

After passing the fort, he came out on a tree-lined road and entered the European quarter with its detached bungalows and white-washed church. Christ Church, built in the 1850s in order to serve the expanding number of local converts, was the church that Mary had chosen for them. Robert liked the idea because its square Saxon tower was a landmark for him on his walk home.

The heat refused to retreat that Friday evening, and he was relieved when he stepped into the comparative cool of his bungalow. A deep portico with round wooden pillars ran across the front of the single-storey building. Inside, a high peaked ceiling, two punkhas and green blinds helped to reduce the temperature. By at least four degrees, he had been informed by his daughter Molly, who had conducted her own experiments.

As soon as he crossed the threshold and sank into a white wicker chair, Mary pecked him on his clean-shaven cheek.

'Tea?'

'Umm.'

Mary returned with a tea tray, placed it on the sideboard and poured. That was one thing that India had over Ireland, Robert reflected. Best tea in the world. They had learned early on in their India experience that nothing cooled the body in hot weather like a steaming cup of tea.

'Tough day?'

'No, not so bad. Das's mother is worse and he's asking for more leave, which I can't afford.'

'Why's that?'

'I already told you.'

Mary winced and he softened his tone.

'Remember? I've got to look into that cattle raid. Last week, a gang of Maravars tore through some village—forget the name—and made off with more than fifty cattle. Everyone lost livestock. Everyone who's not a Maravar, that is.'

'But Das isn't police, is he?'

'No, no. I need Das to take me there, translate and help write the report. And we're behind on the palmyra census.'

'Palmyra census?'

'Hard to believe, but it's true. Every three years, we count the toddy palms. Every bloody tree across the whole district, from Tenkasi to Tuticorin. Part of the land tax, so we've got to get it right.'

Mary was always taken back by the scope of her husband's job. As district collector, he was responsible for virtually every aspect of the lives of almost two million people. Revenue and roads, education and irrigation, public health and public safety—it all fell on his shoulders. He also acted as magistrate and judge in civil and criminal courts. From ten in the morning until six in the evening, six days a week, he signed letters, wrote reports, issued licences, received rupees, fined vagrants and investigated crimes. All that with a clerical staff of three—the dependable Das and two assistants, plus two peons and a sweeper. His house staff, especially the bearer, helped if necessary.

'I see, so the trees will have to wait,' Mary said with a tiny smile. 'By the way, what did you think of the bishop's sermon yesterday?'

She had persuaded Robert to attend Ascension Thursday, which had been celebrated by a man visiting from Madras.

'Good speaker. I liked the way he compared sati to legalized murder. But he lost me in that digression about which Tamil word best translates "god". Your Mrs Solomon might have an opinion, though.'

'No doubt,' Mary said, 'but the main thing is that we all worship Him in our own way. I'm sure Das sees the same divine presence that we do.'

'I'm not sure what Das sees sometimes,' Robert said under his breath. 'By the way, where are the servants?'

'Oh, I gave them the day off. A holiday.'

'Good idea,' Robert said. 'Sheila and Herbert?'

'Already asleep.'

He enjoyed their rare private hours almost as much as Mary did. The punkha man pulling the rope was invisible to them both.

'But cook made us something before he left this morning,' she said and stood up. 'Back in a few minutes.'

Robert looked at the pewter teapot on the sideboard. Its high-angled handle was nicely balanced by the curved spout on the other side. It was Mary's prized possession, given to her as a belated wedding present by her ailing mother, after she and Robert had gone back to Dublin on the long furlough. Mary wouldn't hear of parting from it when they made ready to return to India. 'If Mary goes back,' her younger sister had proclaimed, 'the teapot goes with her.' Wrapped in muslin and laid inside a custom-made wooden box, it had accompanied them on the long journey back.

He looked at it now and saw his reflection in the gleaming grey surface. He might have been six or seven years old. His parents had taken him on holiday in County Wicklow, where they always stayed for a week in August, in a country manor house converted into a hotel. It was a hot afternoon. His parents dozed in the library with the other guests. A sturdy wooden table in front of him held the remains of a high tea, which had followed lunch. Robert stood at eye level with the table and made faces that became distorted when reflected in the polished teapot. He felt embarrassed and stopped, but no one noticed. Restless, he went to a tall window and looked out at the closely cropped grass. He knew that the lawn continued down to a silent river, but he had been told not to go out by himself and his parents were still half-asleep. Sweeping his gaze to the far left, he saw figures on the lawn. Two men in boaters and two women in wide-brimmed hats were bending down and swinging mallets against a little ball. He could tell that they were laughing by the way their heads moved.

'C'mon, Robert. It'll get cold.'

Mary's voice was firm but kind, like his mother's.

'Sorry. Right,' he said and joined her at the dining table.

Over the potato cutlets and fish curry, their talk turned to the two children in Kodaikanal and their annual visit, only a few weeks away.

'You know, we'll need a larger place this year,' Mary said. 'We can't keep cramming them all into one bedroom.'

'Why's that?'

'Well, for one thing, Molly needs her privacy. She's nearly a young lady, you know.'

'Hmm.'

'Hmm nothing. There's a fairly large cottage near the lake. Mrs Wilkinson told me about it. You walk out the door and the lawn leads right down to the water.'

'How much is it?' Robert asked between spoonfuls of curry.

'Not sure. It's only for six weeks, though.'

Over coffee, Mary did the calculations, while Robert puffed on his pipe and mulled over his task for the morning. He hated having to deal with the wretched Maravars, who had recently appeared on the official list as a 'criminal caste'. They were a tough bunch and had formed the core of the local forces that had fought the British in the eighteenth century. When not soldiering, Maravars had exerted control as village watchmen and offered protection from thieves, often their own kin, for a price. They had even developed their own legal system, written laws and set up courts, in which sentencing was harsh and swift, especially for non-payment of protection fees. All that had been swept away after the colonial constabulary was introduced in the 1850s. Now, as gamekeeper turned poacher, they roamed the district, experts in blackmail and theft. Gold and jewellery were the preferred prizes, but cattle were their speciality.

*

In the morning, when Ashe was preparing to leave the office, Das knocked and put his head inside the doorway.

'There's a Mr Walker to see you, sir.

'Damnation. There's no time.'

'He says it's important.'

'Of course. It always is. Right, tell him to come in.'

Ashe tidied his desk and pulled back the corners of his mouth.

The young man who strode through the door was tall and, when he took off his straw hat, displayed a head of thick golden hair. His smooth face was flush from the heat and his linen suit stained with sweat.

'The name's Walker,' he said in an accent that Ashe took to be from Yorkshire. Without waiting for an invitation, he sat in the chair facing the collector. 'I represent Mr Collingwood of South India Cement. Head office in Madras.'

'And your business here in Tinnevelly, Mr Walker?'

'We are interested in building a new cement factory, in the harbour area in Tuticorin. You see…'

Ashe relaxed a little. Cement was produced only in small amounts in a factory owned by the company his visitor had just named, and he was keen to expand the port facilities at Tuticorin. And that meant cement.

'…so, we are looking for a good location.'

'Fine, fine. I can certainly provide you with a letter of introduction to my colleague in Tuticorin, who would be only too happy to show you around.'

'That would be most kind, Mr Ashe. Most kind.'

Minutes later, the collector was bumping along in a jutka, accompanied by Das and a policeman. His eyes were narrowed and his jaw set hard. Something didn't seem quite right about Mr Walker, but he dismissed that thought and tried to concentrate on the task ahead. Although the village where the cattle theft had occurred was only twenty miles away, first they had to pick up a local official, the tahsildar, in a nearby market town.

'He knows the village,' Das had said. 'They might talk to us more openly if he's there.'

When Das escorted Ashe into the tahsildar's office, the young man bowed while extending his hand. Ashe shook it and turned on his heel, but his host had arranged for tea. Pushed to the limits of his patience, Ashe accepted the tepid brown liquid but not the stale biscuits. Having gulped down the tea, he got up and insisted on leaving.

'Yes, yes,' the tahsildar said, 'but I also have something to show you.'

'And what might that be?' Ashe asked curtly.

'Yesterday I received this from the Maravar leader,' the local man said and handed Ashe a palm-leaf manuscript.

About a foot and a half long and two inches wide, the smooth leaves were held together by a string inserted through a hole in the upper left-hand corner. Both sides of the leaves were inscribed in a tiny script.

Ashe passed the manuscript to Das, who said he couldn't read it and handed it back to the tahsildar.

'I'm not surprised,' the man said. 'They use special writing on palm leaves, a sort of shorthand. You see, this letter "a", for example—'

'Right,' interrupted Ashe. 'Summarize it while we ride to the village.'

The first section of the document, the tahsildar explained, provided the history of the local Maravars, including their hereditary rights over a large village and its outlying settlements. It dated back to the time of the East India Company in the mid-eighteenth century, when a 'Jackson Sahib' had granted the Maravars rent-free land in return for keeping the peace in the countryside. They did their job and received their fees, typically a share of the harvest, from the villages they protected. For the past two years, though, they had not received payment. And now they demanded that the village headman send them forty silver coins, twenty sheep and ten cattle to defray the cost of their annual temple festival.

'And when their demand wasn't met, they stole the cattle,' the tahsildar said at the end of his story.

They reached the village at mid-day. Warned in advance of the collector's visit, the headman, who was not a Maravar, had organized a clean-up campaign, making sure that the houses on the dirt track from the main road were white-washed and newly thatched.

'Looks prosperous enough,' Ashe offered as the pony cart took them into the village centre.

A large table and three wooden chairs taken from the local school had been placed under a tamarind tree. By the time Ashe took his seat, with Das to his right and the tahsildar to his left, two or three dozen men had gathered, some of them sitting on wooden benches commandeered from a tea stall. The constable stood well behind the table but made a prominent display of his thick cane stick. 'Just in case,' Das had said.

Ashe tried to look interested as the villagers stood before him and made their statements, which Das worked hard to capture on paper.

It emerged that the refusal to pay the protection fees was the result of a vendetta that had begun months back when the Maravar leader's younger brother had 'mistreated' the wife of a farmer. Witnesses gave animated descriptions, enhanced by gestures and re-enactments, of the arguments and insults that had led to a series of revenge attacks. Huts had been burned, a well poisoned and a young man beaten within an inch of his life.

'Have they attempted to retrieve the stolen livestock?' Ashe asked after an hour of testimonies.

'Not possible,' replied Das, after asking the question and hearing from several men all at once. 'They would have been taken over the border and sold in Travancore, for a high price.'

'And the thieves themselves?'

'No longer in the village. But probably not far away, causing more trouble.'

'Right. That's all,' Ashe said and closed the file folder in front of him. 'I think I've heard enough.'

But the villagers were not finished. When would the new road be built? Last week a child had died because it took her parents two hours to reach the hospital in Palayamkottai. The school building was falling down, the masonry in the irrigation channel had cracks and Untouchables were using the upper-caste graveyard for their burials.

It was late afternoon when Ashe set off on the return to Tinnevelly. He wanted to ask Das for clarification on one or two details of the Maravar protection system, but he was exhausted. The carriage jolted him from side to side, and the heat was heavy. Wiping a layer of dirt from his chin with a knuckle, he moistened his cracked lips and slumped back against the wooden seat. The landscape that moved past him was scrubland, scraped dry and waiting for the seasonal rains. And my new irrigation canals, he said to himself.

Only the toddy-tappers offered diversion for his eye. They shimmied up the tall palmyra trees using a piece of rope looped around their waist and the tree. Leaning back so that rope took all their weight, they gripped the trunk with their hands and pulled up their feet, in a little jump. Then, shifting the weight back onto their feet, they flung the rope further up the tree, leaned back again, gripped the trunk and slid up higher.

Ashe watched the near-naked men scale the trees like insects. Sticklebacks, he thought. No, more like inchworms. He even counted the number of times they repeated their crouch-and-jump move. Eight, nine and sometimes ten throws of the rope took them from the ground to the thick fronds near the top. Once there, they leaned back against the rope, sliced the young flowers and hung small clay pots to collect the juice. Later, they would climb again and pour the juice from the pots into a gourd attached to their belt.

Although a teetotaller, Ashe had sipped the juice once or twice, when his mouth was as dry as sand. Can't really refuse, he'd told himself, it would insult my hosts and I need them onside. It was cool but had a sour taste. He tried to pass off his puckered lips as a smile and did manage to say something in Tamil that sounded like 'good'.

He was still observing the climbing men and wondering why the juice was called 'toddy' when his dust-caked eyelids shut. A damp, green expanse, dotted with soft knolls and bracken, stretched out in front of him. A stream gurgled beside moss-covered stone cottages. The smell of a household fire hung in the air. The sea could not be far away.

The carriage hit a pothole and jolted him awake, with Das dozing beside him. He looked out and saw again the hard-baked land with its tough fibrous trees. Heat, dirt and disease. People struggling to survive. Children dying of malnutrition. It won't always be like this, he said to himself, rubbing the grit from his eyes. Ten more years and we can go home.

*

At noon the next day, he summoned Das to his office. He had read through his clerk's detailed report, covering five foolscap pages, excluding appendices that listed the victims, their losses and the suspected perpetrators. That had taken him only ten minutes, but he waited for an hour before calling him. In fact, he'd made up his mind on the ride back the day before.

'Excellent report, Das.'

'Thank you, sir.'

'Draw up arrest warrants for all eighteen men. And then I want all the information concerning this protection racket. What's it called again?'

'Kaval, sir. Kaval system.'

'Right. Get me every existing law, regulation, ordinance and court case. I'm going to abolish this protection thing—it's blackmail, for God's sake—and make these payments illegal. It's the only way to rid the countryside of this evil practice.'

'Yes, sir.'

'Any questions?'

'No, sir.'

Das did not move, though it was clear that he had been dismissed.

'What is it?' Ashe asked.

'It's just that I think you'll find, sir, that the information you want is with the governor's office in Madras.'

'I see. I'll write to them and ask for it.'

'Very good, sir.'

Das turned to leave when Ashe cried, 'Wait a minute. Which department is it? The one we…I should write to?'

'Legal, I should think, sir.'

'Yes, of course.'

Left alone, Ashe leaned back in his chair and stared at the files on his desk. He picked up the top one, labelled 'Palmyra Census, Ambasamudram Taluk, 1909/1910'. He looked through the figures, scanning numbers and columns, and making notes in the margins. But his mind kept straying back to the letter he would write to the governor's office. He considered various phrases: 'Uproot the cause of criminality', 'Usher in a new era of modern policing', 'Establish trust between the natives and His Majesty's government'. Placing the palmyra census file to one side, he took up his pen and wrote a draft, requesting the information he needed and setting out his intention to abolish the protection system.

After lunch, which he hardly touched because the curd rice had gone off in the heat, he called his head clerk again.

'Here's the letter, Das. Check it and let me have it back.'

'Yes, sir. Right away.'

'Now, tell me. How is your mother?'

'Not well, sir. The pain in her stomach and back is still strong.'

'Right. Here's what we'll do. You'll take leave, starting tomorrow. No, starting this afternoon. Take her to the hospital in Palayamkottai. You know, the new one, near the market. I'll pay for her treatment. Just bring me the receipt.'

'Thank you, sir.'

That had been Mary's suggestion, for him to pay the hospital costs. He had agreed after reassuring himself that he could claim back the costs under 'medical expenses'.

By tea-time, he had signed the letter, largely rewritten by Das, and pulled the census file to the front of his desk. Tapping his fingers on the damp-stained buff cover, he wondered how the governor's office would regard his proposal. His latest title—'The Abolition of Protection Fees'—looked good on paper. A sight better than 'Uprooting Local Blackmail', which had been his first idea. He needed something to show the higher-ups that he wasn't just holding down the fort in Tinnevelly. Though that's just what they did in 1795, he chuckled to himself. Yes, he needed to impress them with his dedication and competence.

He tore off a piece of scrap paper from the bunch hanging on a string over the edge of his desk. Pushing everything aside, he made the calculations one more time. If he gained two more promotions, his pension in 1920 would be so much. And Mary's aging father would surely leave them something in his will. Molly would be married and Arthur probably in the army, but educating even two children back home in Dublin would be expensive. Perhaps he would need to hang on for an extra five years.

*

Das could hardly wait to tell his wife about the collector's promise. Things had worsened between them after he had taken out a heavy loan to pay for their daughter's marriage. His wife had opposed the idea, but Das had been adamant that the groom was a good catch.

'The boy's uncle is a manager in the Bank of Madras,' he said, more than once. 'It's a good investment.'

Das's judgement of people was not as sharp as his knowledge of administrative procedures. After the marriage was concluded, the bride's family turned their backs on their poor in-laws in Palayamkottai, and the terms of the loan saddled Das with huge debt. The interest payments alone ate up most of his monthly salary. And now there would be the extra medical costs for his mother.

Although Ashe didn't know it, Das came from a family of palmyra tree climbers, the traditional occupation of the Nadar caste. His ancestors were among the many who had converted to Christianity a hundred years ago. That, and their business acumen in the cotton boom, had meant a rise in status, but Das was the only success story in his generation. The only one with an education and a salary, the one they all looked to for help. He couldn't ask them for money.

Thank God for the collector, Das thought as he left the office that afternoon. Mr Ashe might be less than meticulous, but he had a kind heart.

Before going home, Das decided to indulge himself a little and approached the paan-seller. His long-established habit was to buy a packet of betel nut every evening on his way home. He certainly did not want to chew it and spit out the juice during office hours. Let Mr Ashe abolish the kaval system; he would abolish the expectoration of red juice outside public buildings.

The paan-seller did a good business, situated as he was across the street from the collector's office. Dozens of salaried men worked there, and scores more went there on official business. Eager, worried, confused or confident, a large number of them sought the pleasure of chewing betel leaves and areca nut shavings, mixed with sweets, spices and a pinch of tobacco. Adapting to his upmarket customers, the paan-seller did not squat on the pavement in a juice-stained tunic, as others did elsewhere in town. Standing in starched clothes and leather shoes, with stripes of ash prominent across his forehead, he looked more like a law clerk than a street-vendor. And though other handcarts under the wide-branching tree sold everything from tea to sweets, his stood out with its large, green image of Hanuman.

'Early today,' he suggested as he prepared Das's favourite mixture.

'Yes. Special day.'

'Good news, I hope.'

'Yes. I'm…expecting a guest at home.'

'Oh?' The paan-seller often knew more about his customers than their employers did.

'Umm. The wife's older brother, from Madras.'

The paan-seller looked up at Das as he folded the leaf into a neat triangle, tucking one corner under another. That was the first he'd heard of this brother.

'What's he do up there?'

'Do? He's a judge in the High Court.'

'Well, who'd have thought?' he said with a knowing smile. 'Might come in handy one day.'

Das popped the paan in his mouth and turned away without replying. I could have had a brother-in-law as a judge, he thought, if only I'd married someone else. In any case, I should be working in the governor's office in Madras and not in this provincial town. I'm smart enough, just don't have the right connections. And the government always favours Brahmins anyway.

*

Superintendent Hartley arrived for their fortnightly meeting at five o'clock sharp. Not seeing Das, he walked straight past the two assistant clerks, who mumbled 'sir', and rapped on the open door.

'Ah, Hartley. Come in.'

Ashe slipped his retirement calculations under a file and gestured to the chair in front of his desk. He looked forward to these conversations, but he didn't feel quite up to it that day. Then his face brightened. Maybe he could sound him out about the proposal to abolish the protection system? What was it called again? Cavil or kabul or…

'Das on leave?' Hartley said as he sat down heavily. He took off his cap, wiped his brow and fitted the khaki-coloured hat over a knee. As always, his sunburnt face looked strained, as if he were staring into a sandstorm.

'Yes. Gave him some leave. His mother's ill.'

They traded comments about their own families' health, while waiting for a clerk to bring in the tea and leave.

'Close the door, that's a good man,' Hartley said to the retreating figure.

He picked up his chipped cup and took a big gulp.

'How's your staff, old man? Loyal chaps, are they?'

Ashe eyed him along the edge of his own raised cup.

'Yes, I think so. Das is superb. Had him in Tuticorin, a few years back. Been in the service all his life, I believe.'

'Good to hear it. But you can never be too careful, mind.'

Ashe was about to launch into a defence of Das but stopped. What did he really know about the man? Or any of the Indians he worked with?

'And the others?' Hartley continued. 'Two clerks, right?'

'Umm. Run-of-the-mill. Steady workers, don't complain. Why?'

'Nothing specific, but we're picking up more and more reports of anti-government activity in the southern districts. One character, name of Nilakanta, has been giving speeches all over the place. Tanjore, Madurai and now here. He's scheduled to speak in Palayamkottai next week, but I'm minded to ban the meeting. With your permission, of course.'

Ashe nodded with a grimace. Sounds like more Chidambaram Pillai nuisance.

'We don't know much about him, yet. This Nilakanta. Seems that he's setting up groups in different towns. He's also a writer, or an editor. Madras proscribed his paper, but he's moved the operation to Pondicherry, where he prints leaflets and sends them down here. We've arrested a few people, but they're small fry.'

'What kind of leaflets?'

'The usual sedition nonsense. Printed by the Bharata Mata Association, whatever that is.'

Ashe's teacup rattled as he put it back on the saucer.

'You said this Nilakanta is setting up separate groups. Does that mean there's a central organization?'

'Yes. We think in Madras or Pondicherry. They've also got support from Germany.'

'Germany?'

'Yes. Good old Kaiser Wilhelm has agents in the country who are in touch with the revolutionaries in Calcutta. There's also some talk about an agent here, in the south.'

'Any names?'

'No. But apparently, he's an Englishman. Off his rocker, of course, but you know these lefties.'

'Right. But these people, what did you call them? Brata…?'

'Bharata Mata.'

'Right. Any idea who might be their leader?'

'That's what we don't know.' The superintendent drew his chair up closer and squeezed his eyes. 'But we've got to infiltrate these groups. Get inside information. Then we can destroy them.'

'You mean arrest them?'

'Course. What'd you think, a wholesale massacre? Now listen, the problem is these small groups. Each one has only five or six men in a village or town. No documents, no address, no headquarters. They're clever.'

'Can't we get a man on the inside? Shouldn't be too hard. We have contacts so—'

'Not that easy, old man. I had one of my best men approach Nilakanta's supporters. Said he wanted to help the "cause". Two days later, his family was threatened with violence. They'd rumbled him that quickly.'

'I see,' Ashe said, though he didn't.

'We may have contacts, but they have informers. We'll have to be smarter next time. Turn one of them.'

'But they're ideologues. Fanatics.'

'Precisely. They're mad. Unstable. And that's why they'll change. We can help them, too, with a little cash. I'm waiting for approval from Madras.'

'Good idea.'

'In the meanwhile, though, I suggest you call in more reserve police. I don't like the way the wind is blowing.'

Hartley rose, and Ashe watched him reach the door before he stopped and spun around.

'Oh, one last thing,' his visitor said. 'I wouldn't talk too openly about your movements.'

'Movements?'

'Holidays, that sort of thing.'

*

Hartley's large frame disappeared and seemed to suck the air out with him. Ashe placed both hands palms down on the table and pressed hard. 'Damn the Maravars and the palmyra trees,' he muttered. He knew he should have told Hartley, but he just couldn't do it. Reaching down and unlocking the top drawer, he pulled out the letter he'd received that morning. Addressed to him personally, it had not been opened by Das.

'Vande Mataram,' it read in roman script. 'We members of the Bharata Mata Association do hereby warn you to the following effect: do not participate in any public matters. If you are stubborn, despite this warning, then your head will be smashed to pieces within a short time. Yours truly, Bharata Mata Association members.'

He had decided to tell no one about the letter. It was the work of fanatics, extremists, who talked a good game. If he told anyone, even Hartley, he was afraid that Mary would find out and demand that they return to Ireland. He couldn't countenance that.

But I will be careful, he said to himself as he folded the letter up again and placed it back in the drawer.

10

Punalur and Shenkottai, 1910

'Good news,' Shankara said. 'Nilakanta wants to meet us.'

Vanchi trusted Shankara. He was older and he was his wife's brother. He had guided him from the very beginning, advising him to go to Trivandrum, persuading him to travel in order to hear Pillai and introducing him to Madasami. Besides, Vanchi had no one else. He couldn't confide in Thatha, who wouldn't understand, or in Dr Raghavan, who wouldn't approve.

He wasn't even sure he understood it all himself. Self-rule made sense when he read about it in the newspapers, and he could still remember the thrill of listening to Pillai speak about 'foreigners trampling over our traditions and enslaving our people'. He knew it was all true, but when he walked into the forest to take his bath in the morning, it seemed distant. Although Pillai had shown him that things were connected, events that happened in Madras and Calcutta and Bombay still felt far away.

He and Shankara had been distributing leaflets for more than a year now. Printed in Pondicherry, the single-page flyers were sent to Tinnevelly, among other places, where a man received a bundle in the train station and handed it over to Shankara. Vanchi took yet another day off work and they distributed the leaflets in one of the major towns in the district. Shankara was no longer wanted by the police, but it was dangerous work, nevertheless.

Last month, they'd almost been arrested. They'd gone to Kovilpatti, a market town north of Tinnevelly, where a teacher had agreed to spread the latest leaflet headlined 'The Deceit of Foreigners'. Inside was a list of a dozen 'heroes' killed by the British in the Mutiny of 1857. Opposite each name was a blank space and the question: 'Who will take his place?'

Carrying fifty of those handbills, wrapped in newspaper and stuffed in a cloth bag, Shankara went inside the school building to find their contact, a teacher named Shanmugam. Vanchi stayed outside, pretending to be a parent waiting for a pupil. The school playground was filled with screaming children and he didn't notice the policemen until they had rounded the corner and confronted him.

'Where's your friend?' one asked.

'Who?' Vanchi prevaricated.

'Your friend, the one with the leaflets. Where is he?'

'I don't have a friend. I'm waiting for my little cousin. Playing over there,' Vanchi said, pointing to the playground.

The police scowled at Vanchi and marched into the building. Soon, Vanchi heard shouts and prepared to run. That was the plan: if one of them were arrested, the other would flee. Instead, he waited.

Ten minutes later, the policemen emerged alone and walked out of the school compound. Then Shanmugam appeared and explained that he had his own 'lookout' who had warned him in time to offload the leaflets to another teacher and escort Shankara out of the building through a backdoor. He would be waiting for Vanchi at the jutka stand.

'Did you meet anyone on your way here?' Shanmugam asked.

Vanchi had thought for a moment before saying, 'Yes. A young man. Said he came from Tuticorin. We mentioned Chidambaram Pillai and he seemed interested.'

'So you gave him a leaflet?'

'Yes.'

'He must have gone to the police. Better be more careful next time.'

*

Now, hearing the excitement in Shankara's voice about the meeting with Nilakanta, Vanchi tried to put his fears to one side. He trusted his brother-in-law, but he wasn't sure he wanted to meet this man who was organising secret cells. That sounded ominous. Vanchi also wondered what excuse he could give to his family this time. They all seemed to be watching him.

'Tell them whatever you like,' Shankara said, waving his hand in the air, 'because this is more important than your family.'

Vanchi told them that he was going to attend a training session for Forest Department guards. His mother eyed him all day, while his grandfather averted his gaze. Ponammal questioned him as she lay by his side that night.

'It's not really training, is it?' she whispered. When he didn't respond, she turned over so he couldn't see the pain in her face.

In the morning, Vanchi and Shankara were on the first train going west through the mountains, to Punalur. A safe place, Shankara assured him. On the way, they talked about the recent crackdown on newspapers, pamphlets and books that supported swadeshi. Owners of presses and publishing houses were now required to pay hundreds of rupees as a security deposit, and many periodicals were banned outright. The most sensational news was that Aurobindo Ghose had sought refuge in Pondicherry.

'He's there with Bharati,' Shankara said, referring to the Tamil writer and editor Subramania Bharati, who had already fled to the French territory. 'Nilakanta's probably met him. Maybe that's what this meeting is about.'

Vanchi looked at him with steady eyes. Bharati was a

name he knew well. He often read his Tamil newspaper, *India*, which reported on national news but also contained a 'Letter from London' written by VVS Aiyar. The last letter had reported on an arson attack in retaliation for the hanging of an Indian revolutionary who had murdered a British official in London. The British had refused to allow the assassin's body to be cremated according to Hindu tradition. Aiyar's final words—'This was revenge taken by Agni, god of fire'—stuck in Vanchi's mind.

Things were coming closer. Tinnevelly and Tuticorin didn't seem so far from Pondicherry, Madras and Calcutta, even London.

'Amazing!' a man next to them cried and pointed.

Vanchi saw a row of stone arches that held up a bridge curving ahead of them for half a mile. He had heard about this 'miracle of engineering', as the papers called it when the railway line had been extended through the mountains six years earlier. But its gravity-defying audacity took his breath away. As the train rattled over the bridge, suspended hundreds of feet in the air, he stared at the white frothing river below.

Pulling his head back inside, he placed a hand at the base of his neck and rubber his skin.

'This Nilakanta, what's he like?' he asked Shankara.

'Dedicated, completely.'

'To what?'

'Swadeshi. Like us, only more.'

The train squeezed through a gap in the mountains, blown out by dynamite and shaped by pick-axes. Soon, it slowed down on the approach to Punalur. Climbing down from the high carriage and onto the platform, Vanchi looked at the station, which hadn't even existed when he had passed through the town on his way back from Trivandrum four years ago. It looked like it had been there for decades, hacked out of the jungle that was reclaiming it. Vegetation sprouted between the cracked roof tiles, and the wooden pillars resembled tree trunks with a patina of green mildew. Patches of the original mustard yellow were still visible on the walls and doors, but everything else had been discoloured by the heavy mountain monsoon.

'Here are the directions,' Shankara said, showing Vanchi a piece of paper, torn from a school notebook. 'It's near the paper mill.'

They walked from the station, passed through the market and continued on the main road leading out of town. Although they had dressed in local fashion and were speaking with a local accent, Shankara swivelled his eyes from side to side.

The rain had stopped, but the red earth road was muddy and filled with puddles. The sky was black and a wind raced down from the surrounding mountains. Vanchi thrust his hands into the pockets of his cotton tunic. They said little, only commenting on the cold and sunless countryside. No houses or shops in sight, and the forest had thickened on both sides.

Going around a bend, they saw the hulking façade of the paper mill. Shankara trudged on, but Vanchi was immobilized by the sound of the machines grinding away inside. Shankara realized that Vanchi was several paces behind and turned to say something when he heard a voice.

'Come with me.'

The man's face was hidden beneath a peaked rain hat of banana tree fronds. He gestured and turned back into the forest without waiting for a reply.

As Shankara and Vanchi followed, the forest turned to jungle, and the man in front hacked away at the undergrowth with a machete. Hearing a river, Vanchi concentrated on its location and the vegetation around him. Thatha had taught him how to retrace his steps in hilly jungles. If only he had told his grandfather what he was doing, he would have talked him out of it. Taken him to the Shiva temple at the end of the Brahmin street and persuaded him to make a vow.

The cackle of a hornbill announced their arrival. In a small clearing ahead of him, Vanchi saw a bearded figure in a shaft of light. He'd seen something like it on Christian calendars sold in shops. But this man had his arms folded across his chest and wore no robe.

'*Vanga, vanga*,' the man cried and spread his arms wide as if to encircle them both, but he looked only at Vanchi.

'This is Vanchi, my brother-in-law,' Shankara said.

'Yes, I know.'

At that moment, the sky opened up and the pent-up rain sent them inside. It was an old Forest Department guardhouse, abandoned years ago, a single room with a cot, a high table and two rattan chairs. A suggestion of warmth came from a charcoal fire smouldering in the grate.

'I'm glad to see you again, my friend,' Nilakanta said to Shankara. 'You are looking well.'

Shankara returned the compliment with a smile, while Vanchi lowered his eyes and shifted his weight.

'By the way, Raman says you weren't followed,' Nilakanta added, gesturing towards the old man who was crouching down to boil water.

Nilakanta sat in one of the chairs and indicated the cot for his visitors. 'Now, you must tell me everything that's happened since our last meeting.'

Shankara gave details about the new contacts they had made in four towns and estimated that they had distributed about five hundred leaflets.

'And in Kovilpatti?' Nilakanta asked.

How did he know about that? Vanchi wondered while Shankara described their close call, admitting that it was their own fault and taking full responsibility for it.

'You learn by experience,' Nilakanta said and launched into a narrative of his own mistakes.

Vanchi adjusted his thread as he listened to the man, who was the unofficial leader of the swadeshi movement in the southern districts. He was younger than Vanchi had expected, though he had no basis for such an expectation. Up close,

Vanchi could also see that he was thin, almost ascetic-looking.

'I came here, to Punalur, because I'd been travelling for months,' Nilakanta said, bringing his story up to the present. 'Normally I stay with friends. But the CID are looking for me, even here in Travancore. And I needed time to think. And to write.'

The old man served tea in bamboo mugs along with stale biscuits dug out of a tin. Nilakanta dropped a biscuit into the steaming tea and took a sip.

'Do you write?' he asked.

Shankara looked at Vanchi. Neither of them answered.

'You should try writing. It helps to clarify thoughts. If I can't explain something on paper, then I know I don't understand it. And our thoughts must be clear if we are to succeed.'

He paused, sipped the tea and looked at the other two.

'Are your thoughts clear?' he asked.

Shankara muttered yes.

'And you, Vanchi? What about you?'

'I think so.'

Nilakanta considered this and said, 'You're from Shenkottai. You live with your mother and grandfather. Your father works for the Travancore State Devaswom Board. You studied in Trivandrum. You work for the Forest Department. You are married and have a young daughter.'

Vanchi looked at Shankara with alarm.

'Don't be frightened, my friend,' Nilakanta said. 'We have to know everything we can about our people. So we can trust them.'

He stared at them, first Shankara and then Vanchi, with an intensity that made them both look away.

'I do trust you,' he said. 'But I asked about your thoughts because you cannot help us if your mind is not clear. Understand?'

Shankara wagged his head in agreement, and Vanchi followed suit.

'The foreigners want to destroy us,' Nilakanta said as he tugged on his bushy black beard. 'That is what must be clear in your mind. They want to destroy our civilization. Not just enslave us economically but mentally, too. They want us to abandon our traditions and denounce our religion. They want to destroy us from within. Without guns.'

A thin smile spread Vanchi's pursed lips. He couldn't explain swadeshi himself, but he understood it when someone else did.

'That's the first thing you must understand—the foreigners want to destroy us,' Nilakanta continued. 'And the second thing is this. We will destroy them.'

'Destroy them?' Shankara asked in a shaky voice.

'Yes. Eliminate them. Remove them from our country.'

Vanchi narrowed his eyes and cocked his head to one side.

'That is why I invited you here. You've heard of the Bharata Mata Association. We are organized in small groups. There are now seven here in the south, but we need more in Tinnevelly District. I want one in Tenkasi and one in Tuticorin.'

He's no older than me, Vanchi thought. But he's confident. It's his eyes. They never move.

'The key to our success is total secrecy. No written communication. Everything is kept inside, in the heart. And blessed by Mother India.'

Nilakanta put his palms together and raised them above his bowed head. Vanchi and Shankara did the same.

'But how can we…destroy the foreigners?' Shankara asked.

'There are different ways. I write books about our ancient traditions. Others write editorials and make speeches. We all teach our people about the truth.'

Nilakanta stood up and went over to a leather suitcase lying against a wall.

'Here,' he said, returning to them and holding out a book. 'This may inform you.'

Vanchi took it and saw the Tamil title: *Sanatana Dharma*. The Eternal Tradition.

'Books are necessary, but not sufficient,' Nilakanta said as he began to pace around the room. 'For that reason we are forming an army. A secret army. Several zamindars have promised men and weapons. But first, we need to show our people that the invaders are weak. That we can destroy them.'

Shankara swallowed hard and said, 'How can we help?'

'I want you to consider your own answer to that. We will discuss it when we meet on Tuesday next week.'

'Here?'

'No. You will meet me at the railway station in Shenkottai. A train arrives from Punalur at 11:25. Do not be late.'

Shankara indicated that he understood.

'Then, you will take me to a place where we can talk. In secret,' Nilakanta said. 'Do you know of a suitable place?'

When Shankara hesitated, Vanchi filled the awkward silence. 'Yes,' he said, with a conviction that surprised Shankara. 'I know a place.'

'Good. If I do not come on Tuesday, you will come here on Wednesday. One more thing: do not speak a word of this to anyone. Secrecy is our salvation.'

*

The next day, Vanchi's daughter fell ill. Spots appeared on Vanni's face and she ran a high fever. Vanchi said he couldn't miss another day at work, so Shankara took Ponammal and his little niece to the new hospital in Palayamkottai.

In the crowded train, the child wailed loudly and Ponammal tried to breastfeed it without success. Clutching the bundled child, she buried her head in her chest and held back her own tears. Shankara wanted to comfort her but could think of nothing to say.

'Try turmeric paste, dear,' an older woman said. 'Rub it on her stomach.'

'And after that,' said another, 'give her an oil bath.'

'But now, just hold her upside down,' said a third.

Ponammal did that and the crying stopped. When everyone relaxed, a man wearing a crumpled white coat over his *veshti* spoke up. 'That's only temporary. If you really want to cure her, tie a two-anna coin in a piece of cloth and hang it near a Mariamman temple.'

Shankara looked at his sister, who was now smiling. Little Vanni was the centre of her life. She had no idea what he and Vanchi were doing. But some day she would.

The Christian missionary hospital, Shankara had to admit, was impressive. An arched entrance in the compound wall led to a three-storey building with wide verandas and corridors. While he and Ponammal waited on wooden benches, Shankara looked down the corridor and saw a man in conversation with a doctor. Short, with cropped hair and glasses, the man looked familiar. Looking again, he remembered that he'd seen him near the collector's office. Nilakanta had told him to pay attention to anyone working for the British.

He stood up, strolled down the corridor and stopped when he could hear their words.

'I'm afraid it's bad news,' the doctor was saying. 'Your mother has a tumour in the lower abdomen.'

'What does that mean?'

'She needs it removed immediately, but we can't do that here. You'll have to take her to the hospital in Vellore, near Madras. They have a first-rate surgeon.'

'But that'll cost a lot of money. I don't have it.'

'The operation can't wait. You'll have to find the money somehow.'

After the man left and disappeared around a corner, Shankara approached the doctor.

'We need to see someone about this child,' he said, pointing to Ponammal and Vanni on the bench.

'You'll have to wait, like everyone else,' the doctor said curtly.

'Of course. Ah, that man you were talking with. Who is he? Looks like someone I once knew.'

The doctor looked Shankara up and down. His clothes were neat and he spoke politely. 'His name is Das,' he said. 'Head clerk in the collector's office.'

*

At noon on the following Tuesday, three men walked west through the market area in Shenkottai. The air was muggy, with rain clouds clinging to the tops of the nearby mountains. One of them carried an expensive-looking leather satchel and wore his *veshti* in the Tamil style, tucked into the waist and reaching the top of his sandals. The other two were more local, tying the long, white garment into a knot in the middle of their waist. They wore leather shoes. The group appeared to be heading out of town to catch some breeze, but the man with the satchel kept turning around as if looking for someone.

Although Vanchi's face was familiar to most of the shopkeepers, no one greeted him. He was the grandson of the herbalist from the agraharam, the Brahmin street. That's all they knew since he kept to himself. Withdrawn by nature, he was now secretive by choice. It suits me, he thought. I'm a nobody.

Half a mile beyond the last shop, Vanchi turned off the main road onto a footpath that crossed the paddy fields and led into the forest.

'Not far, now,' he said, turning back to the others.

Leading them to the spot, he couldn't help a smile slipping across his face. It was the obvious choice, but even he had been impressed by his decision.

Ten minutes later, he stopped in front of his banyan tree. The stone man lay beyond, deeper into the forest. He wouldn't show them that, not now and maybe never.

Vanchi threaded his way through the tangle of aerial roots and waited for the others to follow. The three of them stood up easily in the screened-off space. It hadn't rained overnight and the ground was firm.

Nilakanta indicated his approval, and Shankara, who had

not guessed where Vanchi would take them, gave his brother-in-law an admiring smile.

'Before we begin,' Nilakanta said, 'we will worship Bharata Mata.'

Sitting down, he opened his satchel and took out a lithograph of goddess Kali. It had been cut from a calendar and pasted onto a stiff piece of cardboard. Kali danced on the prostate body of her victim, her red tongue lolling and a necklace of skulls hanging down her blue body. In one hand, she held a head dripping with blood, in the others, a conch, a lotus and a curved sword.

Nilakanta propped up the image against the satchel, leaned forward and put a vermilion dot on the goddess' forehead. He settled himself directly in front of the picture and made sure that Vanchi and Shankara were on either side. He closed his eyes, and they did the same. When he began to chant, Shankara remained silent, but Vanchi recognized the Sanskrit verses and joined in.

As the chanting drowned out the noises in his head, Vanchi's voice became louder and more confident, a stream of syllables without pause or shift in tone. He focused on Kali's sword until it merged with the weapon on the carved stone. The stone man struck and everyone danced.

When he opened his eyes, Nilakanta had already stopped chanting and was looking at him.

'Good. Now we can begin,' he said, sliding himself back from the satchel and gesturing for the others to sit closer to him.

'As I said last week,' he continued, 'the primary goal of the Bharata Mata Association is to drive out the foreigners. Think about what has happened to those who have tried to achieve this by legal means. You know the fate of Chidambaram Pillai, for example.'

Vanchi grimaced at the thought of the man yoked to a wooden beam like an animal.

'And there are others whom I could name. These patriots

used speeches and rallies, and they ended up in prison. The lesson is clear. We must destroy the foreigners by force. Do you understand?'

Shankara narrowed his eyes. 'You mean kill them?'

'Yes.'

Shankara shrank back and looked at Vanchi.

'Are you clear in your thoughts?' Nilakanta asked.

Shankara said he was.

'And you?' Nilakanta asked Vanchi.

Vanchi stared straight ahead, his eyes unfocused.

'It is not a sin to kill,' Nilakanta said. 'Not if you kill to defend our traditions.'

Vanchi fingered his sacred thread.

'You must think of your country, not of yourself or your family. You must dedicate your life to your mother, to Mother India. Worship her and serve her as you would the goddess.'

Vanchi looked at the image of Kali and tilted his head to one side in a sign of acceptance.

'Good. We are clear in our thoughts. Now, to join the association you must make an oath of allegiance.'

Nilakanta pulled a sheet of paper from his satchel and handed it to Vanchi. At the top, Vanchi saw the opening verse of the nationalist song 'Vande Mataram' in a Tamil translation. Below, in the middle of the page, he read the oath of the Bharata Mata Association, also in Tamil:

> To establish self-rule in India we will drive out the white man. For this purpose, we sacrifice our lives and our assets. To achieve this, we will kill white men. Whoever reveals the affairs of the Bharata Mata Association will be killed. When we drink kumkum, it is the blood of white men.

After Shankara also read the oath, Nilakanta opened his satchel again and gave them each a blank sheet of paper and a wooden pen. He told them to write the oath in their own handwriting and produced a small vial of ink. When they had written the oath, he had them read it aloud and sign it with a secret name by which they would be known within the association.

'Good,' Nilakanta said. 'Now, sign it with your blood.'

Vanchi pricked his thumb with a needle and pressed his blood mark beneath the name of 'Ananta'. Shankara did the same under the name of 'Ananda'.

Nilakanta then mixed vermilion powder and water in a half-coconut shell. After both men drank the kumkum, Nilakanta smeared it on Kali's forehead.

'Repeat after me,' he said. 'Goddess, Mother India, we will serve you until we die.'

The two men repeated the words, while facing the goddess, who was streaked with red.

'You are now members of our association,' Nilakanta said. 'You must honour our goals. History will not forgive us if we fail.'

They all looked up. A troupe of monkeys had landed in the upper branches of the banyan tree. Swinging and leaping, they bared their teeth and began to whoop.

'What should we do next?' Shankara asked.

'Continue with the leaflets,' Nilakanta said. 'And try to identify new recruits for your group. But be careful. The government has spies everywhere. When you are sure of a new person, contact me in Pondicherry.'

Nilakanta gave them an address and ended by telling them to keep their written oaths in a safe place and to read it aloud to themselves once a month.

After Nilakanta left, Shankara and Vanchi waited for half an hour before walking back to Shenkottai. Shankara spoke in a flutter of excitement about the oath, the association and its mission. They parted at the station, where Shankara boarded a train to Tenkasi and Vanchi walked home. He turned off the main road onto the dirt road and, a minute later, turned again down the Brahmin street. A corpse was burning in the cremation ground, but he didn't stop to ask who it was.

*

'Anything the matter?' Thatha asked without looking at him.

It had rained hard overnight, and they were sitting side by side in the kitchen having a breakfast of idlis. He had tried to avoid his grandfather ever since the meeting with Nilakanta the day before.

'No, nothing. Just tired, that's all,' he said.

Even lying down with Ponammal the night before, he had been afraid that he might say something in his sleep.

Thatha rinsed his eating hand in the brass plate and leaned back against the wall. He burped twice before clearing his throat.

'Your mother's a little concerned,' he said. 'Ponammal, too. You're away from home a lot, you know.'

'It's work and…things.'

'With Shankara?'

'I'm late for work,' Vanchi said and stood up.

He fled, almost knocking Vanni over on the veranda. When he reached the main road, he didn't turn in the direction of the checkpoint. Instead, he went west, towards the town and the mountains. Passing through the market, he bought a small clay pot and continued walking. After crossing the paddy fields, he reached the banyan tree, where he folded his handwritten oath and pushed it inside the pot.

His eyes searched the base of the tree where the roots twisted together like writhing snakes. Kneeling down, he saw a cavity and explored it with his hand. His whole arm went in, up to the shoulder, and his fingers found moist ground. Using twigs and leaves, he built up a little mound inside the cavity and placed the pot on top.

Nothing will touch it, he told himself. Not the rain and not the sun. And he, too, would stay away. Nilakanta said he should read it every month, but he wasn't sure he could do that. He didn't want to remember that he had taken an oath to kill.

11

Pondicherry, 1910

As the shoreline came into sharper relief, VVS Aiyar allowed himself to smile. The whole escapade had been a conjuror's trick. He had slipped over borders in disguise, ridden incognito on trains and disembarked from ships undetected by the British authorities. And it had all begun when he'd recruited an Indian fakir into a revolutionary cell in London.

Aiyar had arrived in the capital to study law but soon joined a group of young Indians dedicated to the violent overthrow of British rule. Led by Vinayak Savarkar, another law student in London, the radicals lived in a student residence called India House, from where they published political pamphlets calling for self-rule. Casual surveillance by the Home Office turned serious when the group staged a public event to commemorate the fiftieth anniversary of the failed 1857 Mutiny against the British Raj. They vowed that the next revolt would succeed.

Aiyar joined the group in 1908, a year after his arrival in London. His first contribution was to employ the talents of Amar Nath Dutt, a renowned 'Hindu sorcerer' who was performing in the capital. That profession, Aiyar realized, was the perfect cover for their clandestine activities. Resplendent in a red-tasselled turban and gold robes while juggling firebrands and wrestling cobras, Dutt could deceive the police as easily as an audience. Having recruited the fakir, Aiyar sent him to Paris for training in firearms and then to San Francisco to set up a revolutionary group.

More trickery followed when Aiyar befriended a new student at India House. Mr Kirtikar said he had come to London to study dentistry, but his movements aroused suspicion. One day, when Kirtikar had gone out to watch a stage play with his English girlfriend, Aiyar used a bent hairpin to open the locked door to his room. Inside, he found a report in the man's handwriting that summarized the discussions at the India House group's most recent meeting. The would-be dentist was a government informer.

Rather than expose and punish him, Aiyar persuaded the others to utilize him as a double agent. In exchange for his safety, Kirtikar continued to send his reports to the Home Office, but Aiyar himself wrote them, supplying the government with irrelevant names, inaccurate information and false leads. Although this ruse was successful, the seditious material printed by the group and their suspected involvement in the assassination of a high-ranking official in London, prompted the government to issue an arrest warrant for Savarkar, the group leader. Aiyar was next on the list.

*

During his eight months on the run, Aiyar had been in danger only once. On the first leg of his journey, by boat from London to Amsterdam, he was disguised as a Sikh but had forgotten that his initials 'VVS' (for his Hindu name of Varahaneri Venkatesa Subramaniam) were embossed on his suitcase. When the British secret police questioned him, he found inspiration from somewhere and answered that, of course, the initials represented his name, 'Vikram Vivek Singh'.

Aiyar continued by train to Paris, where he spent two months planning his escape route to India and perfecting the art of impersonation. Living in seclusion with Madame Cama, a Parsi woman at the centre of the Indian revolutionary group in France, he grew a thick beard and learned how to act and speak like a Parsi man. He even perfected his pronunciation of

Old Persian in order to say prayers. He had to be meticulous because the British authorities were searching for him everywhere and intercepting his letters. To confuse them regarding his whereabouts, he wrote to his father informing him of a decision to emigrate to Brazil. He also gave Madame Cama a number of post-dated letters, which she would send after he had left Paris.

Despite this careful planning and subterfuge, travelling from Europe to India was still dangerous. The British police were swarming over the port of Marseilles, where Savarkar had just been arrested. The same was true of Port Said and other stops on the sea journey to India. Knowing this, Aiyar travelled on another route.

One rainy morning, a man strolled out of Madame Cama's house with a long beard, silver hair and an ivory-handled cane. In his coat pocket were business cards printed in Urdu announcing himself as Mr Rustum Sait, a Parsi. Mr Sait travelled by train to Rome, where he bought a copy of Dante's *Inferno* and an Italian-English dictionary, which he packaged up and sent to an address in Pondicherry. Sait also purchased an expensive pair of leather shoes, something he had set his heart on for a long time. From Rome, where Sait spent days admiring the ruins of a culture that he knew well from his study of Horace and Virgil, he went by ship to Constantinople and on to Cairo.

While in Egypt, he obtained a new set of business cards, printed in Persian with a Turkish name, and introduced himself as a Muslim returning from the pilgrimage to Mecca. On the ship from Cairo to Bombay, he read the Koran and prayed five times a day on deck with others returning from the Haj. When he disembarked at Bombay, he was spotted and followed by two British intelligence agents. After an hour's surveillance, they decided that he was another harmless Muslim pilgrim. Minutes later, he was met by a friend and given a ticket on a ship sailing to Colombo.

From Colombo, he boarded a vessel bound for Calcutta, handing around the business card of a Hindu jute merchant in that metropolis. When the ship anchored off the coast just south of Madras, the man of many names slipped onto a small fishing boat, which ferried him to a pier projecting out beyond the treacherous surf.

*

Aiyar walked down the three-hundred-metre-long pier and stepped onto French soil with his smile still in place. Inspecting the slender stone pillars standing in a circle at the juncture of the pier with the land, he knew that they had been stolen from a temple. That's the French for you, he chuckled to himself. The British would have put them in a museum. He pivoted around and saw a lighthouse, the town hall and other impressive buildings. Pondicherry would suit him just fine.

Aiyar headed north along the main road, which was lined with statues of horse-mounted generals. Although he had replaced his Haj pilgrim clothes with a traditional south Indian *veshti* and tunic, he kept the bushy beard and fine Italian leather shoes. The wide esplanade ran parallel to the seafront, but it was protected from the unpredictable sea by a masonry wall. The boulevard led to a circular space ringed with imported trees, where the colonial government held ceremonial events, flew the tricolour and sang 'La Marseillaise'.

Turning inland, Aiyar passed the imposing governor's mansion and stopped to compare its architecture with what he had seen in Paris. He had never before been to Pondicherry and was struck by its imperial design in contrast with the muddle that was Madras. He was studying the sculpted pillars at the gated entrance when an armed soldier ordered him to move on.

Pondicherry had been traded back and forth several times before it was finally ceded by the English to the French at the end of the Napoleonic wars. Relations between the two

European powers on the subcontinent remained cordial until the turn of the twentieth century when the city became a haven for anyone threatened with arrest in British India. Close to Madras and with access to the sea, it was French, where revolutionaries were safe.

And it was as French as Madras was English, exuding a charm that took its residents back to the glories of the early nineteenth century. It was also a colonial city, its French and Tamil quarters separated by a canal of stagnant water. Ville Blanche, or White Town, stretched for two miles along the seafront, with mansions featuring tall compound walls, ornate wrought-iron balconies and high wooden doors. Inside, wealthy French merchants and officials enjoyed dinner parties and afternoon soirees, with little adjustment to the world beyond their drawing room. When they did venture out on the streets, men wore pith helmets, white coats and trousers, while the women sheltered under broad-brimmed hats and long, white muslin dresses. If the heat was too intense or the distance too great, they had themselves pulled in rickshaws by stringy men naked to the waist.

Leaving Ville Blanche, Aiyar crossed the canal into Ville Noire, where Rue Dumas and Rue de Bussy gave way to Kannappa Mudaliar Street and Kamatchi Amman Street. The crowded Black Town was inhabited by Indians, mostly Tamils, but also others from the south. The houses and shops were small, except for the cotton mills and their sprawling warehouses. Every other street had a temple after which it was named.

Eswaran Dharmaraja Street took its name from a small temple dedicated to Dharma Raja, the god of justice and death. Aiyar turned down that street and found what he was looking for, a single-storey building with a tile roof and small veranda. Dharma Alayam, or Dharma House, took its name from the happy coincidence of its physical location and the political purpose of its occupants.

As Aiyar stood in the street, the front door opened and a man rushed out.

'Welcome, sir! So happy that you are finally with us.'

'You got the books?'

'Oh, yes. When they arrived, we knew you were on your way,' the man said. 'Who else would send such crazy things?'

Dante's *Inferno* and an Italian-English dictionary, with letters concealed inside, had indeed been a signal. Although Arumugam Chettiyar had never met the well-known writer and nationalist, the two had corresponded through letters when Aiyar was in Paris. Fearing the authorities would open and read any letters to and from him, Aiyar had devised a simple yet effective code. He assigned the numbers one through ten to the letters in 'Subramonie', the French version of one of his names. 'S' was indicated by 1, 'u' by 2 and so on. Plus and minus signs were added to indicate other letters: for example, 'c' was 3+1. The system proved especially useful when he wrote to Madame Cama in Paris requesting a dozen Browning automatic pistols.

The plump Chettiyar ushered Aiyar into the front room, which was lined with bookshelves and furnished with wicker chairs and a broad table strewn with newspapers, pamphlets and papers.

'We call it the reading room,' Chettiyar said. 'But it's also where we meet every Monday afternoon. Then it becomes the argument room.'

Aiyar acknowledged the humour but did not respond.

'Most of the books and papers are the gifts of well-wishers. Particularly the zamindar of Singampatti, who sends us a money order every month.'

Aiyar scanned the book spines, mainly history, literature and science, with some fiction, primarily in English and some in Tamil. The newspapers were also in English and Tamil, with one Bengali weekly.

'You can work here,' Chettiyar said. 'I've arranged a separate place for you to stay, just a few houses further down the street.'

'My wife is also coming.'

'Yes, it's large enough for you both. And your daughter.'

'Thank you,' Aiyar said but did not add that his daughter had died a year earlier.

Aiyar was pleased to see the pedal-operated printing press standing on sturdy legs in a small back room. Running his hand over the black metal surfaces, he wondered if it would print as clearly as the machine in London. He also glanced with approval at the reams of paper and cans of printer ink stacked in a corner.

'How many copies do you print of *India*?' he asked, referring to the Tamil daily edited by Bharati.

'About eight hundred. It's down from last year because the British—'

'I know. What about the leaflets?'

'Usually a thousand for the first run, depending on the content.'

'Good,' he said, though he was already planning to increase those numbers and add a new publication.

The rest of the house did not interest him. A makeshift kitchen, barely more than a broom closet, had been added at the back under a sloping roof. Upstairs, two identical rooms each held a cot, small table and wooden chair.

'We put people up there, when necessary,' Chettiyar said. 'But they're mostly used when someone wants peace and quiet.'

The first thing Aiyar did was to write a letter to his wife in Bangalore. During the nearly four years of separation, she had grown increasingly anxious about their future. She had attempted to join him in London and then in Paris but didn't have the money. A cousin who had planned to take her to Paris fell off a horse and the trip was cancelled. She returned to her parents' house after Aiyar's father denounced his son and spoke cruelly to her. A month later, her young daughter died of dysentery.

Aiyar's letters had only contributed to her desperation. 'I

have given up hope of ever returning to India,' he wrote. 'You might never see me again.' His last letter, sent from Paris, left her even more worried. In it, he had announced his plan to emigrate to Brazil and asked her to organize a group of families to join him there as emigres. Anxious to explain everything, including the fake emigration plan, he now wrote a long letter and begged her to join him in Pondicherry.

Only when that letter was posted did he agree to eat. Following a short nap upstairs, he took tea downstairs with a group of men who had also sought political refuge in Pondicherry, either as writers or activists. They all lived within minutes of the Dharma House and had been waiting for the news that Aiyar had arrived.

The small group included Nilakanta and Madasami, but the most prominent person was Bharati. Bharati often disagreed with Aiyar's radical political views but published them anyway, which was one reason that his Madras-based newspaper had been banned and a warrant issued for his arrest.

Born a year apart, in 1881 and 1882, the two men had an uncanny physical resemblance. Although Bharati was thinner and Aiyar had a strong Roman nose, both had a smooth oval face, high forehead, full beard and dark brown eyes. And they were both Tamil Brahmins with a love of literature and a passionate commitment to Indian independence. They met for the first time in Dharma House that afternoon.

'You didn't expect a rugby player, did you?' Aiyar said to Bharati, mocking his own robust physique.

'On the contrary,' countered Bharati, 'anyone with your energy would need an athletic body.'

Aiyar laughed and, when prompted, launched into an account of his journey from London to Pondicherry. Speaking at length in his native language, something he hadn't done for months, he found a voice more expansive than the English of his legal writing and journalism. For the best part of an hour, he entertained Bharati and the others with stories of his adventures and assumed identities.

'And now that I'm here, I want to go swimming,' he said at the end. 'If the authorities will permit it, of course.'

The tea things were taken away, and Aiyar changed his tone.

'Now, tell me the news here,' he said to everyone but looking at Bharati.

'The British have strangled our publications,' Bharati said. 'Just a few months ago they proscribed every one of our papers—not only my *India*, but also *Vijaya*, *Karma Yogi* and *Suryodayam*, edited by our friends here.'

'Can't you smuggle them into British India?'

'We've tried,' said one of the others, 'but the postal authorities seized the bundles and handed them over to the police, who burned them. Besides, the newspapers need subscriptions, and all those payments have been refused at the post office.'

The speaker was Nilakanta, the youngest of the men in Dharma House that day.

'That's one thing you can count on with the English—they understand money,' Aiyar said with a gentle smirk. 'But what about the leaflets?'

'We've had more success there,' Nilakanta said, 'at least in the southern districts, where most of our supporters are.'

Aiyar listened to the details of the 'southern network', as it was called.

'That's excellent,' he said. 'But the problem with the newspapers seems to be money.'

The faces around him showed grim agreement.

'Well, I have a plan to start a new paper, with money they can't touch. I suggest we call it *Dharma*, after this house and our movement.'

Everyone began to talk at once, bubbling over with ideas and expectations. Aiyar was not only an insider, but he had come back after years abroad, living with radical thinkers in London and Paris, bringing with him a confidence that had been draining away from those exiled in Pondicherry.

'What about Aurobindo Ghose?' Aiyar asked after the voices quieted down.

Ghose, the prominent political radical, was also in Pondicherry. Although a Bengali, he had taken a keen interest in the nationalist movement in south India and even bought shares in Chidambaram Pillai's shipping company. Aiyar had counted on his intelligence and support.

'He's withdrawn from radical politics,' Bharati said. 'Ever since he came last year, he's devoted himself to spiritual matters.'

'That's a great loss,' Aiyar said. 'And what do you hear about Pillai?'

Bharati sighed and said, 'He's been transferred to the central jail in Cannanore.'

No one spoke for a long minute.

*

When Aiyar's wife joined him in Pondicherry, they began their new life in a small house lent to them by a supporter of the swadeshi cause. Her joy at the reunion was not without regret. She had expected her husband to come back from London as a lawyer who would make a good life for her and her daughter. Instead, he had fled England, escaped the police, been dispossessed by his father and exiled himself in French territory. Also, she had been used to a high standard of living, and now she and Aiyar depended on the fifty francs sent to him each month by a friend in Paris. Within weeks, though, she had accepted their situation and began to take a keen interest in her husband's political work.

Every morning, he dressed with meticulous care. Clean white *veshti*, white tunic, white shawl and shiny black shoes. Built like a sportsman, he moved gracefully, even over the pot-holes and dung piles in the streets of Ville Noire. Ten minutes brought him to the Dharma House, where he had organized the small group of radicals into a team that would publish

Dharma as a weekly paper in Tamil, with Bharati as co-editor. The other men scoured every available periodical, newspaper, pamphlet and leaflet in English and Tamil, and wrote down a weekly summary of the relevant news. Aiyar himself read both the Bengali and French press. Those summaries formed the basis of a discussion between Aiyar and Bharati as they planned each issue and wrote their joint editorial.

Aiyar also set to work on writing a biography of Napoleon in Tamil and translating the *Tirukkural* into English. The latter book, a compendium of maxims composed nearly two thousand years ago, was often called the 'Tamil Veda'. It had already been translated by an English missionary, but Aiyar felt that he could reveal deeper layers of meaning in the gnomic verses.

'That's important work,' Bharati said when he found his friend bent over the translation one afternoon.

Aiyar laid down his pen and looked up.

'I mean, those ancient texts can show us the way forward today,' Bharati explained.

'It's not like that,' Aiyar said softly. 'They teach us nothing about our revolution.'

'Nothing?'

'Nothing. But they show us what we will lose, if we do nothing.'

The more time the two men spent together, the more pronounced their differences became. If they discussed a Chekhov play during one of their long walks on the beach, Bharati sympathized with the landowner, while Aiyar condemned serfdom. Aiyar was a fast walker, who easily outpaced his friend during their evening outings and grew impatient when he had to wait. The same was true in chess playing, where Aiyar's boldness triumphed over Bharati's caution.

The personality gap soon widened into a political breach. Nearly every day the men in Dharma House discussed not only the news but also the means to achieve self-rule. If Aiyar spoke of the bomb and the bullet, Bharati spoke of freedom and independence. Even when they agreed, for example, on the power of goddess Kali, Aiyar saw blood and Bharati saw sacrifice. Bharati quoted poets, while Aiyar relied on historians. As Aiyar told the group, 'India is like Italy before Garibaldi set it free. If we study his strategy, we see that only violent action achieves radical change.'

*

Things came to a head in early 1911, two months after Aiyar's arrival, when he called a special meeting at Dharma House.

'I've come to a decision,' he said in his usual calm voice. 'You all know my views. But now I have decided to act.'

Bharati and the others waited.

'It has been announced that the king will be coronated in London in June. On 22 June, to be exact. Less than six months from now.'

'Are you thinking of an action in London?' Bharati asked.

'No. We can't stop that ceremony, but we can do something here to counteract it.'

'Counteract it?'

'Yes. We must demonstrate that the king is not our emperor. That we are a free people.'

'Good point,' Bharati said. 'We can hold mass rallies in Madras, Calcutta, Bombay and right across the country. Thousands and thousands of people.'

'No, not that.'

Aiyar's sharp tone silenced the murmur of approval that had followed Bharati's suggestion.

'No, it must be a single action that has irreversible consequences.'

'What exactly do you mean?' Bharati asked.

'I mean an assassination.'

Two hours of heated argument ended when Bharati left

Dharma House. He never again worked with Aiyar, but neither did he denounce him or withdraw from politics. He simply continued to work for swadeshi with a passion confined to the printed page.

'I regret losing a great friend and dedicated patriot,' Aiyar said to those who remained with him. 'However, the time has come for us to act.'

His eyes slid across the room, resting for a second on each man in turn.

'In order to mark this moment,' he continued, 'I propose that we call ourselves the Young India Society. And also that we give a new name to our press. It will be called the Feringhi Destroyer Press.'

*

The following morning, Aiyar met with Nilakanta and Madasami. Rather than talk in Dharma House, he summoned them to his own house. Aiyar had observed the two men closely over the past weeks. Nilakanta was articulate and outspoken, while Madasami displayed a mute determination. Neither of them, he noticed, had sided with Bharati in the argument about the merits of violent action. Aiyar had also been impressed by their success in distributing leaflets and setting up the Bharata Mata Association. It was the perfect southern companion to his northern Young India Society. And he, Aiyar, was about to marry them.

He asked about their organization, and Nilakanta described the secret cells.

'This oath to kill white people, how many people have taken it?' Aiyar asked.

When told the number was approaching forty, Aiyar revealed his plan. He would set up a furniture shop in Pondicherry and receive genuine articles for a few months in order to establish the cover of a legitimate business. Then he would instruct his contacts in France to send chairs and tables that concealed pistol and rifle parts in false legs and tops.

'But won't the authorities intercept your letters?' Nilakanta asked.

'They might,' Aiyar said, 'but they will be written in code.'

'Code?'

'A system of letters and numbers,' he said, and waited for the inevitable question. 'No,' he replied, 'but I can help you devise your own.'

Madasami spoke for the first time. 'The guns you mentioned. Our people need them.'

'Yes, but I need to know what kind of people they are.'

Nilakanta said that they were mostly young, some of them students and many of them Brahmins. All were dedicated.

'And some are naïve, too, I suspect. Misguided and unstable,' Aiyar said.

Madasami agreed, and Nilakanta did not contradict him.

'Is there anyone who is both committed and reliable? Someone who will obey orders?' Aiyar asked. 'Think hard. This is important.'

'Yes, there is someone,' Madasami said. 'In Shenkottai.'

12

Palayamkottai, 1911

The new year brought no respite in revolutionary activity. Despite the crackdown on the press and tough talk from Calcutta, bombs were still thrown and government officials, both British and Indian, were still shot and injured. If one newspaper was shut down, another emerged.

In Tinnevelly District, there was restlessness without release. No repeat of the violence three years earlier, but the pent-up anger had not dissipated. Meetings were held, speeches made and pamphlets read throughout the district, even in the smallest towns. Although careful not to express seditious ideas, the writers and speakers urged people to 'oppose the government' and 'fight for freedom'. CID officers had stepped up surveillance and the police continued to make arrests.

The public appetite for news was voracious, but two annas for a newspaper was expensive and most people couldn't read. Determined to follow events, small groups gathered in public places and listened while someone read the news to them. One such open-air reading room was the paan-seller's stall under the tree opposite the collector's office in Palayamkottai, where the sagging benches now held more customers than ever. Proximity to the headquarters of local government seemed to confer extra credibility on the newsreader.

Before office hours on a morning in early February, the usual mixture of labourers, farmers, clerks, shopkeepers and the unemployed had gathered to hear the headlines from one of the previous day's Tamil papers. The reader was a junior lawyer who prided himself on his correct pronunciation and knowledge of the world beyond the ken of his audience.

A story about a new dam to be built on the Cauvery River triggered the most reaction. Until the punctilious man came to the main political news.

'In Calcutta, yesterday,' he read in his high-pitched voice, 'a bomb was thrown into a car entering Dalhousie Square from the Writers Building.' Having explained that that was the main government office in Calcutta, he went on, 'The incendiary was apparently aimed at Mr Denham, head of CID, but it landed in the wrong vehicle and, in any case, failed to explode.'

'Ha!' cried one of the listeners. 'Those revolutionaries can't even get the right car.'

Everyone laughed.

'Should have killed the bastard!'

The speaker was a labour contractor well known for being sympathetic to swadeshi. He glared at the others, whose muttered responses were a mixture of shocked disapproval and grudging acceptance.

*

Mary's runny nose and cough persisted for more than a week before her husband noticed.

'It's nothing, really, Robert. Just a little cold.'

Ashe chewed on his pipe at the breakfast table and looked hard at his wife.

'No, Mary, you've got to do something. It's this blasted climate—even the so-called winter here can make you ill.' He summoned the cook and shouted at him in English to make 'medicine tea for memsaab'.

It was almost a year since he had received the threatening letter, which remained locked in his desk drawer. Although there had been no second letter, he had accepted Hartley's conviction that the danger was real. All the children, including six-year-old Herbert, had been sent to Kodaikanal. He would never forgive himself if any harm came to them. Without revealing the nature of his concern, he had argued with Mary for months.

Wasn't it better, when you looked at it in the round, that all the children should go to school in Kodai? It was healthy. They loved it. They had friends there.

Mary had conceded that it was the right decision—what's more important than the children's health? But the daytime quiet in the Palayamkottai bungalow had begun to unnerve her. She almost wished the servants would talk louder. Taking tea with other ladies from the small British community was pleasant enough, though the gossip was enervating. And while Mary Braddon and Edwin Bulwer-Lytton rescued her from endless hours of afternoon ennui, even their melodramas could not dispel her loneliness.

Robert loved her, she was certain of that, but he was away all day and sometimes late into the evening. Even after dinner, he usually put in an hour or two with his insufferable files. Sunday was their only day together, and she especially liked their walk to the nearby church. Giving thanks to God, singing His glory and praying for His providence always buoyed her up, but underneath she could not forget that Monday was just around the corner. And then there was Robert himself. Supportive and kind, yet more and more distant. She blamed it on his demanding and so often unrewarding work, but she suspected there was more to it.

What was it? she wondered as she sipped her tea mixed with crushed cardamom, grated ginger and honey. Mary was especially fond of that thick, strong honey and kept a good supply. It came from the hills near Shenkottai, from an area known as Thenmala, or 'honey mountain'. She had first tasted it when she and Robert had stayed in a hunting lodge as guests of a Hindu raja.

That expedition resulted in another discovery, as well. They were out trekking in the high hills, when they ran into an old man, to whom they offered a taste of coffee from their thermos. In return, he had found and given her a special plant that he said cured headaches. Or, at least, that's what she thought he was trying to tell her. Taking a leaf back to Tuticorin, she had a local herbalist prepare a concoction, which did, in fact, relieve her migraines. She had never been without the herb since, even when she travelled back to Ireland.

Holding her teacup in mid-air, she thought of her sister in Dublin. Their mother had died four years earlier, and only this month her sister had written to say that their father had also passed away. Her sister was ten years younger and always made Mary feel like an 'old maid'. At twenty-eight and still unmarried, she would now have a difficult time finding a husband. Their uncle would look after her, give her a home and so on, but there was no father to bestow an income on her. Maybe she should go back and see what she could do.

'Mary, I said I must go.'

'Yes, of course, dear.'

'Be back as soon as I can, but it might be late.'

She watched Robert brush breadcrumbs from his neatly trimmed beard and rise from the table. He was in one of his 'anxiety phases', as she put it to herself. Edgy, short-tempered and chewing hard on his pipe stem. One day, he'll munch right through it, she thought. They brushed cheeks at the doorway and he was gone.

*

The driver looked different, and Robert paused for a moment. Surely Hartley would have told him, but the carriage was the same. Although he had accepted Hartley's stricture, he still resented being driven to his office. He appreciated that the horse-drawn carriage was larger and more comfortable than an ordinary jutka, but he missed the physical sensation of walking.

Even when the road was filled with bleating goats or splattered with cow dung, he liked passing people, catching a scrap of unintelligible conversation and thinking that life was normal.

When the carriage rolled up in front of his office, he straightened his coat and climbed down. Followed by his file-burdened bearer, he strode up the steps, where lounging peons and sweepers rose and tried to look alert. They adjusted ill-fitting khaki shirts and pulled up trousers that threatened to slip from their hips. Lined up along the corridor inside, supplicants bade good morning to the collector.

Acknowledging no one, Ashe marched past and through the ante-room, where the clerks' greetings resembled a military salute. He allowed himself an almost imperceptible twitch of his lips and proceeded into his own office.

'Das?'

He found head clerk bent over his large desk.

'Good morning, sir,' Das said, spinning around. 'I was… looking for a file I left here yesterday.'

Ashe advanced and Das retreated, so that they crossed in the centre of the room.

'And what file is that?' Ashe asked.

'The palmyra census, sir.'

'It was here yesterday,' Ashe said. 'Do you need it this morning?'

'No, sir. Not now. I just wanted to check something. I've done that.'

That's funny, Ashe thought when he was alone and sitting down. The palmyra census file was still buried beneath the others and looked as if it hadn't been touched for days. Swivelling from side to side in his hard-backed chair, he considered and dismissed the idea of questioning Das. Instead, he dabbed his forehead with a handkerchief and looked at the punkha-man, who reacted by pulling harder on the cloth fan hanging from the ceiling.

A peon brought his tea on a chipped lacquer tray and he

stopped writing. He was scheduled to open a new veterinary hospital that afternoon and was hoping he could bluff his way through a short speech and evade the contentious issue of animal slaughter. More pressing was the impending civil case against the estate of a recently deceased landowner whose son, a ward of the court, had amassed a mountain of debt. Someone needed to look carefully at the documents detailing the revenue of the estate.

He summoned Das and asked for those files.

'Yes, sir. I also think you should see these,' Das said, holding out a clutch of leaflets.

Ashe pursed his lips and took the single pages printed on cheap paper. The only part in English was at the bottom, announcing that the leaflets had been printed by the Feringhi Destroyer Press.

'I can't read this, Das. It's in Tamil.'

'I have prepared rough translations, also, sir,' Das said and gave him two pieces of paper in his handwriting. 'But I thought you would want to see the originals. As evidence.'

Ashe nodded, took the translations and smoothed them out on his desk.

'Two different leaflets?' he asked, without looking up.

'Yes, sir. But the same press, same paper, same language and similar content.'

Beneath the heading 'A Friendly Word to Aryans', Ashe read the first sentence: 'We exhort all Indians to cherish rancour and swear to God that you will remove the sinner of a feringhi [foreigner].'

'Where did you get these?' he asked.

'People brought them in from all across the district, sir. These two came from Tenkasi.'

Ashe swallowed hard and read on: 'Kill the foreigner, even as you would a dog, with a knife, a stick, a stone or even the hands given by God. The ancient sage Vyasa has predicted that the "white empire" will be destroyed in the period between Nandana [1892] and Andana [1914].'

The second leaflet also called for the violent overthrow of the British government and the death of its representatives. It then reminded 'all Indians that the task begun in 1857 is yet to be accomplished. Let us finish it once and for all. Cherish rancour'.

'Send for Superintendent Hartley,' Ashe ordered Das. 'Tell him I want to see him as soon as possible.'

The police chief arrived just before noon, placed his cap on his knee and sat opposite the glum-faced collector.

'So, what's the good news?' he said, looking around with his habitual squint.

Ashe showed him the leaflets and translations, and explained where they had come from.

'They're prolific, I'll give them that,' Hartley said.

'Is it the same group as before? The leaflets, I mean?' Ashe asked.

'Hard to say. They changed their name, though. Now it's Abhinav Bharata Society. How did Das translate that? Oh, yes. Young India. That seems about right.'

Hartley had served in India for more than twenty years and had a reputation as a linguist.

'What does "feringhi" mean?' Ashe asked. 'I know it's us, but what exactly?'

'It's Urdu for "foreigner". Or, more accurately, "European". It's from the Arabic. Not cognate, funnily enough, with our word "foreign". That comes from Greek and Latin for "Frank". You know, the people who conquered Gaul in... Sorry, old man, can't stop once I've got rolling.'

'Foreigner, eh?' Ashe said with an arch smile. Taping his forefinger on the bottom of one of the leaflets, he asked, 'What about this Feringhi Destroyer press? Sounds like a joke to me.'

Hartley screwed up his face even more tightly. 'It's no joke. My guess is it's in Pondicherry.'

'Pondicherry? Anything we can do there?'

'Not much, I'm afraid. Request surveillance, but they usually don't take any notice.'

'Blasted French!'

Hartley's lips spread into a thin smile. He was about to make a comment about French political exiles in London in the 1790s but thought better of it.

'Pondicherry's become as important as Calcutta for the revolutionaries,' he said instead. 'It's the only place these people can print their leaflets now.'

'This Nilakanta and his ilk, I suppose,' Ashe threw in.

'Exactly. And there are others, who you probably know. One named Bharati writes flowery stuff about swadeshi. Another one, Ghose, is something of a sadhu.'

Ashe nodded.

'But we're more worried about a recent arrival. Chap called Aiyar. VVS Aiyar, to give the pretentious nigger his full name.'

'Aren't they all called Aiyar or Iyer or Iyengar?'

Hartley snorted and said, 'He's a special one, though.'

Ashe listened to a wildly inaccurate account of Aiyar's escape from London and flight to India.

'CID are keeping an eye on him, even in Pondicherry,' Hartley added at the end. 'Could be he's printed these vile things.'

Ashe picked up a leaflet and waved it about.

'Did you ever read such rubbish? "Cherish rancour." "An ancient sage predicted the end of the white empire." For God's sake!'

Hartley smiled again. 'Typical of our gentlemen revolutionaries here in the south,' he said. 'More mythology than ideology, if you ask me. They have extremist views all right, but they don't throw bombs like they do in Bengal.'

Ashe frowned and looked at the drawer with the hidden letter.

'Aiyar's one of those Brahmins educated in London,' Hartley went on. 'Proper wog, he is.'

'Maybe,' Ashe said, 'but Das says these things are all over the district.'

'Don't worry, Robert,' Hartley said as he rose to leave. 'We've got everyone here under surveillance. We know what they're up to and we'll move on them before long. As soon as we have more intelligence.'

Ashe cancelled his appearance at the veterinary hospital and pushed the court papers aside. He swung back and forth in his chair and wondered who 'everyone' was.

*

The following day, Ashe made his monthly inspection visit to the prison in Palayamkottai. Accompanied by the warden, he walked down the line of prisoners and watched as another member of staff used a short stick to lift their tattered tunics and look inside their flimsy trousers. 'Checking for any dangerous objects,' the warden explained, with a wink. Most of the men were shaven-headed. All had sunken eyes. Ashe asked if anyone had ever been found with a knife or a gun.

'No,' the warden said. 'That's the proof that our routine is an effective deterrent.'

Ashe also observed the prisoners as they received their mid-day meal. They filed past a waist-high table filled with cooked rice. One prisoner was given the task of scooping up two handfuls of rice and depositing it in a metal bowl held out by the prisoners. Any excess rice was scraped away and knocked back onto the table by running a wooden ruler over the edge of the bowl. A second prisoner ladled vegetable curry on top. Two scoops of rice, one ladle of curry. No more and no less for each man, who squatted and wolfed down the food.

The prisoners were then allowed to wash. Off came the tunics and trousers. Clad only in a loin-cloth, they knelt by the side of the trough and, using the same bowl as that for eating, poured water over their head. They scooped out the water as fast as possible. After thirty seconds, an officer blew a whistle and the next batch of bathers took their place.

Back in his office, Ashe recorded his visit, noting the

satisfactory condition of the cells and the prisoners. He had yet to supervise a hanging, but he knew that day would come.

He came home a little early that evening with a plan to visit another institution in Palayamkottai. And when Mary said she was feeling better, he revealed his idea to take her out to dinner at the European Club.

'Something to cheer you up,' he said. 'Besides, it's almost your birthday.'

They hardly ever went to the Club, except when invited by others, but Mary realized that Robert needed a break, too.

'Oh, Robbie, that is sweet. But I can scarcely believe it. Nearly forty years old.'

'Well, you know what they say?'

'What's that?'

'Be wise at forty because a fool at forty is a fool indeed.'

'And in six months' time, when you cross that golden threshold, know what I'll say?'

'No.'

'Every man over forty is a scoundrel.'

They both laughed aloud, which caused the cook to poke his head around the screen that separated the kitchen from the sitting room.

The European Club had been established in the 1880s, though it occupied a much older building. In addition to the bar and dining room, it included a good library and playable tennis court. As a local resident, Ashe paid an annual subscription of eight rupees, while others coming from nearby towns paid only five but were limited to two visits per month. Membership was also restricted by class rather than race, which amounted to the same thing, as the only Indian member was the chief medical officer of the district.

The austerity of the squat building was relieved by an extensive garden and flower pots on the shaded veranda. Set back from a tree-lined road, it was approached by a semi-circular drive bordered by white-painted stones. Most evenings, the thwack of racquet on ball could be heard mingling with bursts of laughter echoing out from the veranda.

When the horse-drawn carriage stopped, Robert leapt out and held Mary's hand while she negotiated the drop to the ground. Walking arm in arm up the steps and through the reception area, they chatted away like schoolchildren. Inside the dining room, their voices fell to a whisper as Robert nodded to acquaintances and led her to a table with a view of the veranda.

The set meal was predictable yet satisfying. After the mulligatawny soup, which again produced grins on both their faces, they feasted on a joint of beef, fish curry and several side dishes. Throughout the meal, their pleasure in each other's company was enhanced by the cheerful atmosphere, and they took special delight in painting a portrait of each of their children, discussing how they had changed and what their futures might bring.

Only when the tarts were brought for dessert did Robert's face change. Idly looking around the crowded room, he saw the blond-haired Mr Walker seated with managers from the cotton mill in Tuticorin.

'Anyone you know?' Mary asked.

'Oh, just someone I met the other day.'

After Mary excused herself to use the ladies' room, Ashe lit his pipe and pretended to enjoy the view of the garden beyond the veranda. From the corner of his eye, though, he kept watch on Walker's table, and when the newcomer left, he sauntered over.

'Good meal, eh?' he said to the three men, whom he knew not only from his time in Tuticorin but also from more recent interactions in Tinnevelly.

'Indeed. And you? Wife and children all doing well, I hope,' said one of the managers.

'Yes. I see you know our friend, Mr Walker.'

'Who?'

'The chap you were talking to just now. Walker. Down here representing a Mr Collingwood. South India Cement.'

The men looked at each other and shook their heads.

'He said his name's Pemberton, a journalist from London.'

Ashe furrowed his brow.

'Right…I guess he just looked like someone else. Interesting conversation?'

'He asked about our plans to build the new factory. Knows we'll need cement and wanted to do business.'

'I see,' Ashe said. 'Oh, there's the wife. Why not come into the office one day? I'd like to hear more about those plans.'

*

When Mary's cold worsened, he urged her to go away and stay with the children in Kodai. He felt it was better if all the family were up there while the situation in the plains remained troubled. He didn't want to use the word 'dangerous', not even to himself. She would only be going a few months early, and he would join them sometime in June, when things would surely be resolved. Hartley reckoned that it wouldn't be long before the CID arrested whoever was distributing the leaflets. Stop that and the whole thing would collapse. Back to normal, so I can get on with counting palmyra trees, Ashe said to himself with a snicker.

He wanted to trust Hartley's judgement but still hadn't shown him the letter from the Bharata Mata Association. Out of sight, out of mind, he hoped. Except it didn't work like that. He was lucky if he managed to get through a whole day without looking at the letter.

'I'm not going, much as I'd love to see the kiddies early,' Mary said when he raised the topic again at dinner. 'This silly cold will die off soon anyway.'

He wasn't unhappy that she had refused to take his advice. He never liked being alone, and now he felt he needed her strength more than ever. He wasn't sleeping well and during the day his mind often spun around and around. The letter, the leaflets, Pillai, Pondicherry, Walker. Even Das.

'I suppose you're right,' he said, and that was the end of it.

Although she seldom contradicted him, she went against her own judgement even less frequently. It had been that way from the very beginning, he realized, as they sat in separate chairs after coffee. She worked on a jumper that she was croqueting for eight-year-old Sheila, who never seemed to be warm enough in the mountains. He puffed on his pipe and ran his eyes over revenue reports for salt production:

> The recent reduction in excise of Rs 2.80 to Rs. 2 per maund had mostly likely led to the increased production in the four factories in the district, but the illegal salt-making from the sea had...

He glanced at Mary, head bent to her task. She wasn't a beautiful woman, he admitted, but she had character. That's what had attracted him in the first place, all those years ago in Dublin. Her candour had surprised and delighted him, especially the letters she had written to him after he'd been sent to India and before they were married. She was clever, using a secret language, a sort of love code, that only he understood. 'Pussycat' wrote to 'Mr Walrus', telling him that 'worms wiggled through the wet soil' and that 'leaves on the plane trees grew warm in the sunlight'.

Those letters, too, were kept in the locked drawer in his office. He read them sometimes, when Das was away.

13

Shenkottai, 1911

When Ponammal heard the moaning, it was pitch black on a muggy night. Rolling over onto her stomach, she propped herself up on her forearms and looked out through the kitchen doorway. She could just make out the hammock hanging from the beams in the front room, where her daughter slept. She saw that it was motionless and relaxed.

Vanni was not a healthy child, everyone could see that. She ran around, played and laughed like a normal little girl, but she often had a high fever and the spots remained on her skin like a permanent stain. Ponammal went to the goddess temple every Tuesday to pray for her, and Thatha supplied her with special potions. She also hung another wooden cradle on the tree, telling herself that Vanni would like to have a brother or sister. Deep down, she wondered if she were hoping for a replacement.

She turned over and was half-asleep when she heard the moaning again. Not at all child-like. It was coming from her husband lying in another corner of the kitchen, a position he had taken up for the past several months. No explanation had been given and none asked for.

'Hey,' she whispered. 'Quiet.'

But the low moan continued and became a growl.

'What's the matter?'

No response, so she crawled over and shook him hard on the shoulder.

Vanchi screamed.

'It was the head,' he told her after the others in the front room had been assured that nothing was the matter.

'What?'

'I saw his head. The one I...' He stopped and stared at the wall. 'What day is it?'

'Can't see in the dark.'

Vanchi lit the kerosene lamp and held it close to the calendar hanging on the wall. It was a thick pad of small square sheets, one for each of the days of the Tamil year. He didn't read the astrological information and ritual instructions, or even notice the English date of 30 January. It was enough to know that it was the full-moon day. And he wasn't surprised.

Almost a year had passed since he had taken the blood oath. He and Shankara continued to distribute leaflets sent from Pondicherry, though Vanchi's excuses were beginning to wear thin at home and at work. He had also recited the oath once a month, as Nilakanta had ordered, but he couldn't bear to do it while looking at the blood-stained paper hidden in the banyan tree. Instead, he had memorized the words and repeated them on each full-moon day, on his walk to the bathing pool in the morning. That way it all stayed inside his head, where it was safe.

'Here, take this,' Thatha said in the morning and handed him a concoction of ground ginger root and senna leaves. 'You're not sleeping well, she says.'

They were sitting on the veranda after breakfast. The women were eating inside with Vanni, their laughter audible. Men and boys were moving in the narrow Brahmin street, coming and going from their bath and other morning business. Towels were slung over their shoulders, wrapped around their waists or turban-like on their heads. The early morning sun had cleared the tree tops, and steam rose from the ground with a hiss.

Vanchi drank the concoction and looked at the *kolam* on

the ground in front of the veranda. It was a complex design, made only on that full-moon day. Large circles connected by broad stripes formed a ring around a grid pattern in the centre.

'Afternoon shift today?' Thatha asked.

'Yes.'

'Why not come with me then? I'm going towards Thenmala, to get some honey.'

'Ah, I can't.'

Thatha raised a bushy eyebrow. 'Then come to temple with me,' he said.

Thatha led the way down the street. The gauze-like mist had burned off, letting the sun warm every bone of Thatha's thin body. He carried a small, round brass pot of cooked rice mixed with spices and milk.

Together, they ducked inside the dank space, just big enough for them to stand up in and hold another two or three people. The air smelled of coconut oil. In front of them, Shiva sat cross-legged on a raised plinth, his dark body festooned with a garland of bright marigolds. Red hibiscus flowers, with phallic-like protruding stigma, lay scattered on the ground.

Vanchi watched as Thatha moved forward and placed his pot on the edge of the plinth, close to the god's feet. Stepping back, but still facing the god, Thatha stood beside Vanchi. They chanted verses that celebrated the marriage of Shiva and Parvati and blessed their sons, Murugan and Ganesha. After they prayed silently for a few minutes, Thatha poured the rice mixture over the god and both men withdrew.

'You know, it's not just Shiva's marriage we honoured in there,' Thatha said as they walked back to the house. 'It's every marriage, all husbands and wives.'

Vanchi looked straight ahead, avoiding Thatha's eyes and trying to ignore his words.

As soon as they reached the house, Thatha buckled on his leather belt and picked up two jute bags. 'Right, I'm off,' he said. 'You should go to temple more often. It's good for you.'

Vanchi watched his grandfather walk away. He's right, he thought. I do feel better when I'm chanting and praying. When it's all under control. With lines that mark beginnings and endings.

Vanchi waited until Thatha had disappeared into the jungle behind the temple before he set out for the bathing pool. Fifteen minutes later, he had passed through the market and turned off the main road onto the path through the paddy fields. Once inside the forest, he recited the oath. Neither aloud nor in a whisper, this time his voice found a rhythm in the phrases, a regular pattern of rising and falling tones, which carried him to the end: 'When we drink kumkum, it is the blood of white men.' The oath had become a chant.

*

When the summons came, it had the mystique of the ordinary. A stranger came to the Forest Department checkpoint and said, 'Meet your friend at the same place as before. At sunrise tomorrow.'

'Shankara, too?' he'd asked.

'No. Just you.'

At home that evening, Vanchi was quieter than usual. He barely spoke, though he played with Vanni and laughed when she tried to climb up on the veranda and fell back. Later, when he ate, he squeezed each handful of rice into a perfect ball before popping it into his mouth.

His early departure aroused no suspicion—he was on the early shift that day anyway—and the town was half-asleep in the grey light as he walked through the market. Out on the main road, he could just about trace the crooked line of the mountain tops as it began to separate from the sky. When he entered the forest, bird calls rang out with cut-glass clarity.

His first surprise was to see Madasami, not Nilakanta, waiting for him beside the banyan tree. He had grown a beard and put on weight, though he was still the same dark little man that Vanchi had met three years ago in Tuticorin. They greeted each other without ceremony.

'You came alone, right?' Madasami said.

'Yes.'

'No one knows you're here?'

'No one.'

Madasami drew closer to him and took his hand.

'You are a lucky man,' he said. 'You're to go to Pondicherry immediately. Nilakanta wants you.'

Vanchi let out his breath. Not a killing, then. Not in Pondicherry.

'He needs help with a newspaper he wants to start,' Madasami explained. 'And there are others there who also need your help.'

*

Vanchi took two months' sick leave, telling everyone at home and the checkpoint that he had work in Madras. That a friend from college in Trivandrum had contacted him and would pay him to help publish his newspaper. He didn't like lying to his grandfather, but that was as close to the truth as he dared go.

'And after two months?' Thatha asked. 'What then?'

'I'll see. Maybe I'll come back. Maybe I'll stay there.'

'What's his name, this friend?'

'You don't know him.'

Thatha fixed him with a stare. 'What's his name?'

'Subramania. From Thanjavur. He's a writer now, and a journalist.'

'He's not like Shankara?'

'No, he's not like Shankara.'

His mother was not happy to see him leave for so long and with such vague prospects. Ponammal wondered if she should try to stop him.

'I don't like it,' she said to her mother-in-law. 'He's been so strange lately. Moody and distant.'

'Don't worry,' the older woman said while the two of them sat outside and patted cow dung into flat cakes for the fire. 'He'll come back. Just like his father.'

'But that's different. You know what Father-in-law is doing, with his government job. My husband is secretive.' She'd been searching for that word for some time. 'And Madras is a long way away.'

14

Pondicherry, 1911

Vanchi had no need to travel by boat and wear a disguise, as Aiyar had done when he fled to the French territory. He simply bought a second-class train ticket in Tinnevelly and rode the length of the Madras Presidency from south to north.

He brought with him a small cardboard case, containing an extra set of clothes, a bar of soap, a copy of the *Tirukkural*, which was a gift from Dr Raghavan, and a small tin box filled with Thatha's concoction for headaches and nerves. His mother provided him with a packet of cold rice and half a dozen idlis.

Madasami had warned him to be careful and look out for suspicious people, but Vanchi dozed most of the eighteen hours of the journey. The carriage he rode in on the overnight trip was largely occupied by families with children of all ages. Clutching his case, he sat on a hardwood-slated bench, leaned against whoever was beside him and drifted into sleep. No one spoke to him, except to say 'move over' or 'what's the next station?' No one paid any attention to him—a young Brahmin man heading north, probably to Madras—not even the policemen lounging on the station platforms.

At Villupuram, close to Madras, he got down and boarded a slower train that took him east towards the Bay of Bengal. It was mid-morning when it stopped at the border, an isolated station that Madasami had warned him about. Vanchi held his suitcase tight against his stomach.

'Tickets! Tickets!' cried the uniformed official who was working his way down the aisle of the crowded carriage. Vanchi was glad to see that he was Indian, though the man swore at anyone who took more than a few seconds to fish out the creased piece of paper. Vanchi found his and looked at the handwritten details, now smudged by the damp heat of his body. A passenger in the middle of the carriage was told to get off and report to the stationmaster. Vanchi pressed hard on his case, until the surly official glanced at his ticket and passed on.

He couldn't relax, though, because everyone was ordered out of the carriages and onto the platform. He and the rest of the passengers were lined up by officials wearing a box-like red hat with a small black visor, a white shirt and white shorts. Must be from Pondicherry, Vanchi thought. Although they spoke Tamil, somehow it didn't sound the same. They looked like police, but he couldn't be sure.

As Vanchi shuffled forward in the queue, he kept telling himself that he possessed nothing suspicious. No revolutionary pamphlets, no banned books, no seditious leaflets. Madasami had been adamant. Tell them you are visiting your uncle.

Inside the room at the end of the platform, a foreign man with the little red hat commanded a desk beside an Indian in office clothes. Behind them stood two Indians in the French uniform. They were definitely police.

'Open your suitcase,' he was told in Tamil by the plain-clothes man, who translated the foreigner's words. The man opened Thatha's tin, smelled and dipped a finger into the herbal mixture.

'Medicine?'

'Yes, sir.'

'Why are you going to Pondicherry?'

'My uncle.'

'Who is that?'

Vanchi hesitated. Madasami hadn't provided any further details. Looking behind the desk for an answer, he noticed piles of confiscated goods against the wall. Sacks of rice and other grains, clusters of coconuts, areca nuts and toddy palm fruits.

'Well?'

'He has a shop, a fresh fruit shop, and—'

'What's his name?'

'Madasami.' It came out without thinking.

'Address?'

Vanchi stared at the man and bit his lower lip.

'It's in Pondicherry, sir. Near the railway station. He will meet me there, at the station.'

'Next.'

An hour later, the whistle shrieked, steam hissed from the engine and the train clattered across the border into French territory. He had been to Trivandrum and Tuticorin, but now he was more than four hundred miles from home. All around, he saw rice fields, palmyra trees, some scrubland and the occasional hamlet. But no mountains.

*

He exited Pondicherry railway station in bright sunshine and felt a ripple of excitement for the first time on the long journey. Gripping his case, he walked towards a water fountain mounted on a low plinth in the centre of the dusty square. He cupped his hands and drank from one of the four taps. Jutkas, pony carts, bullock carts and pedestrians passed by him as he stood and tried to find his bearings. Spotting someone who did not look intimidating, he asked a sweets-vendor for directions to Eswaran Dharmaraja Street. 'Don't ask for Dharma House,' Madasami had told him. 'We're the only ones who call it that.'

Following the route described, Vanchi headed north in the direction of a church, indicated by its twin spires. He began to notice more and more white people and street signs in a foreign language that was not English. The streets were laid out in a grid pattern, with squares every quarter mile or so. The elegant, pristine buildings had high-arched doors and ornate railings on the balconies. Everything seemed monumental and modern, like Trivandrum. Unlike the red-brick of the Travancore capital, though, the colour scheme was white and ochre-yellow, picked out with gold trim. The smell of the sea was strong.

He heard voices and realized that he had been standing still. They must be talking in French, he thought and moved on, wondering why he had been summoned. Was there no one in Pondicherry to help Nilakanta with his newspaper? Besides, he had no experience with printing or writing.

The next landmark was an older and smaller church. Also gleaming white and gold, with three sky-blue doors, it drew him close. He'd never been inside a church.

'Everyone's welcome,' he heard a woman say in formal Tamil. She was all in white, with a headdress like a shawl and a large cross hanging down the front.

'Yes, I—'

'You may visit us whenever you like.' She beamed a beneficent smile at the young Brahmin and walked past him towards the blue doors.

Vanchi turned inland and crossed the canal into Ville Noire. Looking for a temple, he found himself in a street full of shops selling household items, woven mats, baskets, chairs and tables. 'Which temple?' a shopkeeper asked when Vanchi sought his help. There were three in the neighbourhood, but only one on a corner, as described.

He stood with his suitcase and looked down Eswaran Dharmaraja Street. One side was lit by the late afternoon sun, where dogs lay in the dust, while the other side was half in shade. In the mixture of one- and two-storey houses and shops, the houses had shallow verandas, some with white wicker chairs and flower pots, though there was no sign of children.

'Move it!' The voice came from a thin-chested man pushing a cart piled high with coconuts. Vanchi stared as the man shoved the heavy load past him. 'And don't ask,' he shot back, 'because I don't know.'

Vanchi found number 43, squeezed between a dry goods shop and a prosperous-looking house. The shuttered windows were open, but no sound came from within. The tiled roof of the veranda was in disrepair, and the wooden support posts looked crooked. Dharma House.

He turned and walked back to the corner. He could easily retrace his steps back to the station. Board a train and return to Shenkottai. He'd say his friend in Madras didn't need him. No questions would be asked. Ponammal would be happy, and Thatha relieved. Nilakanta would find someone else to help him.

He heard a handbell ring and saw a procession of women carrying brass plates of fruit and flowers. It was Tuesday. He watched them move together, barefoot, damp black hair hanging down their backs, their voices low. They would worship the goddess in a nearby temple. They would place their offerings at her feet, hiding their face with a corner of their sari. They would mouth words that had been spoken for a thousand years, asking for rain to soak the earth, fields to flourish with grain and women to give birth. He could hear their muffled chanting as they passed. Not the words, but the rising and falling sounds. A rhythmic chant, like his own.

*

The front door was flung open as soon as Vanchi stepped up to the veranda at Dharma House.

'Come in.'

Entering the front room, he saw several men at a large table, who seemed to be reading something as a group. They all stopped and looked up at him without speaking. He didn't see Nilakanta or Madasami.

'Is Nilakanta here?' Vanchi asked quietly, still only two steps inside the house.

He was told that he had gone away for a while and that no one knew when to expect him. Vanchi withdrew and looked around with startled eyes.

'Don't worry. You're among friends.'

The deep voice carried across the room from the bottom of the stairs near the back. The man came forward, took Vanchi's hand and said, 'We've been expecting you.'

His long black hair was parted straight down the middle, brushed close to the skull and tied in a knot at the back. He wore a long-sleeved tunic with a breast pocket large enough to hold a book. And his black leather shoes shone beneath an immaculate white *veshti*.

'You're Vanchi, aren't you?' he said with a smile that peeked through his bushy beard and thick moustache.

'Yes, but—'

'I know. Nilakanta sent for you. He'll be back soon. First, we'll get you something to eat. Then you'll need a good night's sleep. We will talk in the morning.'

Vanchi slept in one of the upstairs rooms, on a cot and mattress for the first time in his life. Waking in the early morning, he sat on the edge and looked around. Only a small table and chair, with his suitcase against the wall, but it seemed large because he was alone. He barely heard a sound in the house and wondered again why he was there.

He crept downstairs, found a water pump in the back courtyard and took a bath. It had been more than two days, and he scrubbed hard, using the bar of Pears he had bought in the market in Shenkottai before he left.

'Hey! You won't become a white man just by scrubbing, you know.'

Vanchi turned and saw one of the men who had been in the room when he'd arrived. He stood with a smile on his face and a towel around his expansive waist, waiting to bathe.

'I tried it, and look at me,' he said, this time with a big laugh. His name was Perumal. He was the cook and the printer, and he was as black as coal.

Vanchi ate breakfast with him and three others, though he wasn't sure if they slept in the house or outside. The idlis and sambar, which Perumal prepared, were nothing like those in Shenkottai, and he found it difficult to eat at a table. His right elbow kept knocking against the hard surface as his hand moved to his mouth.

'Aiyar will be here later,' Perumal said. 'Till then you can help with the printing.'

About the height of a man, the black letterpress machine was compact, its large wheel, numerous gears, levers, handles and plates neatly arranged like human organs. On a nearby table, the metal types were stored in a wooden tray with rows of little square compartments. One for each of the more than two hundred Tamil letters.

'We'll start by setting this line,' Perumal said and pointed to the first sentence handwritten in Tamil on a piece of paper: 'Foreigners decide how you live; but you can decide how you die.'

One by one, Perumal found the metal types and laid them into one of the thin metal trays, or composing sticks. After a short time, Vanchi began to help with the task of hunting down the correct letter. By noon, they had set the entire text, which ended with the exhortation: 'If you cannot be a man in life, become one in death.'

They lined up the sticks, making sure that they were correctly spaced, and used a roller to spread a thin layer of ink over them. Finally, they laid a piece of paper on top and stepped on the floor pedal, which brought down a flat plate and left an inked impression on the paper. By the time they stopped to eat two hours later, they had printed close to a hundred leaflets.

When Aiyar arrived in the late afternoon, Vanchi had been released from printing duties by Perumal and was reading at the table in the front room. Aiyar sat down beside him, and Vanchi stood up. Aiyar gestured for him to sit down, but only half-heartedly, and Vanchi remained standing.

'Your full name is Vanchinathan, isn't it?' he said.

'Yes.'

'Do you know what that means?'

Vanchi was about to speak when Aiyar answered his own question.

'The Lord of Desire,' he said, 'that's what it means. Not necessarily the sexual urge, but something deeper. A passion for what is right. We have another word for it. Dharma.'

Despite Aiyar's stocky build, his voice was soft, almost liquid.

'Yes, sir.'

'By the way, what are you reading?'

Vanchi showed him his copy of the *Tirukkural*.

'Excellent choice. Do you have a favourite verse?'

'No, I—'

'Mine is this: "What separates the great from the ordinary is their ability to do the seemingly impossible." Does that make sense to you?'

'I think so, sir.'

'Good. I want you to remember that verse.'

Over the following days, Aiyar spoke with Vanchi at length every afternoon. He gave him history lessons, starting with the ancient south Indian kingdoms followed by the incursions of the Portuguese, the Dutch, the French and the English. He reserved one day to narrate the story of local resistance to the foreigners, ending in about 1800.

'People of all kinds fought the outsiders,' Aiyar said. 'Not just powerful rulers, like Tipu Sultan, but also small groups in the countryside. Especially in the southern districts, where you come from.'

Thatha would like his man, Vanchi thought. He might even know the name of the stone man.

'That is our task,' Aiyar continued, 'to resist enslavement. It's the lesson of another of my favourite verses in the *Kural*. It reads: "One man carrying another man in a palanquin cannot be the result of a previous moral act." You understand?'

Vanchi said he did, though he was relieved that he had not been asked to explain.

After a week, Aiyar plunged into world history, explaining the revolutions in Italy, France and Russia. When he stood or paced around the room and delivered these impromptu lectures, Vanchi sat cross-legged on the floor with hands in his lap. If Aiyar sat on a chair, Vanchi stood beside him. Others might be listening, but it was clear that Aiyar was directing his words at the young man from Shenkottai.

The history lessons were followed by an examination of current events. Aiyar would tell Vanchi to read the front page of a Tamil daily and summarize the news. Aiyar did the same for an English paper, after which Vanchi was encouraged to ask questions.

'Gandhi is a great man, no doubt,' Aiyar said in answer to one query. 'He's doing good work in South Africa, but his belief in non-violence is foolish. More than that, it is a diversion. A dangerous diversion from our goals.'

Vanchi and the other young men under Aiyar's tutelage were also given physical training. Every morning they met at first light in a park where an instructor led them through a series of exercises, and twice a week they were made to run along a sandy beach. Panting and coughing, Vanchi always came last. He collapsed once and began to wonder if physical training was the 'seemingly impossible' thing mentioned in Aiyar's favourite verse.

Printing the leaflets made it all worthwhile. He liked everything about the meticulous business and looked at the neat stacks with pride. In the evening, the stacks were tied into bundles and hidden in jutkas and bullock carts, which carried them across the border. Once inside British India, the bundles travelled by train and cart before being distributed by hand, just as he and Shankara had done. Now, though, Vanchi appreciated the scale of the network that linked a single press in Pondicherry with every major town and city in Madras Presidency. A beginning and an end, with firm boundaries.

Aiyar was equally determined that Dharma House should disseminate books that had been banned in British India. His favourite was a special edition of Savarkar's *India's War of Independence*. Written in London, printed in Amsterdam and disguised with a dust jacket for Dickens's *Pickwick Papers*, hundreds of copies were concealed in the bullock carts that creaked through the night and over the border.

*

Although satisfied, Vanchi was restless. Nilakanta and his newspaper had been forgotten. He sensed that Aiyar had a plan. Alone in his room at night, he turned over the possibilities in his mind. It was time to recite the oath again.

When Nilakanta did appear, he offered no explanation for his absence. He slept in the other cot in Vanchi's room and told him about Shankara.

'He's found another person to help with the leaflets. And he said to tell you something.'

'What?'

'Everyone at home is fine.'

'That's all?'

'Yes.'

Vanchi wanted to write a letter back home. He had promised to write to his grandfather, if only to give them his address. But he'd said he was going to Madras and couldn't post a letter from Pondicherry. Besides, letters were not allowed. 'No one should know you're here,' Aiyar had said on the very first day.

'I can take a letter for you,' Nilakanta said, reading his thoughts. 'I'm going back next week.'

As he drifted off to sleep that night, Vanchi saw the hills above Shenkottai. He heard Vanni laughing on the veranda and watched his mother draw her *kolam*.

'Dear Thatha,' he wrote in the morning. 'I am fine and hope the same for you. I am with friends and working well.

Do not worry about me, please. The work is important. I will come home when it is finished. Vanchi.' He did not include an address.

Nilakanta took him on walks through Pondicherry, showing him the historical monuments and statues, but Vanchi did not like going into White Town. The massive stone buildings that had impressed him on arrival now frightened him. People gave him odd looks because he didn't appear to be a servant or a government clerk or a rich native.

Madasami soon arrived and slept on the floor. The three of them were together now, allowing Vanchi to connect the past with the present. What he was doing was the result of what he had already done. Still, he waited.

Vanchi wasn't sure how it happened, though he noticed that Nilakanta did not respond to Aiyar's impromptu afternoon lectures. Instead, he began to quote from the *Gita* and let his hair grow matted like a holy man. In their bedtime discussions, Nilakanta also disagreed with Madasami and voiced doubts about Aiyar's methods. One night, he told them he had attended one of the spiritual talks given by Ghose.

The final break came when Aiyar told the others about his choice of a headline for the next leaflet.

'It will be this: "We will destroy them with a bomb, the bomb of Kali".'

'We shouldn't use Kali's name that way,' Nilakanta objected. 'She is a divine force, not to be sullied by violence.'

Aiyar countered by saying that the energy of the goddess should always be used 'to achieve righteous ends'. Vanchi and the others listened as the two men argued late into the night. The next morning, Nilakanta left Dharma House.

*

Again, it was Madasami who delivered the message. The little dark man who rarely spoke during political discussions had become Aiyar's most trusted lieutenant. He told Vanchi that Aiyar wanted to see him at his house.

'You know where it is, right?' he said. 'Four o'clock tomorrow afternoon. Don't be late. Or early.'

Why not here, in Dharma House? Vanchi asked himself as he lay on his cot. And why am I still here? As long as Nilakanta had remained in Dharma House, he had assisted him. But now that Nilakanta had left, he could go back to Shenkottai. He could help Shankara with the leaflets. He could look Thatha in the eye and say that he'd gained experience. They'd all be proud that he'd worked in 'Madras' for a while. Besides, Vanni was growing up and Ponammal wanted a second child. He could resume his job at the checkpoint. It might be a dead end, but it was convenient and the pay was regular. With a decent pension.

He knew it was Aiyar's house because the door was painted a bright red. 'For the revolution,' his mentor had said with a twinkle in his eye. His wife ushered Vanchi inside with a warm smile as if he were a favourite cousin. The small room was filled with books, jammed on shelves, piled on tables, toppling off chairs and stacked on the floor. A dark green curtain was drawn in front of the rusty iron bars of the only window. Aiyar was writing, head bent over a table.

'Ah, come in,' he said, without looking at him. 'I'll just finish this.'

Five minutes passed before he spoke again. 'How would you say *arul kadal* in English?'

Vanchi stood mute.

'Sorry, I forgot. You don't know English very well, do you? Just a minute.'

His wife entered the room with a tray, cleared a table and arranged the teacups and pot.

'You better stop now,' she said, 'or poor Vanchi will think you are ruder than you really are.'

She could be an older sister, he thought. He'd like that.

He noticed that there were three cups, not two, and was a little surprised when Aiyar's wife sat with her husband after serving. Vanchi remained standing and did not drink until they had.

'How long have you been with us here?' Aiyar asked.

'Two months, sir. I came in February.'

'How do you like the work? The printing and so forth?'

'It is important.'

'But is it enough? That is the question I constantly ask myself.' Aiyar fixed Vanchi with his large brown eyes. 'You have taken the oath, is that right?'

'Yes, sir.'

'Good. Tomorrow morning, you will not go to the park for physical training. Instead, Madasami will take you to another place. For training in firearms.'

*

The dry paddy field was the size of a tennis court. Tall coconut trees separated it from a stream running along one side. On the three other sides, mud-packed bunds separated it from adjacent fields. Together, the dozen or so fields formed a mosaic of unequal sizes and shapes, though most were rectangular. There were no houses in sight. It was two hours before daybreak.

When Vanchi and Madasami stepped down from the bund and onto the cracked earth, a man emerged from behind the trees.

'This is our friend,' Madasami said to him, gesturing towards Vanchi, who stood behind him.

The man was both older and taller than them. White puffs of hair stuck out from his temples and his skin was pitted. He eyed Vanchi as he might a chicken in the market.

'Right,' he said, with a rasping voice. 'I don't have a name and neither do you.'

Vanchi didn't speak or move.

'Ever seen one of these?' the man said.

The gun lay flat in his palm. Black and sleek, it was

compact, though the metal ring surrounding the trigger looked disproportionately large.

Vanchi shook his head to say no.

'Well, it's easy to use.'

Vanchi watched as the man detached the magazine from behind the handle.

'This new model takes six bullets,' he said. 'You just pull the trigger and another bullet is fired. You don't have to load them or anything.'

He slammed the empty magazine back into the grip and handed the pistol to Vanchi. It was heavy, like the brass pestle that Thatha used to pound leaves and bark. But the metal on the handle was textured and easy to grip.

'Go on. Point it at something.'

Vanchi raised his hand.

'Higher,' the man said.

He aimed the short barrel at the trees on far side, though they were barely visible. In a few seconds, his arm grew tired and dropped.

'There's one thing, though,' the man said and took back the gun. 'The safety catch on the grip has to be pressed hard. Otherwise it won't fire.'

He lifted a handful of bullets from the pocket of his tunic and showed them to Vanchi. They used a smokeless powder, he explained, so your sight is not blurred. He slotted them into the magazine, one by one, and banged the magazine back into the handle with the heel of his palm.

'Right. When you take aim,' he said, 'raise it slowly. To this point.'

He stopped with the gun held just above the line of his shoulder.

'And don't hold your arm out straight. You can't control it that way. Hold it like this.'

He retracted his arm by bending the elbow, until the gun was about a foot from his shoulder.

'Then, press hard on the safety and squeeze the trigger. Slowly but firmly. Like this.'

Vanchi winced. It wasn't an explosion, but a crash. Two in quick succession, like metal hurled against metal. Followed by a faint echo and then a silence amplified by the deafening sound that preceded it.

They headed back to Pondicherry before any sliver of light appeared on the horizon. They saw no one and heard little until they reached the edge of a village, where dogs barked. Vanchi smelled a frangipani tree, plucked one of its delicate white flowers and tucked it behind his ear. The waiting was over.

A pale grey light was seeping in from the east when they reached the outskirts of the town. Most shops were still shuttered, though people were moving about. Street vendors were setting out their wares, schoolchildren were heading to the city centre and women were returning wet-haired from the river. In the tea stalls, day labourers sat on sagging benches, naked except for a loin-cloth and a towel wound around their head. They sipped, smoked and chatted about the weather, their wages and someone's wife. Behind them, a store sign in English announced 'Tip Top Fancy Goods'.

Vanchi wanted to stop for tea, but Madasami said no. Someone might ask what who they were and what they were doing at that early hour. CID did not operate in Pondicherry, but they had informers.

'You did well,' Madasami said in a low voice when they turned the corner and approached Dharma House. 'I mean, it's only your first day.'

Vanchi mumbled something about the heavy pistol.

'But it looked good. Aiyar got it from France only last week.'

*

Everyone at Dharma House knew that Vanchi and Madasami were going out early, but no one knew why. Aiyar came every afternoon, as usual, to discuss current news, plan the next leaflet and oversee the printing of the in-house newspaper. But he was less expansive, abandoning the history lessons and concentrating on an entirely new publication. It was to be an eight-page pamphlet that would be distributed free of charge every month. Aiyar would write all the content, in English, with an emphasis on traditional Hindu literature, philosophy and religion. There would also be a special insert narrating a 'critical event in India's history'. Newspapers received at Dharma House were still read closely, but the long-established practice of summarising their political content had been dropped.

In the dark paddy field, Vanchi's hand shook, his arm ached and his grip slipped. He was allowed four bullets each morning, in order to conserve ammunition for others, Madasami told him. 'But don't worry,' he added, 'we have enough for you.'

He and Madasami didn't talk much about his training. There were too many questions in Vanchi's mind, and Madasami had his instructions from Aiyar. 'Don't let him dwell on it,' he'd been told. 'Keep it natural, like you're still going out for physical exercise. Because that is what it is.'

On the eighth day, Vanchi hit the trunk of a coconut tree from thirty feet.

'Good,' the trainer said. 'Now, we'll bring you a few steps closer each day. And narrow the target, too.'

The next morning, he took aim at a thinner coconut tree. Then it was an even thinner areca nut tree. Finally, he stood at a distance of six paces from a palmyra fruit, which had been thrust onto the sharpened tip of a bamboo pole. On the first attempt, he missed with all four bullets, but on the following morning he shattered the fleshy purple fruit with each squeeze of the trigger.

*

After two more displays of similar accuracy, Madasami told Vanchi that Aiyar wanted to see him at his house. Again, four o'clock sharp. All through that day, Vanchi's mind kept running around in circles. I am ready, he told himself, but Aiyar still wants to test me. He doesn't trust me.

He wished that Shankara was with him. Madasami was supportive, but distant. He didn't talk much, looked angry half the time, and Vanchi didn't know what to say to him. He could talk to Shankara about anything. He was his *machinan*, his wife's brother.

He had seen the bullet smash the fruit and knew it would sink deep into flesh. But how many times would he need to fire? He might miss. His hand might shake. Maybe the man himself would—

'Vanchi, watch out! You've ruined it.'

They were running a test print of the front page of the new monthly journal. The paper that he had placed on the flat plate was askew.

'Tell you what,' said Perumal, the printer, 'we need more ink. Go get some.'

Vanchi approached the shop with hesitation. He hated the smell of the nut oil boiling in a large vat in the back room. Hamid, who owned the place, sat at a greasy desk in the tiny front room. The wall behind him was covered with lithograph prints of mosques.

'More ink?' Hamid asked, opening his thick lips to reveal a row of red-stained teeth. 'You boys are busy.'

Hamid had had a visit from undercover CID officers earlier that week. Who were his customers? Where did they live? No, of course, they wouldn't mention his name. They just wanted information. Calculating that inaccurate statements were information, and that inaccuracy was not a crime, Hamid had misled the officers with names and addresses. It wasn't that he supported the people at Dharma House. He didn't care what they printed because they were good customers and didn't run up debts.

Vanchi paid for a large can of ink, took a receipt and was

stepping outside, when Hamid said. 'Next time, come early in the morning before I open. I sleep inside, so just knock.'

The ink can was loaded onto a handcart and pushed by a little boy. Vanchi followed a few steps behind until they got close to Dharma House. After watching the boy deliver the can, Vanchi walked back and entered the temple on the corner.

In the centre of the compound stood a life-size stone image of a humped bull. At rest, with its legs folded underneath, the bull faced the entrance to the main shrine dedicated to Shiva. Smaller shrines to other gods were built into the compound walls. Reconstructed after a partial demolition by attacking French troops in the eighteenth century, the temple had never regained its symmetry. Looking around, Vanchi sensed a misalignment without knowing its cause.

He washed his feet in a little rectangular pool and walked clockwise around the courtyard before stopping at one of the wall shrines. Inside, the black image of a god sat cross-legged on another bull. He held a noose in one hand and an axe in the other. This was Dharma Raja, the god who had given his name to the temple, the street and the house where Vanchi now stayed. He stood before the flower-strewn image and prayed to the god of death and dispenser of justice.

15

Pondicherry, May 1911

Aiyar stared at the English words he'd just written as part of his translation. They made perfect sense, but they were wrong. Completely wrong! He banged his hand flat on the table and tossed his pen to one side.

'What's the matter?' his wife asked, from the other side of the room, where she was reading a Tamil novel.

'Nothing. Nothing,' Aiyar nearly shouted. 'I just don't think you can translate these maxims into English. The ideas are too embedded in our culture.'

'But it's not about that, is it?' she said, closing her book. 'It's about that young man.'

Aiyar looked at his wife with affection. She was and always had been his confidant. During his long stay in London, before his letters were intercepted, he wrote to her in detail about his ideas and plans. She wrote back and pledged her unwavering support, even while their infant daughter suffered from dysentery. And when the little girl died, she still found the strength to offer him advice. Now, she was the only person to whom he had divulged the details of his plan.

'You're right,' he said and pushed his chair away from the table.

He was confident, he told her, but one always had to second-guess one's decisions. The man had to be a high-profile target in order to ensure maximum publicity. Some of the public reaction would no doubt be negative. It might prompt the authorities to mount even greater surveillance. Men who had been silent or disinterested might turn against the nationalist cause. On the other hand, it would spread fear. A paralysis far more destructive to British rule than any publication. The Russians had used it and so had the French. It was time for Indian patriots to show courage.

'But why this Ashe, the one in Tinnevelly?' she asked.

Aiyar reminded her of the riots in 1908, of Chidambaram Pillai's unjust trial and his cruel treatment in prison. There were other legitimate targets, he conceded, but Pillai himself had claimed that Ashe was the worst of the lot.

'Besides, targets choose themselves,' he said. 'They are ambitious and climb into prominent positions in the colonial administration. And when they destroy our culture, what do they expect? Love and admiration? None of them would be surprised by anger or even hatred. But few will expect a bullet.'

She grimaced. Although she had never accepted the necessity of violence, she had long ago ceased to argue with him about it.

'It has to be bullets,' he continued. 'Bombs are too imprecise, messy and unreliable. Just look at that fiasco in Muzaffarpur and the earlier one in Calcutta. The wrong people were eliminated or the right ones only injured. A pistol is easy to carry and conceal. And it's deadly at short range.'

'And this young man? The one from Shenkottai. Why him?'

Aiyar admitted that it had been a difficult decision. 'For a long time, as you might have guessed, I wanted to do it myself. It was my plan, so I should execute it. But I might be recognized. I could go in disguise, but I'm better known now. Too risky. And, of course, I need to carry on the work, afterwards.'

Afterwards, that was the hardest part. They looked at each other with grim resignation.

'I had to decide what kind of man was best for this task. Someone with passion for the revolutionary cause? Or someone who accepted its political logic? Fire in the heart or ice in the veins.'

'A soldier or a sadhu.'

'A little of both. A man with courage but without self-regard.'

'Someone with nothing to lose.'

'Perhaps. But there were other considerations. Madasami, for example, was a possibility. He is reliable and determined, but then I realized I need him as an assistant. After all, he's the one who told me about Vanchi.'

'But are you sure he's the right one?'

'I need to decide if he has sufficient resolve. He'll be here soon. I want to know what you think.'

*

Vanchi left for Aiyar's house at three o'clock. Too much time, he knew, but he wanted to walk about and gather his thoughts. Inside Dharma House, there was always something that had to be done with printing the leaflets and sending them off. Leaving all that behind, he set off in the opposite direction from the sea and went further into Ville Noire. Smaller houses, fewer shops and more animals on the road. Like home, but without the mountains. He looked down to avoid landing his leather shoes in cow dung. He glided along, passing people whose chatter sounded far away. They didn't look at him because they didn't know him, but soon they would. His aim was good. He overheard a woman singing a lullaby on a veranda enclosed by a slated screen. She was invisible, the child, too, but the words floated in the air. Vanni was almost six. Time for the ear-piercing ceremony. He had told Ponammal he would return in time, but now he wasn't sure.

Three men appeared wearing skirts and turbans. Double-headed drums were slung over their shoulders. One of them led a stunted cow with a threadbare embroidered cloth decorating its back and forehead. Metal bells and faded strips of cloth hung from its horns. Catching Vanchi's eye, the sullen-eyed men slipped wordlessly into their routine, singing in falsetto voices and banging their drums with little, curved sticks. No one in the street showed any interest, but they played on and performed a dance, swinging their long skirts around their skinny legs. They were tribal men, of no caste and no village.

Vanchi tossed them a coin and turned back towards town. He worried that he might not understand what Aiyar would say to him. He'd often been lost in his maze of ancient Tamil poems, English phrases, French words, Sanskrit allusions and historical references.

Or he might ask him to tell a story. 'Imagine you are a tree,' Aiyar had said one day. 'Not just any tree. But a huge peepul tree.'

'A banyan tree,' Vanchi had said.

'OK, a banyan tree. You have stood there, by the side of a village pool, for many years. Decades. Centuries. Now, tell me, what you have seen?'

Vanchi had let his imagination roam, mixing things Thatha had told him with things he had read and dreamed. Aiyar had liked the story of the stone man with the sword. That part of our history, he had said, must be told and retold.

Vanchi turned back. He asked someone the time and walked around for ten minutes. Seeing the red door, he unfolded his clean white *veshti* so that the hem touched the tips of his black shoes. He tightened it at the waist, smoothed down his tunic and adjusted his thread.

Aiyar's wife opened the door.

'Vanga, vanga,' she said. 'Have you eaten?'

He entered and she bent down to light the wick in a tall brass lamp just inside the door.

Aiyar was again seated at a table strewn with papers and books. His eyes glowed and his body bristled with energy.

'Come in,' he said, pushing his papers aside.

Vanchi removed his shoes and stood at the doorway. The dim room was still except for the dark green curtains fluttering in the breeze. Noises could be heard coming in from the street. Aiyar lit one kerosene lamp and then another, which cast overlapping circles of light on his table and halfway up the wall.

'Take a seat,' Aiyar said and gestured towards a wicker chair.

Vanchi moved closer but remained standing. On the wall behind Aiyar, he saw a map of the world and a lithograph portrait of a foreign-looking man. He feared that he would ask him a history question.

'If you prefer to stand, that's fine,' Aiyar said, 'but I need you to relax so that you can concentrate.'

'Yes, sir.'

Vanchi's shoulders fell a little and he folded his hands together in front of him.

'Your marksmanship is excellent, I'm told.'

Vanchi mumbled something.

'Speak up. How is your accuracy?'

'Good, sir.'

'And the pistol?'

'Good, sir.'

'Come, now, Vanchi. Tell me about the pistol.'

'It's reliable. At least, so far, I mean. At first, it was heavy, but not now.'

'And you?' Aiyar asked, fixing Vanchi with his powerful eyes. 'Are you ready?'

Vanchi said yes but swallowed the words.

'Speak up,' Aiyar said again.

'Yes, sir.'

Aiyar rose and began to pace around the cramped room like a tiger in a cage.

'Now listen carefully,' he said. 'You will strike a major blow for our independence. You will do something that will make the whole country wake up and listen to us.'

Vanchi held his breath, and Aiyar's wife leaned forward in her chair.

'You will shoot Mr Ashe, the Collector of Tinnevelly.'

Vanchi went rigid. He had signed the blood oath, but now it had a name.

*

A week later, everything was in place. New leaflets had been printed and tied in bundles. The pistol had been oiled and tested again. Aiyar spoke to Vanchi one last time at his house.

'Do not doubt yourself, or the success of this plan,' he said. 'Maniyachi Junction is an isolated station. There will be little or no commotion. He'll be exposed and more or less alone while waiting for the Boat Mail from Tuticorin. An interval of twelve to fifteen minutes. Unless there's a delay.'

'When, I mean, what day, sir?'

'The exact date is out of our hands. It depends on when he makes the journey to Kodaikanal. It should be sometime next month, hopefully in the second half. That's important because the king will be coronated in London on 22 June.'

Vanchi looked perplexed.

'I want our action to take place as close as possible to that date.'

Again, Vanchi waited for an explanation.

'It will send a message. The whole world will know that George V is not king of India.'

More details followed. Vanchi would take the pistol and most of the leaflets back to Shenkottai. Madasami would leave Pondicherry the next day with the rest of the leaflets and the bullets, but he would take a different route and travel to his family's home near Tuticorin. It was better that way, Aiyar explained, separating the pistol from the bullets. If one were confiscated, the other would still be safe. When they had reached their homes, Vanchi and Madasami would behave as normal. They would stay with their families, but they would not distribute the leaflets. No risks should be taken.

Vanchi acknowledged each element of the plan with a slight movement of his head. Aiyar spoke in a flat tone, as if describing the salient points of one of his editorials.

'You will wait in Shenkottai. When we know the date of his train journey to Kodaikanal, you will receive a telegram telling you when to meet Madasami in Palayamkottai. He'll give you the address before you leave here. The rest of the details will come from him. You don't need to know them now.'

Vanchi's mind was reeling, trying to remember everything.

'Any questions?'

'No.'

Vanchi wanted to know if Ashe would be alone but he dared not ask.

Aiyar fixed his dark eyes on the young man's face. 'There is one last thing,' he said. 'Be sure to load the pistol completely. All six bullets.'

'I can do it with one, sir. Or two, at the most.'

'You can't be sure,' Aiyar said. 'And you will need more than one bullet in any case.'

Vanchi narrowed his eyes in confusion and waited.

'Because after you kill him, you will turn the gun on yourself.'

Vanchi heard the words but did not react. One corner of his mind worked out their meaning, while the rest refused to comprehend.

'It's the only way,' Aiyar continued. 'Think it through. Even if you manage to escape from the station, you won't get very far. It's in the middle of nowhere. No place to hide. They'll arrest you and they'll torture you. We know that from other cases. They'll make you tell them everything you know about us. It will mean the end of our movement.'

Vanchi's head tilted to indicate agreement, but his mind was blank.

'And after some time, after they have broken you, they will hang you. Of that there is no doubt. Probably a public execution. So, it's better that you control things. Defy them. Shoot yourself. Keep our secrets.'

Vanchi looked down at his hands clasped at the waist.

'Don't think about yourself or about him,' Aiyar said in conclusion. 'Our ancient texts have taught us that there is no "self". No slayer and no slain. Don't think about individual lives. Think about the whole, the reality that connects everything. Our culture and our history. You will help to preserve that.'

Vanchi raised his head and murmured, 'Dharma.'

16

Palayamkottai, May 1911

Ashe chewed on the stem of his pipe and spun around in his chair. If only we could do what doctors do, he thought. It was now edging towards the end of May, the height of the hot season, and there was no respite. The whole district was crying out for rain, the leaflets were proliferating and he'd sprained his ankle after falling off a horse on a village tour. 'Never going to ride one again,' he'd sworn to himself.

There was also Das, who'd been moping around all week. When he finally got him to talk, his clerk explained that he'd had bad news about his mother. There was a reasonable chance—but no more than that—that she would recover from surgery. Too complicated for the local hospital, but the hospital in Vellore, near Madras, could do it. Ashe sanctioned a week's leave, which Das could take whenever he wanted.

On top of all that, Mary had gone back to Dublin because her health had deteriorated. She complained of nausea and indigestion, which they had both put down to the heat and food. But then her whole body started to ache and she had long dizzy spells.

'Don't worry about me, Robbie,' she had said the evening before she left. 'I'll be back in no time. Then we'll go and stay with the children.'

'Yes, let's look forward to that.'

Catching the uncertain note in his voice, Mary said, 'Really, I'll be fine. Just a bit of rest. That's all.'

'You know, dear, I'm also looking forward to something else.'

'What's that?'

'Retirement.'

'What do you mean?'

'Well, if we can manage to stay alive in this hell hole for nine more years, I'm entitled to a pension.'

Although Mary feigned surprise, she had noticed a change in her husband over the past few months. He cursed the climate regularly and was short-tempered, even shouted once or twice at the servants. From a letter written by an old Trinity classmate, he had selected a rapturous description of Spring in Dublin and read it aloud to Mary. Three times. The younger children deserve a better education, he said. And they themselves could both do with an easier life.

She knew it was his work. He looked anxious and worn out, but she had promised herself never to question him again about office matters. Not after that controversy over the caste restrictions at the waterfalls.

'Yes, I know,' she said, referring to the pension. 'But can we afford it?'

'I think so. It's nearly £1,000 a year. In 1920, Arthur will be nineteen, probably with an army commission. That's what he says he wants.'

'Molly will be a young woman, probably married or employed,' Mary said, warming to the idea. 'Only Herbert and Sheila would still be in school.'

'That's right. Just think, Mary. We could all be together. En famillie. No more long separations, like we have to go through here every year.'

'It's a nice thought. By the way, when's your next long furlough?

'Eighteen short months, January 1913.'

*

Five weeks had passed since that conversation, and the loneliness had worn him down. He sighed and placed the cold pipe in a little wooden tray on his desk. It was shaped like a leaf, curling to a tip at the bottom, a gift from a carpenter for sorting out an inheritance dispute.

Pulling out his diary from his inside jacket pocket, he checked the dates one more time. Her ship would leave Southampton on 28 May and reach Bombay on 11 June. Two days later, he would meet her when her ship docked at Tuticorin. And two days after that, on the morning of 15 June, they would be on their way to Kodaikanal to join the children. Only three more bloody weeks.

He unlocked his desk drawer and reached for the packet of letters, the ones she had written to him when he first came to India, more than fifteen years ago. Choosing one at random, he unfolded it.

> Dear Mr Walrus,
>
> Mother had one of her tea parties yesterday and I sat quietly thinking of you all the time. I saw your sweet smiling face, your lips and eyes, and remembered when we talked. It was delicious, that night when we spoke. So close and warm.
>
> 'Well, dear, how is your nursing school?' One of mother's bejewelled crones interrupted my dreams, but I recovered and managed to put the old bitty off. Then I returned to my memories of you. It's cruel that you must be so far away. I almost burst out in tears.
>
> I don't think mother or father really understand us. Father keeps asking if you've 'bagged a tiger'!
>
> I long for the day when we can speak again, at night in the garden.
>
> Do keep yourself safe and remember your devoted Pussycat, who sends her love.

*

From his outer office, Das heard the silence. The collector was in one of his moods. Having worked together for many years, he knew that Mr Ashe was not one of those 'rock solid chaps', like Superintendent Hartley, for instance. His boss was more volatile, and more erratic. He did things quickly, too quickly sometimes, which meant that Das had to undo his actions, rewrite reports, revise figures and redirect correspondence. Although he didn't admire him as an administrator, Das liked him as a man. He was not overbearing and treated him as an equal, insofar as that was possible.

Das continued to follow Hartley's instructions and kept an eye on him when he walked home from the office on Fridays. He never had anything to report, except that Ashe did not vary his route as he had said he would.

Today, he was unusually quiet. He hadn't called for papers all morning. His wife had gone back home and wouldn't return until the middle of next month. Das had made a special note of that in order to prepare for her arrival and to make arrangements for their departure to Kodaikanal.

Das was ploughing through the latest batch of reports and statistical tables, when he pursed his lips. He snatched at a piece of scrap paper and studied the column of figures he'd written down earlier. The operation itself, plus the cost of a hospital bed for several days, the train tickets and his own accommodation in Vellore. He'd been right the first time—his salary would definitely not cover it. None of his relatives could give him what he needed, and he couldn't ask the collector, not for that much.

His wife had recommended that he 'seek assistance'—that's how she put it—from the church.

'Scrape and bow to them, you mean?' he had said in reply.

'Oh, no. Nothing like that,' she had said. 'Just ask the Charity Committee if they can help. That's all.'

Das had rejected her advice. He would not, under any

circumstances, supplicate the church authorities. He would not beg from those sanctimonious officials.

*

Ashe put away Mary's old letter and took out a crisp piece of his own stationery. He had decided that he should write it all down.

'My Dearest Mary. Yesterday was the worst day I've ever had here,' he began. 'My only consolation is that you were not here to share in my disgust. I cannot begin to tell you how appalling it was.'

He had arrived at the prison at ten-thirty in the morning. The warden didn't hold with the custom of hanging men at first light. Best to keep office hours, everything nice and normal, he explained. Once inside the heavy gates, Ashe had been escorted to the cell where the four condemned men were kept. He asked them, one by one, if they had anything to say. They did not.

Later, he stood with the warden and the district medical officer on a shallow veranda. He looked out at the courtyard already heavy with heat. Less than fifty feet away, a tall tree was still in leaf, with yellow flowers and long brown pods. From a thick projecting branch, two ropes hung down and dangled above a square wooden platform. The tree cast a circle of shade on the platform and its five steps.

The four men were led out of a low-lying building, which stood at a right angle to the veranda. They were dressed in a thin shirt and three-quarter length trousers, the same uniform he had seen on his monthly inspection visits. Except that these clothes looked new. They also wore a curious white hat on their head. Ashe wished that the light was not so bright, that it was dawn, when the shapes would have blurred.

'Murderers, all of them,' the warden said to him. 'Trial was last year, before you came. They used machetes to kill their cousins, or something like that. A land dispute.'

The medical officer nodded. 'If it's not caste, it's kin, likely as not,' he said. 'In this case, their own wives turned them in. The victims were the wives' brothers.'

The men were led to the gallows in pairs. The first pair were guided up the steps, where the hangman, who looked twice their age, tied their feet and hands and fitted the white hood over their heads. On the ground below, a Hindu priest chanted. Ashe shifted his weight and waited. The chanting seemed to go on for a long time, and he began to sweat.

The hangman slid the nooses over the heads and tightened them. The medical officer had already confirmed that the ropes, which were made by the prisoners, were the correct length and of sufficient strength.

The hangman turned and looked at the veranda. The medical officer whispered to the warden, who nodded to the collector. Ashe dropped a white handkerchief and the trapdoor opened. The first pair were dispatched without incident. But when the trapdoor opened a second time, the head was nearly ripped from one of the bodies, and blood shot up in a spray that splattered the hangman and the priest.

Shooting would be more civilized, Ashe thought as he struggled not to avert his eyes.

17

Pondicherry to Shenkottai, May 1911

They couldn't do anything about the bright moon. If others could see them, at least they could see where they were going. The ground underfoot was dry, but they still might stumble and fall into a paddy field, now a foot deep in water.

Crossing the border would not be easy, even at night. There were guards at checkpoints on all the main roads leading into British India. By sticking to dirt paths, they could avoid those roads, but not the bridges at the end of the journey. Looking at the two men in front, Vanchi wondered if either of them carried a gun.

Another problem was that they couldn't always know what territory they were in. The border between French and British India zigzagged through the countryside without topographical logic. Individual villages were said to be on one side or the other, depending on which government was entitled to collect the land tax, but where the line ran between those fixed points was anyone's guess. If they happened to run into a police patrol at any time, they would be searched and the contents of his suitcase would land them all in jail. The plan would have failed, months of preparation wasted. Aiyar would find someone else, he was certain of that, but he would be a failure.

The first few miles went quickly. They reached Villianur, the only town on the route, by following a well-maintained road that ran due south. Soon, they crossed a shallow river, but the bridge had no checkpoint or guards because it was too far from the border. On the other side of the river, they dropped off the main road and walked along paths that skirted the paddy fields. Frogs croaked and the moonlight reflected off the water.

Vanchi was struggling to keep up. The guides turned around from time to time to glare at him. He could see all right, but his leather shoes didn't grip well and his arms ached. The suitcase held the heavy pistol, four bundles of leaflets and half a dozen books, mostly gifts from Aiyar. He cradled it in both arms, like a kid goat.

A light flickered in the distance, probably a watchman's lantern or a campfire. Under the vast, open sky, everything seemed far away. Only the silhouetted coconut trees gave definition to the flattened landscape. Suddenly, the frogs stopped gurgling and the countryside went quiet. He heard an animal sound off to his left, a bleating or a growling.

Then he stumbled and fell face first on the hard ground. Although the case flew out of his hands, it didn't open. Madasami had seen to that by securing it with a thin rope. The guides turned but said nothing. 'Only one rule,' Aiyar had said. 'No talking. Not even a whisper. Not until you reach the train station at Cuddalore.'

After two hours, they regained the main road not far from their destination. But two more rivers lay ahead. The Ponnaiyar river was too wide and deep to wade across, even now in the dry season. The newly built bridge was lit by a lantern in the guard's hut on the far side.

Vanchi followed his guides as they ducked off the road and edged their way down to the riverbank. A boatman appeared and beckoned them forward. Vanchi went first and stepped into the boat, more like a raft or canoe, made by lashing three logs together. It was long and narrow, with an upturned prow, and lay low in the water. He sat on the only cross-piece, clutching the case to his chest, and held his breath as the man poled them across.

Vanchi heard voices on the bridge and saw the shapes of men, with pinpricks of light from beedis. Water slapped at the side of the boat, and the boatman grunted each time he thrust the long pole into the riverbed.

The prow of the boat slid up the sandy bank and they all climbed out. The boatman took his money and pointed the way. Bent forward, they sank in the sand as they made their way up the high bank, passed through a bamboo thicket and reached a dirt road. The guides gestured to him to keep to the verge, in the shadows of the trees. He sensed that they were close to the station, but he knew there was another river.

The red-brick bridge over the Gadilam was the main crossing point into British India. Rebuilt after floods and supported by eight low arches, it stretched for nearly four hundred feet. Both ends had checkpoints, which even at that predawn hour were staffed with customs officials, watchmen and armed police.

The sky was beginning to lighten, and from the approach road Vanchi could see men patrolling the bridge. Again, he followed the guides down the bank, where a boatman was waiting for them. His boat was longer and wider, and they lay down as flat as possible. But the boatman had to stand as he pushed the pole down and then lifted it above his head.

'There! There!'

Men shouted from the bridge when the boat was only halfway across. The boatman changed course and poled furiously downstream. No one spoke. All eyes were on the men scrambling after them along the bank. After a sharp bend, the river flowed faster and mangrove forests appeared on both sides. Hoping their pursuers couldn't see them through the thick foliage, the boatman steered them into a cove, where they waited, hidden in the dense tangle of roots and leaves.

With the sky reddening along the horizon, Vanchi slept alongside the guides in the boat while the boatman walked to the nearest village and brought back fruit and fried snacks.

When evening came, the boatman gave them directions. In the semi-darkness, he pointed out the ruins of an old Dutch fort near the mouth of the river.

'We're on the south bank,' the man said with a grin. 'In British territory.'

The guides paid him and led Vanchi out of the mangrove forest and onto the main road, where they kept their voices low. The only change in plan was that they took him to the old railway station, the one in the centre of Cuddalore. When they parted, Vanchi tried to express his gratitude, but they cut him short. 'We got you this far,' they said. 'The rest is up to you.'

Exhausted, he rested his head on his suitcase and slept on the station platform along with dozens of others. Drifting off to sleep, he kept repeating Aiyar's instructions. Wait for the telegram. It will tell you when to meet Madasami in Palayamkottai. He will tell you the day.

The first train south in the morning was crammed with families travelling to a temple festival in Thanjavur. In his second-class carriage, high-backed wooden benches faced each other across a narrow aisle. With no overhead storage space, the floor was covered with trunks, bundles, bags and squirming children. Vanchi put his case on his lap and held it to his chest with both hands.

The man next to him, apparently travelling alone, began to whistle. He had rucked his *veshti* halfway up his thighs and sat cross-legged on the bench, chewing away on a wadge of paan. Without moving his head, his eye strayed sideways. Vanchi edged away and tightened his grip. It didn't work.

'Nice old one,' the man said and ran his hand over the linen covering of Vanchi's case.

'Umm.'

'You some kind of salesman?'

'Umm.'

'My father was a salesman. Pears soap. Travelled everywhere. Bombay, Rangoon, Colombo. What do you sell?

Ladies' underwear, I'd guess, by the way you're squeezing that case.'

He let out a loud roar of laughter. When Vanchi didn't reciprocate, the man sized him up. He didn't look like a salesman. Too young and too scared.

Eight hours later, the train eased into Maniyachi Junction, which felt like another kind of border. Vanchi had barely noticed the station when passing through on his way up north three months earlier, but now he studied every detail. He walked up and down the main platform. He found a toilet at the end of the platform and checked the lock on the door. That's the place, he decided. He looked inside the first-class waiting room and stood beside a first-class carriage. He was thinking that the step was too high when the whistle blew.

Leaving the station, he tried to picture the man called Ashe. He'd seen few Englishmen in person and never looked at them closely. Madasami would do the reconnaissance and identify him, but he wondered if he had a beard and wore a helmet, like he'd seen in newspapers and books.

It was dark when he arrived in Tinnevelly, too late to catch the last train to Shenkottai. Again, he slept on the platform and, in the morning, bathed in the river. He crossed over the bridge to the Palayamkottai side, where the pools were deeper, and edged his way down the bank. Having washed and laid his clothes out to dry, he sank into the cool water. Bobbing up and down, he kept an eye on the case, which he had placed in the shadow of a large rock. He hadn't opened it since leaving Pondicherry and he wondered if, like his shoes, the pistol had taken on any water during his flight. Good thing the bullets were with Madasami.

When he stepped out of the water, he glanced up at the bridge and thought he saw someone looking down at him. Aiyar had warned him to be on his guard. But it was too far away and couldn't be sure. Walking back across the bridge to Tinnevelly station, he didn't want to go home. He wanted to go to the 'rendezvous' house in Palayamkottai. That's what Aiyar had called it, and he had to explain the word to him in Tamil. Vanchi knew the address—43 Rajakkal Street—but not the day. He had to wait for the telegram.

*

He bought his ticket and stood on the platform, waiting for the train to Shenkottai. Only he wasn't really there; he was at Maniyachi Junction, holding a gun. He heard the shots in the paddy field and looked straight ahead. His face hardened into a mask. People beside him on the platform looked the other way, repelled by his hollow eyes staring into space.

Coming out of the station in Shenkottai, he turned towards the mountains, went through the market and out into the countryside. The case felt heavy, but he didn't mind. When he was about to step down onto the footpath, he stopped. All around him, he saw paddy fields bursting bright green, with young stalks swaying like ribbons. When he had left three months earlier, the heat was peaking and the fields were broken clumps of earth. It was now late May, with heavy clouds bunched high up on the mountains. A breeze brushed his face and a drizzle fell. The blazing sun and vast sea of Pondicherry were far away. He would never see it or Aiyar again. He was home, but he was alone.

At the banyan tree, he took out the pistol and pushed it deep into the hole beside the pot with his oath. Even if the heavy rains began before he needed it, he thought it would remain dry. He was about to leave when he heard a shrill chirping in a clump of bushes. Although well hidden by the foliage, a pair of red-whiskered bulbuls were betrayed by the twitching of their sharp pointed crowns. Watching as they hopped from branch to branch and pecked at tiny white flowers, Vanchi's face slipped into a sad smile.

The suitcase was lighter when he retraced his steps back through the market and past the station. Turning off the main road onto the dirt road, he bent down and brushed the dust from his shoes. When he reached the top of the Brahmin street, he noticed a figure behind the houses on the right. A man was squatting down in the cremation ground, raking with a long stick. His head was shaved.

Going closer, he saw that it was his grandfather and his mind raced through the possibilities.

'She died two days ago, in the morning,' Thatha said. 'We lit the pyre that afternoon. She's only five, but she is the first-born.'

Vanchi let his suitcase drop and fell to his knees beside the shallow pit. The acrid smell of burnt bones and flesh kept him from fainting. He felt his grandfather's hand on his shoulder.

'Ponammal?' he asked.

'She's fine, my boy. And your mother. We didn't send a telegram because we had no address.'

Vanchi's body crumpled up in pain.

'C'mon, my boy,' his grandfather said. 'Take a bath and get your head shaved. I need your help.'

Bathed and bald, Vanchi joined his grandfather at the blackened pit. Thatha had fashioned a stick for him, and together they stirred the charred remains. Perhaps it's better for her, he thought, as they raked and sifted without speaking. After two hours they had collected small bone fragments, a few teeth and clumps of skeletal ash. Thatha placed it all in a brass vessel and they walked back to the house.

In a plain sari, Ponammal sat in a corner of the front room, her hair uncombed and her face twisted in grief. She turned when Vanchi entered, and he saw that she wore no kumkum on her forehead and no bangles on her wrists.

His mother was in the kitchen, crouched over a fire, cooking rice balls for the dead.

'I can't offer you any food,' she said. 'Not yet. But at least you're here.'

They both heard Ponammal sobbing softly in the next room.

'She's exhausted, poor thing,' his mother said. 'Only one child and now it's gone. But I keep telling her that she can have another. That's right, isn't it, son?'

*

Early the next day, Vanchi and Thatha, along with Shankara and his father, walked behind a young priest down the main road towards Tenkasi. Wearing a dull orange *veshti* and shawl, the priest held a brass vessel at his waist and led them to the banks of the Chittar. After going inside a small temple, he re-emerged and stood near the water, chanting in Sanskrit.

'Yama, Dharma Raja, do not harm our sons and daughters. Fold them to you, like soft wool.'

Vanchi saw the black stone image in the temple in Pondicherry. God of death and god of justice. With the noose and the axe. The sword and the pistol. The brass vessel, held high above the priest's head, glinted in the sunlight. Vanchi willed himself not to shake. Death is a passage, he told himself, a journey to the world of the ancestors.

From the corner of his eye, he saw an egret take flight. Three heavy flaps lifted it into a long glide. White wings outstretched, dark legs pulled back in a line, it floated out of sight. We expire, but dharma is eternal.

In the afternoon, they all sat on the veranda. The house had been scrubbed clean, Vanchi's mother said. A neighbour had told her that they could cook in her house. Shankara spoke about the priest, his calm demeanour and the clarity of his chanting. Thatha told them what he needed to collect from the hills during the long mourning period. Shankara's father was worried about Ponammal, who would not come out of the kitchen.

'She's not strong, you know. She might lose her mind after this. Can't we do something?'

Shankara looked at Vanchi, who kept his eyes lowered, and said that she would be 'well cared for in this house'.

'You've sent word to Raghupathi?' Shankara's father asked, referring to Vanchi's father.

Thatha assured him that they had, and the two older men entered into a discussion about dietary restrictions and preparations for the ceremony on the last day of mourning. After Vanchi's mother went inside to comfort Ponammal, they changed topics.

'I hear you've found a new job, Vanchi,' Shankara's father said, trying to cheer everyone up. 'Is that right?'

Vanchi tilted his head to indicate yes.

'C'mon, tell him about it,' Thatha said.

Vanchi explained that he had resigned from the Forest Department and that the permanent job in Madras—'with a friend's daily newspaper'—would start in a few weeks. He had come home to settle things and prepare for his departure.

'What about Ponammal?' his father-in-law asked.

'It's better if she stays with you. Let me make some money first and find a place. Then, if things work out, she can come.'

'But you can't leave before the thirteenth day,' Thatha said. 'You're the father. You should be here for the final feast.'

Vanchi did some quick calculations in his head. 'I hope I can stay until the end,' he said. 'The people in Madras will send a telegram, telling me when I have to leave.'

'It's all settled, then?' Thatha asked.

'Yes,' Vanchi said. 'Everything's settled. Except the date.'

It was dusk when Shankara and his father left to return to Tenkasi. As the older man was saying goodbye to Thatha and Vanchi's mother, the two younger men walked away from the veranda and stood in the middle of the Brahmin street.

'I need your help,' Vanchi said. 'I've got new leaflets. But I can't distribute them now. Not during the mourning period.'

'Don't worry,' Shankara said, 'I've got two new people to help, from Tenkasi. We can spread them around in no time.'

'Good. Madasami said to put them in as many places as you can,' Vanchi told him. 'We need support, now more than ever.'

Shankara looked at him for an explanation but received none.

'All right,' he said. 'We'll do it as soon as possible. But you've got to tell me all about Pondicherry. Nilakanta and everything.'

'Nilakanta's no longer in charge. It's Aiyar.'

'I see. But what's all this business about a telegram?' Shankara had grasped his hand and moved close.

'It's something important.'

'What?'

'I can't tell you. Just keep repeating the oath and distribute the leaflets.'

*

Thatha and Vanchi's mother slept on the veranda that night. Everything felt suspended. No food had been cooked in the house that day, and none would be for the next twelve days. Vanchi drank water from the terracotta pot standing in the corner of the kitchen and sat down on his mat. His suitcase was pushed against the wall behind him.

A flame spluttered in the half-coconut shell. He refilled it with coconut oil, tweaked the wick and lit it again with a twig from the smouldering ashes. He sat down again and looked over at Ponammal lying on the other side of the room. They hadn't exchanged a single word since his arrival the day before. She had squeezed her body into a tight ball, knees drawn up to her chest. He looked again and saw that she was trembling. He found an old shawl and draped it over her. He lay down on his mat and closed his eyes.

She will not have another child, he thought. There isn't enough time. But perhaps it's best that she lost Vanni. A girl without a father has little chance of attracting a good marriage offer. And even less when the mother is a widow.

'Plop!' He heard the dreaded sound and searched in the poor light until he saw the hooked tail waving in the air. Less than a foot from Ponammal. He fixed it with his eyes, daring it to move, as he inched himself towards the hearth. Still staring at the crab-like creature, his hand found what he wanted. He raised the brass mortar and smashed the scorpion.

The period of mourning suited him. The death of his daughter had made him impure, separating him from the normal world. The many obligations and restrictions also brought more discipline to his routine. Each morning he went early for his bath, checked the pistol in the banyan tree and slipped behind the aerial roots. Prohibited from entering a temple during the mourning time, he prayed and chanted in that private place. Then he repeated Aiyar's instructions: Wait for the telegram. Go to Palayamkottai. Meet Madasami.

As he walked through the town one morning after his bath, Vanchi saw that Shankara and his associates had been busy. A new leaflet had been nailed to trees, pasted on walls and left on tea stall benches. It was headlined 'The Discipline of Dharma'.

Passing by a tea stall, he heard someone reading the leaflet aloud to a dozen other men. Vanchi stopped close by and bent down, pretending to tie his shoes. The reader was dressed in all white and looked like a teacher or government clerk. Spectacles obscured his pinched face, as he struggled to articulate Aiyar's literary Tamil:

'What is needed is a cadre who will renounce worldly attachments and sacrifice themselves for the nation, their mother. Let us make every village and town an outpost of selfless men and women. We will furnish them with a bomb, the bomb of Mother Kali.'

After the man read it more clearly a second time, his audience burst out in voices of condemnation. Vanchi couldn't hear much, only phrases like 'playing with fire' and 'reckless numbskulls'. He straightened up and walked away with a dry smile. Aiyar's right. They don't understand. We need to wake them up.

18

Palayamkottai and Shenkottai, June 1911

The driver thought it was odd. He'd had strange passengers before. Only last month there was an old man who fancied he was a poet and kept pouring verses into his ear. But this one was the exact opposite. A young man, impeccably dressed, who had not said a word during the entire two-hour journey. He'd made several attempts at small talk, but the man in the passenger seat behind him had not spoken. Had not even smiled.

Family trouble or money was his guess. Probably both. Not that he cared much. He'd been paid well, and in advance, and was now considering what he would buy in Palayamkottai before returning in the evening. One of those new style *veshtis* with a broad green border would be nice. A sari for his wife and a bag of boiled sweets for the children. Pulling on the reins to slow his horse in the crowded town, he glanced once more at his passenger. The man's stony stare looked menacing in the bright afternoon light.

Madasami told the driver to stop near the market. That way he could disappear in the crowd before making his way to his uncle's house. He always stayed there. No questions asked. His uncle knew but didn't know. One of the supporters who did not want to get involved.

As he walked through the rows of stalls, he wondered about Vanchi. If anything had gone wrong on his journey back to Shenkottai, he wouldn't know. No one would. Not even Aiyar. Aiyar wasn't as smart as he thought he was. He'd chosen Vanchi, but Madasami had his doubts. He was trustworthy, yes, but there was uncertainty in his eyes. Pillai wouldn't have chosen him.

The next morning, in an upstairs room, Madasami took out the little tin, prised open the lid and counted. Picking up the six bullets, he jiggled them in his hand. They were small, no larger than the top joint of his index finger, with a nickel coating that shone like gold. Small, but capable of changing the course of history. He rubbed them in his hands, in case moisture had formed on the snub-nose casing, placed them back in the tin and hid it under his rolled-up mat.

He ate his breakfast alone and made his way towards the river. Sitting at the tea stall under the tree, he had a clear view of the collector's office across the road. It was nine-thirty. The one-storey building had a wide, porticoed veranda with three arches. A peon in khaki shorts and shirt sat on the wide front steps. A sweeper brushed debris into dusty piles, scooped them up with his hands and deposited them in a gunny bag hanging from his waist. A steady stream of bullock carts, pony carts and pedestrians passed in front of him, but Madasami could see everyone who entered the building.

Although one or two other white men might have business in his office, Ashe would be accompanied by his bearer. More than that, everyone would react to him in a particular manner. Madasami was more worried about being able to identify the head clerk. If anyone knew Ashe's travel plans, it would be him. Shankara had told him his name was Das.

'And he's short of money,' Shankara had added, remembering the conversation overheard in the hospital corridor. 'His mother needs an operation.'

Madasami sipped his tea and opened yesterday's *Swadesamitran*, the Tamil daily from Madras. He held it in front of his chest with two hands, keeping his line of sight clear across the road.

'What's the news, eh?' the stall-holder asked as he prepared tea for other customers.

'Oh, they say the monsoon is weak again this year,' Madasami answered.

'I can see that,' said a man sitting beside him. He was a burly man in his thirties or forties. Three broad stripes of white ash on his forehead called attention to his high, bald crown. 'Read me something I don't know.'

'Right, here's something. Yesterday CID officers found a cache of bombs and weapons in the village of Kanheri, near Satara in the Bombay Presidency. They arrested a man, who is now in detention.'

'Name?'

'Ah…Gangadhar Kulkarni.'

'Hope they hang him.'

'Why's that?'

'You can't run a country with people making bombs everywhere. Killing officials and that. It's wrong.'

Madasami didn't respond. The burly man left and others came, while Madasami kept watch over the top of his newspaper. Five or six Indians had gone into the office, but none looked right. Maybe the clerk is on leave, he thought. Ten minutes later a man trudged up the steps. About fifty, with short-cropped hair and glasses, just as Shankara had described him.

Bang on ten o'clock, a carriage pulled up in front of the office and the peons and sweeper stood to attention. Madasami put down his paper and saw the sour face of the white man who entered the building with his bearer in tow.

'What time is their morning break?' Madasami asked, gesturing towards the collector's office.

'Varies,' the stall-holder said. 'Most of them come out about eleven or half past. Who are you looking for?'

'Oh, no one really, just wondered,' he said, paid for his tea and wandered off.

Not very far, though. He needed the information as soon as possible. It was now early June, and Ashe might be going any day. He walked along the river and kept an eye on his watch.

*

Das entered the building in a foul mood. He'd just had a row with his wife. Their youngest child, a sixteen-year-old boy, wanted to enrol in the Hindu College in Palayamkottai. It was the most prestigious institution in the district and, despite its name, was open to all students. His son was qualified, no doubt about that, but the fees were high and they had already spent some of their savings on his mother's medicines. When she said that they should focus on the children's future, he flew into a rage and accused her of neglecting his mother. He had rarely spoken with such anger, and felt ashamed, yet did not apologize and hurried off to work.

He never regained his equilibrium that morning. Ashe mislaid a file and blamed Das. Rather than protest, Das undertook a search of every drawer, cabinet and desk in every room. The file was found under a pile on a side table in Ashe's office, but Das pretended that it came from his own office. He knew that the collector, too, had not been himself recently. It was not only the strain of the political tensions in the district—new leaflets had been found—but also his wife's illness and absence.

Hoping to clear the air, Das decided to go outside at the tea break and buy his paan. At least that would cheer him up. He could look forward to a good chew when he went home in the evening. And buying it now meant he wouldn't have to stand in the queue at the close of office hours. He was on his way back to the office, betel leaf mixture tucked into his coat pocket, when a man approached.

'Excuse me, are you Das?'

Das was a genial person, but he didn't like the look of this young man.

'Yes,' he said curtly. 'What do you want?'

'Ah, I'd like to know when the collector is going on summer holiday. You see, my boss in Madurai wants to meet him.'

'I can't give you that information,' Das said with a whiff of self-importance.

Superintendent Hartley had impressed upon him the necessity of keeping all travel plans confidential. Considering the current situation, he'd said, we need to ensure the collector's safety. The fewer people who know such things the better.

'But the collector goes to Kodaikanal, I believe,' the man continued, 'and my boss is prepared to travel up there to meet him. You see, it's important business.'

'What kind of business?' asked an imperious Das.

'Oh, it's important all right. Investment in the scheme for improving the port at Tuticorin. Surely, the collector would be interested.'

Das considered this but repeated his refusal and started to turn.

'Wait,' the man said. 'I can offer you something in return, something to help at home.'

Das pulled up.

'One hundred rupees.'

Das pursed his lips and walked away, but not before the man said, 'Think it over. I'll be here every morning when the office opens.'

Walking home that evening, Das went at a leisurely pace and chewed methodically on the betel leaf mixture. A hundred rupees was almost six months' salary. After all, it was innocuous information the man wanted. Holiday plans, not some confidential government document. He spat out a stream of red juice and made his way through the market, totting up the figures in his head. Even after the operation and the school fees, there would be something left over.

He reached the residential quarter north of the market and turned down his street. Children were playing cricket between the two rows of small houses with thatched-roof verandas. A good neighbourhood, where people respected him. A red-tiled roof on his veranda would look nice.

When he bounded up the two steps and pushed through the weathered wooden door, his wife looked up from her church pamphlet. Seeing his face, she beamed with affection. During their long marriage, they had rarely quarrelled and he was a good father to their children. True, he'd made a mistake in selecting a husband for their daughter, but those things happen. Their older son was a bank clerk, and the younger one would be a success, too.

Discovering what was for dinner, Das chided her on her obsession, calling her his 'Rice Queen' and saying he would only get his chapatis once he was in heaven. Later, after enjoying her coconut rice and eggplant curry, he sounded out his younger son about his reasons for wanting to study at Hindu College. It was a perfunctory question, which told everyone at the table that he had made his decision.

Calm down, he told himself as he lay in bed that night. It's only the departure date. Hartley's overcautious, and no one will ever know. Besides, the district needs investment in the port scheme. He'd be doing a good thing, and why shouldn't he benefit from his insider knowledge? He'd worked for the government for almost thirty years and never stolen a paisa.

In the morning, the atmosphere at the breakfast table was almost gay. His two sons bubbled over with excitement about the cricket. For the very first time, an all-Indian team was touring England and scoring runs against the county cricket clubs there.

After his sons had left, Das tried to sound as casual as possible.

'I'll be taking Mother to Vellore soon.'

'When?' his wife said, cocking an eye at him.

'Two or three days, I think.'

Her suspicious eye did not relax.

'Don't worry,' he said. 'There's a mandated rise in my salary. I'll have extra cash.'

*

That same morning, Ashe ate another solitary breakfast. He barely tasted the watery eggs and had long ago given up trying to tell the cook to serve his tea hot. Only nine more days, he kept telling himself. He'd meet Mary at Tuticorin, and, two days later, they'd be on their way to the mountains. Her last letter was so cheerful. The doctors had diagnosed her condition as thrombosis of the heart and prescribed a regimen of nitrate medicines and exercise. She said she felt better already.

He pictured the cottage they had rented for that summer's holiday in Kodaikanal. It was called 'Lake View'. A grey-stone bungalow surrounded by eucalyptus trees and a lawn in front that sloped down to the water. Not County Wicklow, perhaps, but a welcome relief from the heat and dust of Palayamkottai.

They both knew that the cottage would not really be big enough for the six of them. The two girls would have to share a room and a single bed, as would the two boys. Twelve-year-old Molly was sure to raise a fuss about her 'privacy'. Still, they agreed that a little family tension was a price worth paying for such a wonderful spot. After all, there was a good-sized sitting room with a fireplace, where they would warm themselves on cold nights. What a thought that was!

During the day, the older children could go riding with them, while the younger ones could play by the lake, supervised by the ayah they would hire in Kodai. In the late afternoon, he and Mary would take long walks, beside the lake and through the forests. There was a new path, Mary said, from where you could look straight down to the plains.

*

While Ashe was readying himself to leave the bungalow that morning, Madasami had already taken up his post on the bench opposite the collector's office. A heavy rain had been falling since daybreak and, though he borrowed his uncle's umbrella, his damp *veshti* stuck to his thighs and his sandalled feet were muddy. The scowl turned his face black in the poor light. Suppose Das refused? He sipped his tea, held up his paper and wondered who else could tell him what he needed to know.

The rain stopped and he looked up to see Das approaching the tea stall. He tried to read his eyes, but the man's glasses were too large. Gulping down the last of the tea, he rose and met him in the middle of the road.

'Good morning,' Madasami said. 'At least, we're getting some rain.'

'Morning,' Das replied without smiling.

Madasami led him to a lane that ran down to the river. It was innocent enough, him talking with the collector's head clerk, but when the man was shot dead, someone might remember. He wasn't sure what the prison sentence was for an assassin's accomplice.

'He's leaving on the 15th,' Das said.

'Morning train?'

'Yes.'

'Alone?'

'No, with his wife. She's away now. Returns on the 13th.'

'Anything else?'

'No.'

'Thank you. My boss will write to him and make the arrangements.'

Madasami slipped the cash into Das's hand and they parted.

Returning to his uncle's house, Madasami was exhilarated but also worried. The presence of the wife was a detail not anticipated in Pondicherry. He deliberated about whether or not he should inform Aiyar. No, he concluded. Aiyar wouldn't change his plan. Should he tell Vanchi? Again, no. Better not disturb him with anything new.

*

In Shenkottai the next day, a man in a red coat, royal-blue sash and dark blue turban appeared at the top of the Brahmin street. Before he had taken three steps, a gaggle of residents attached themselves to the visitor and began to speculate. Swaminathan, the temple priest? Or possibly Srinivasan, the retired judge? The field narrowed with every house passed over by the liveried employee of the Travancore State Postal Service. Until he stood in front of the herbalist's house.

'Must be the death of a relative somewhere,' said one bystander.

'The father, probably,' said another. 'No loss, there.'

It was with astonishment that the crowd heard the man call Vanchi's name, reach into his leather pouch and hand over the folded message.

'It's about a new job,' Thatha announced to his neighbours, having joined his grandson on the veranda. 'He's going to Madras.'

Vanchi signed the man's notebook and went back inside the house. Facing a corner, he opened the telegram and read the words handwritten in English: 'Chandran arrives 12 June.'

Less than a week. It would happen, as planned. He had known it would, and the telegram made it official. But it was hard, all on his own in Shenkottai. It was easier in Pondicherry, with Aiyar and the others.

He turned around and spoke to Thatha.

'I'm going to Palayamkottai next Monday.'

'Not Madras?'

'No. I have to go to Palayamkottai first. My friend is coming down to find agents for the paper. I'll go a few days early, to see what I can set up for him. Talk to some existing agents, look for new ones.'

'And then?'

'I'll go to Madras with him.'

The remainder of the mourning period passed slowly. Vanchi felt everyone was watching him. He ate little, spoke less, and spent long hours at the bathing pool and banyan tree. He checked the pistol and the written oath. Both were dry, despite the occasional downpour. In the secluded space behind the screen of aerial roots, he lifted the compact gun and pointed it at imaginary targets. Nearly three weeks had passed since leaving Pondicherry and he would have liked to practise, just to make sure. He knew places in the hills where he would be alone, but Madasami had the bullets.

The mourning period ended with a mid-day feast, attended by Shankara and his parents and several distant relatives. No one spoke about Vanchi, but they all knew he was to leave in the morning. That night, he brushed his shoes hard with a tuft of coconut fibre and hung his clothes on a thin rope tied to rafters in the front room.

He awoke earlier than usual and went to the bathing pool carrying his suitcase. After his bath, he put on the freshly laundered white *veshti* and tunic and walked to the carved stone. From his case, he took out a little vial of vermilion mixed with water. He smeared it on the man's forehead and watched as the red streaks dripped down, animating the grey stone. He sat on the ground and chanted the oath. On his way back, he retrieved his pistol from the tree and placed it in the case. He left the oath behind.

At home, they were waiting for him. Thatha was pounding leaves on the veranda with Shankara, who had spent the night. As soon as Shankara caught sight of him approaching the house, he hurried out to meet him. He grabbed Vanchi's hand and held him where he was, in the middle of the street. Searching his brother-in-law's face, he spoke in a pleading voice.

'Vanchi, tell me what's going on. There's no job in Madras, is there?'

Vanchi looked down and did not answer.

'You trust me, don't you?'

Vanchi raised his eyes and stared at Shankara. 'Yes, but I can't tell you.'

'Please, Vanchi. Think about it. I know you took the blood oath, we both did, but that doesn't mean—'

'Shankara, I don't want to talk about this.'

'But you're my sister's husband. She needs you. Even more now, without Vanni.'

He squeezed Vanchi's hand and said goodbye. Vanchi watched him disappear at the end of the street and struggled to stay calm. He would never see him again.

'Morning, my boy,' Thatha said without much enthusiasm, after Vanchi returned to the house. 'Breakfast's ready, I think. Eat well.'

Vanchi left his suitcase on the veranda and went inside. He ate in near silence while Ponammal served him. His grandfather had persuaded his mother that the married couple should be left alone in the kitchen that morning. They hadn't spoken directly to each other since his return from Pondicherry and the death of their daughter.

When Vanchi had finished, Ponammal brought him a bowl of warm water to wash his hands. Then she gave him a cloth to dry them. He was about to get up when she spoke.

'I hope it goes well, in Madras and all.'

He looked at her, thin-cheeked and hollow-eyed.

'I do, too.'

'And... I hope I can join you.'

He didn't reply.

'When you're ready, I mean.'

'It might be some time.'

'I know. But it will be a new thing, won't it?'

Again, he kept quiet.

'I mean, a new start and...well, maybe another baby.'

Vanchi didn't look at her again. He rose and crossed the threshold to the veranda, where his grandfather was waiting for him.

'I did a special puja for you,' he said, angling his head towards the Shiva temple. 'To ensure success in your job.'

Vanchi responded by kneeling down and touching Thatha's feet. 'Get up, my boy, get up,' he said with a shaky voice. 'I know you'll do your best.'

Vanchi rose and leaned over to pick up his case.

'Nice one that,' Thatha said. 'Good and sturdy.'

Vanchi froze.

'Picked it up just now, while you were eating.'

It was time to go, but Vanchi didn't move. He wanted to stay with his grandfather, to walk with him into the hills and hear him talk about the trees and flowers. He wanted him to tell him the story of the stone man one more time. Vanchi would tell him the truth and he would understand.

'Best to get going, my boy.'

Vanchi stepped off the veranda and stood beside his mother, bent at the waist. She moved her hand swiftly, and Vanchi watched the dots and loops whirl into another pattern. The wind scattered some of the white powder, and she redrew it.

Then she straightened up and looked at him.

'It's a *sikku* pattern,' she said. 'The twisted one. Can't tell where it begins and where it ends.'

But it's all connected. It has boundaries, he said to himself and left.

19

Palayamkottai, June 1911

Vanchi alighted at Tinnevelly, turned left outside the station and crossed over the long bridge to Palayamkottai. He did his best to shield his suitcase from the light rain that had begun to fall. On his way through the market, he saw a foreign woman dressed in an ankle-length white dress with crossed swords on a high red collar. He wanted to shout 'Vande Mataram!' Hail Mother India. But he had been told not to attract attention and only glowered when he passed her, though she appeared not to notice.

Rajakkal Street turned out to be a narrow lane, running at a right angle away from the market and towards the old fort. The two-storey house stood at the end close to the market, where hawkers shouted and carts rumbled by. Newer and more substantial than the house in Shenkottai, it had a double front door, which confused Vanchi. After knocking on both thick wooden panels, he was greeted by a young girl, only a few years older than Vanni, who told him that her cousin was waiting for him upstairs.

He stepped into a square, open-air courtyard with rough stone flooring. Carved wooden pillars held up the roof, which sloped in towards a shallow, sunken washing area in the centre. Clothes were drying on a rope stretched diagonally across the courtyard.

Vanchi walked along two sides of the courtyard and found

the stairway. Upstairs, Madasami greeted him, though neither of them showed emotion.

'This is our room,' Madasami said.

Two mats were rolled up against a wall. A single window with thin iron bars overlooked the street.

'We'll eat by ourselves in the kitchen. Don't talk to anyone you might meet in the house, except to be polite.'

'Your uncle, what does he know?'

'That you are a friend of mine. That we are campaigning for swadeshi.'

'Nothing more?'

'Nothing more. Let's see the pistol.'

Vanchi opened his suitcase and gave him the gun, wrapped in a cloth. Madasami slotted the bullets into the magazine and the shoved it back into the grip.

'Seems fine,' he said. 'What do you think?'

Vanchi let the loaded gun lie in his palm. He had never held it inside a room before, so close to someone. Would it be like this in the train? He raised the gun and pointed it at the window.

'Don't,' Madasami hissed.

Vanchi smiled and handed him the weapon. Madasami separated everything again, and Vanchi wrapped up the gun and put it back in his case.

'Right. Now listen carefully,' Madasami said. 'He's travelling on Thursday morning.'

'Three days,' Vanchi mumbled.

'Yes. Tomorrow, we go to Maniyachi Junction, to prepare.'

*

Vanchi hardly slept that night and woke up in a sweat. He was trying to imagine what it would feel like to get up in the morning and know you would be dead by noon.

Do everything as you would on the actual day. Perfect all your movements and your thoughts. Those were Aiyar's instructions, part of his final words to him before his midnight flight. And do it only once. More than that might look suspicious and might make you nervous. But everything should be the same. Except that you won't have the gun and he won't be there.

'What about the letter? Should I write that, too?'

Vanchi had waited until Madasami got up before asking the question. He needed to know, to get everything right. Realising it was another detail overlooked in their preparations, Madasami didn't answer at first. He wondered what else might have been missed. He thought hard about what Aiyar had said to him. Everything must be the same on the practice day, but don't force things.

'Get the pen and paper ready,' he said at last. 'But don't write it. Not until the day.'

Vanchi stuck to his morning routine, but nothing was the same in that unfamiliar house. No veranda. No Thatha. No Ponammal. Going downstairs to bathe, he heard voices coming from various rooms. He saw an older woman washing dishes in the open-air courtyard. Servants stepped aside as he walked to the men's bathing area, a small space behind the kitchen.

An hour later, they left the house carrying cloth bundles, like ordinary train passengers. Madasami had thought of that at the last minute. They walked through the market and reached the bridge, where Madasami checked his watch. It had taken thirty-seven minutes. He said they should leave a little earlier to make sure they didn't have to rush.

They crossed the bridge, entered the station and bought their second-class tickets. Before boarding the Madras-bound train, Madasami noted that there was only one first-class carriage and that it was near the front. The train left four minutes late, but Madasami said that didn't matter.

After disembarking at Maniyachi Junction, Madasami told Vanchi to look inside a first-class compartment, to study the seating. Just a glance, he said. Don't attract attention. Vanchi already knew that he was too short and the windows too high, though he hadn't told Madasami about his reconnaissance when returning from Pondicherry. Madasami wouldn't like that but he didn't have to know. Vanchi stood beside the wood-sided and steel-framed carriage, hoping that the step up into that compartment might be lower. It wasn't.

He joined Madasami and together they walked past the first-class waiting room. Although the door was closed, the windows were open and Madasami managed to look inside. He didn't like what he saw. Too large and too many people. They crossed over the footbridge to the platform where the Boat Mail from Tuticorin would halt.

'Poor devils. They look lost,' the stationmaster said to himself as he watched the two men wandering about on the platforms.

The Boat Mail came and went, and they took the first train back to Tinnevelly. They didn't speak about it until they were alone in the house in Palayamkottai.

'Perfect,' Madasami said. He decided not to say anything about the waiting room. And Vanchi didn't mention the high step.

*

The next morning, Madasami left Vanchi in the house and walked to the tea stall opposite the collector's office. He wanted to have another look at the man, to make sure he could identify him quickly. There wouldn't be much time and to make the same mistake that others had made would be disastrous. He hid behind his newspaper, *The Hindu*, which was the only one he could find that morning. Although his English was limited, he could make out the gist of the lead article on the front page. Arthur Lawley, governor of Madras for the past five years, was leaving his post and returning to England. A smug smile crossed Madasami's face. A lot more will be returning, if we can get this right.

He checked his watch. It was nearly ten o'clock, but Ashe had not appeared. Could he have left for Kodaikanal earlier than planned? Had he been summoned to Madras?

He put down his paper when he saw Das come out of the office and approach the tea stall.

'What's happened? Where's the collector?' Madasami asked.

'He's inside. Came early to tidy things up for his departure.'

Madasami relaxed but then noticed Das's face.

'What's the matter?' he asked.

'I have some information for you.'

Madasami steered him away from the tea stall and into the lane leading to the river.

'What information?' Madasami demanded.

'The kind you want and will have to pay for.'

Madasami promised another ten rupees.

'It's been delayed,' Das said.

'Delayed?'

'His wife's ship was late getting to Bombay. It won't reach Tuticorin until Thursday. She won't get here, to Palayamkottai, until that afternoon or evening.'

Madasami tried to remain calm. After all, he was just asking for a departure date.

'I see. But when—'

'They're going on Saturday morning. Same train, same time. I already have the tickets.'

Walking back, Madasami mulled it over. A two-day delay. Saturday rather than Thursday. The platform at Maniyachi Junction might be more crowded, but there was nothing he could do. Ashe was the one controlling the day. At least, he would die on a day closer to the coronation in London, which is what Aiyar wanted. He sent a coded telegram to Aiyar in Pondicherry.

Hearing someone enter the house, Vanchi put aside the *Tirukkural* and waited. Madasami entered and sat beside him on the mat.

'There's been a change of plan,' he said. 'Not tomorrow. It's Saturday.'

Vanchi didn't ask for an explanation. He brought his hands together in his lap, interlaced the fingers and closed his eyes.

*

All afternoon, Vanchi lay on his mat, thinking of the final day. Madasami was a perfectionist, like Aiyar. He liked to be in control, always looking at his watch. That was good. Vanchi kept playing the final scene over and over in his mind's eye. Leaping into the compartment, getting out the gun and shooting. All within a few seconds.

Madasami went out again and came back with a small, custom-made wooden box.

'Let's see the gun,' he said.

Madasami placed the pistol inside the box and closed the unlatched lid. A good fit.

'You'll carry this,' he said and gave him the box. 'The cloth bundle shows too much and takes too long to untie.'

Vanchi put the box under his arm and stood up.

'Right. Take a few steps, see how it feels.'

Vanchi crossed the room.

'It's fine,' he said. 'But there's something else.'

Madasami screwed up his face.

'I need to practise.'

'No!' Madasami's loud voice startled them both. 'Aiyar said no. It's too risky.'

'It's been more than three weeks.'

Vanchi's lips trembled. Everything had been set. Then the delay, and now this box.

'Just one or two shots,' he said. 'To make sure I'm ready.'

Madasami saw his point. He frowned and opened the tin.

'There's six in here,' he said, half to himself. 'That's all we have.'

Following the routine they had established in Pondicherry, they left the house two hours before daybreak. But they didn't have a local guide and didn't know where they might find a good spot. After half an hour, they had left the town behind and were walking along a country road. Paddy fields lay on both sides, but they were a foot deep in water.

'There,' Vanchi whispered, pointing towards a small hillock lying beyond the fields.

Turning off the road and going closer, they found a group of palmyra trees. No houses or huts in sight. Vanchi walked up to one of the trees, turned around and marked off six paces.

'Let me have two,' he said in a low voice.

He pushed the bullets into the magazine and shoved it back into the grip. The wind picked up, threatening rain.

'Be quick about it,' Madasami urged.

Vanchi raised his right arm and drew back his elbow until the gun was a foot from his shoulder. He raised the barrel and held it steady for a long moment. He fired twice and missed.

'Two more,' he said, turning to Madasami.

'No.'

'I've got to hit the target today. That's the only way I know I won't miss.'

Madasami heard the desperation in his voice and handed over the bullets. He held his breath and watched Vanchi raise the gun again. Two crashing sounds followed by the thud of metal sinking into wood.

'Hey! What're you doing?'

A man emerged from the darkness waving a thick club.

'You can't fire off guns around here like that,' he said in a wheezing voice. He was now less than fifty feet away.

Madasami grabbed Vanchi and pointed. 'Go that way,' he said. 'I'll go the other. Meet me at the house.'

Vanchi ran, slipped and fell into a field but managed to hold the gun above the water. He hauled himself up just as the man reached the other end of the field, swinging the staff above his head like a circus performer. Vanchi sloshed through the field and scrambled onto the mud bund before turning around to see that the man had not moved.

Two bullets left, he said to himself as he regained the main road. That's all I'll need.

20

Tuticorin and Palayamkottai, June 1911

Mary leaned on the railing and strained her eyes, willing the land to appear. She had been at sea for nearly three weeks and spent two extra days stewing in her cabin during the delay at Bombay. At least the monsoon had held off for much of the voyage, but there was only so much shuffleboard and badminton one could endure. Not to mention her female travelling companions, most of whom prattled on about the adventure of 'going out east'. Mary found herself in demand as she offered advice to governesses, brides-to-be and young ladies in search of a husband among the office class. Dear me, she thought, I've become an old India hand.

Having reached Colombo the previous night, she had disembarked from the P&O steamer and boarded a smaller vessel for Tuticorin. The food had been awful and made worse by the rough sea crossing, all sixteen hours of it.

'There it is!'

She shifted her eyes in the direction indicated by the soldier's finger. Although this was the first time she'd sailed to Tuticorin, she had expected to see the familiar outline of the harbour, not a raised wooden platform sticking out from the shore. Still, she viewed it as a lifeline, flung out to rescue her. Bowing her head, she repeated her silent prayer. A telegraphic message about the delay in Bombay had been sent to all government offices, and she could only hope that Robert had been informed.

She was taken to the pier in a launch boat with the other first-class passengers. The dangling rope ladder cut into her palms, but she managed to climb up without damage to her dress or shoes. Straightening her hat and pinning her hair, she waited for her trunk and cases to be hoisted up and shouldered by porters. Only then did she allow herself to look at the small crowd gathered at the far end of the pier. Dear God, she pleaded again, please let him be there.

She squeezed her eyes like a marksman and tried to pick him out among the waving hands and hats. But, in the end, it was he who broke cover, pushed past the customs officer and rushed up the pier, shouting, 'Mary! Mary!'

Both were embarrassed when they thought about it later. But at the time, they revelled in the pleasure of their bodies fused through kisses and embraces. Mary cried and Robert pressed his lips so hard that they hurt. Still wordless, they turned and walked arm in arm to the quayside.

He led her to a two-horse carriage and opened the half-door for her to step inside its elegant box.

'Robert, what's this?'

'Oh, just a little treat for you, my dear,' he said. 'Welcome home.'

Mary smiled. Home, that's what she, too, had called it during the long journey.

'However,' he added, 'if you'd rather we boarded the train here, changed at Maniyachi, went to Tinnevelly and then took a jutka, well, just say so.'

'Certainly not! Cinderella will travel in the prince's coach.'

The road was bumpy and torrential rain slowed their progress, but they didn't notice. Delighting in each other's company inside the coach, they giggled like children hiding in a cave. Robert assured her that their own children were fine. That they would see them soon. And that he, too, was feeling well. When the carriage hit a deep pothole and flung her on top of him, they howled with laughter.

'Tell me, honestly,' he said after a brief silence and with a change of tone. 'Are you feeling better?'

'Oh, yes. Dr Simpson, you know, the one who treated mother and father. He has a new machine. A cardiograph. He used it to measure my heartbeat and then catheters to stimulate my arteries.'

Robert listened with waning interest as she described the rest of her treatment: mustard plasters on the chest, vigorous rubbing of limbs and wrapping of feet in thick flannel.

'But the worst part,' she said in conclusion, 'was when he put me on a strict diet for the rest of my stay. Nothing but soup, fruit and vegetables. And, oh, yes, a small glass of brandy and water before bed.'

'I see, that explains it. Your hollow cheeks, I mean. We'll have to fatten you up here!'

'I shall look certainly forward to whatever cook serves up. The P&O food was indescribably horrible. And the people, well, the less said the better. I wouldn't have survived the voyage if it hadn't been for Miss Foster.'

She told him about the young girl she had befriended as soon as the ship passed Gibraltar.

'She's so sweet, Robbie. Engaged to a tea-planter in Assam and completely innocent. Problem was she couldn't abide her chaperone, an old Tartar of an aunt.'

'I see. So, you stepped in to plug the maternal gap.'

'But she was so frightened. Didn't know what to expect.'

'And you told her how to avoid the tigers, cholera and spear-throwing natives.'

'Don't be facetious. I gave her some very practical advice about housekeeping and…husbands.'

Robert took her hand and said, 'You didn't fail to mention, I hope, that your own Prince Charming would meet you with a chariot.'

They both laughed so loudly that the driver turned around. White people, he thought, smiling to himself. Sometimes they're funny.

*

By the time the coach pulled up in front of their bungalow in Palayamkottai, the rain had stopped. Stepping out into the blazing sun, the air felt light and Mary instinctively looked for a rainbow. Robert took her arm as she held the hem of her dress above the puddles and together they approached the house. Only then did she notice the servants. Bearer, assistant bearer, cook, cook's assistant, gardener, water man and sweeper—all of them had gathered by the door. Dressed in clean clothes, they greeted her with phrases that she still understood. 'Vanakkam, amma.' Welcome home, madam.

'Robert, you shouldn't have told them to,' she said when they were inside.

'But I didn't. It was their idea entirely.'

Mary looked surprised.

'Honestly. I wouldn't have known how to tell them even if I'd wanted to. But, you know, they really are good people. Not always trustworthy, mind you. But deep down, they're kind and affectionate.'

The bedsheets had been washed and ironed, the furniture dusted, and fresh flowers arranged in a pitcher on the dining table. The highlight of Mary's homecoming, though, was a butter-soaked fish biryani, her favourite dish.

After eating, they sat down and faced each other in the sitting room.

'Now, listen. Tomorrow is your day of rest. Sleep as long as you like and I'll come home early so that we can pack everything for the journey on Saturday.'

'Oh, Robert! It's going to be wonderful.'

'Yes. You'll recover even faster in the mountains.'

'You've got the tickets? The new ones, I mean.'

'Yes. Das has them.'

'Dear man. How is he, by the way?'

'Das? What do you mean?'

'Didn't you say his mother was ill and needed an operation?'

'Seems he's taking her to the hospital in Vellore, near Madras, after we leave.'

'Good. He must be happy.'

'Umm. He's been acting a little strange lately.'

'Strange?'

'Distant, withdrawn. Of course, he's always been formal with me, but never like this.'

Mary slept for twelve hours and woke near mid-day. On the dining table she saw a note: 'Cinderella is to have two eggs, porridge and honey tea. Prince to return at four.'

She spent the rest of the day making preparations but found it difficult to select clothes for both the hot journey by train and the cool weather in the mountains. Closing up the bungalow was also demanding. She had lost a little facility with the language and struggled to tell the servants what to do. Then came more detailed instructions to the gardener and sweeper, the two who would remain as watchmen sleeping on the veranda. By late afternoon, she felt a migraine coming on and sent the cook's assistant to the market to buy a fresh supply of the senna leaf concoction.

*

Hearing the neighing of a pony, she rearranged herself with a series of pats and pulls before Robert came bounding through the door.

'Right,' he said, loosening his tie and taking off his coat. 'No more office for this boy. Not for a long time.'

He clapped his hands and told the bearer to bring their dinner as soon as possible. During Mary's absence, Robert had taken on some of her domestic duties, though he tended to use the bearer, who spoke rudimentary English, as an intermediary with the other servants.

He was not disappointed when the man brought in the special meal that he had ordered for their dinner on this, their last day. A clear gravy soup was followed by tinned salmon, boiled potatoes with herbs and another fish curry.

'You liked it?' he asked when the plates had been cleared and coffee served.

'You're spoiling me, Robert. I guess I should go back to Ireland every year!'

They sat and talked about Kodaikanal. Robert read aloud Molly's latest letter, which chronicled the 'exploits of the gang', as she termed her siblings. Both parents commented on their daughter's witty turn of phrase, and Robert pledged to find a suitable English tutor for her next year.

Then it was Mary's turn. She went into the bedroom and came back with a case that had accompanied her all the way from Dublin. She reached in and, one by one, brought out gifts for the children: a turtle-shell backed hairbrush for Molly, a set of toy soldiers for Arthur, a music box for Sheila and a teddy bear for little Herbert. Plus new clothes and shoes for each of them.

'What's it called again?' Robert asked, picking up the soft brown animal and moving its limbs.

'Teddy. After the American president, Roosevelt.'

Robert said they should get to bed early.

'Tell me again,' Mary said, after he had risen to his feet, 'what time do we leave? I just can't wait.'

'We'd better get off by 8:30, to be on the safe side. The train leaves at 9:30. Das will meet us at the station.'

'And we have the cottage until the end of July, right?'

'Right. End of July.'

'Six whole weeks. All of us together.'

Robert sank back down in his chair.

'Yes,' he said with a weak smile, 'let's hope so.'

'Robert, whatever do you mean?'

'You can certainly stay for six weeks, but I may have to return early.'

Mary stared at him in disbelief. He picked up his cold pipe and began to chew it.

'Hartley's warned me, that's all,' he explained. 'Says things are hotting up again. More leaflets and now a whole pamphlet. All the work of those self-styled revolutionaries in Pondicherry.'

'And?'

'I'll have to come back down, if necessary.'

'Why? What does he think will happen?'

'I'm not sure. Maybe a riot. Or some other kind of violence.'

21

Maniyachi Junction, 17 June 1911

The station was surrounded by silence. Goats nibbled the branches of spiky trees and snow-white egrets balanced on one leg in stubbled fields. The slightest movement caught the eye, as when one of the birds jumped on the back of a water buffalo and pecked at the insects burrowing in the tough black skin. If the bulky animal ambled off, the egret stood like an erect sailor on a slow-moving ship. The only sound that carried was the occasional creaking of high-swaying palmyra fronds. Even the wind seemed to struggle, gusting now and then, before giving up and dying out without a trace.

The nearest village was two miles away, a dozen thatched and mud-brick houses clustered around a small temple. A dirt track led out of the village to the station. Passing the temple, it skirted a dry riverbed before straightening out and running through scrubland. Some of the fallow fields were bordered by bushes pinpricked with yellow flowers. There was no paddy or sugarcane. This was the 'black country,' where only cotton and millet grew in its dark soil.

The landmark for anyone walking or driving a cart to Maniyachi Junction was a single palmyra tree. In its shade stood a terracotta image of a woman, crunching the head of a child with her protruding teeth. She had been a temple dancer, betrayed, murdered and transformed into a goddess. Still carrying the man's child, she tracked him down to a deserted temple, ripped out his heart and drove a stake through his chest. The clay statue was weather-beaten and cracked, but in the winter, when her story was sung, the goddess entered the bodies of dancing women, merging her fury with theirs and bringing them solace.

Viewed from the distance of the palmyra tree, the raised platform, the water tower and the station buildings looked like abandoned monuments of an ancient civilization. A drought or a flood might have left them unoccupied and sleeping in the hot sun. But they were barely ten years old, a slab of modernity, complete with telegraph lines, laid on the land in the age of the bullock cart.

That Saturday morning, the stationmaster paid the jutka driver, straightened his coat and stood for a moment. All he heard was the wind. 'That place is dead,' he often complained to his wife. 'Like a cremation ground.'

The air was heavy, but it didn't look like rain. Still, it was just after eight o'clock, and anything could happen before he locked up and went home. He'd had his uniform washed and ironed because the collector was passing through in a few hours. That's also why he'd hired the jutka rather than walk the two miles. Can't greet the collector wearing mud-splattered shoes and trousers, he'd said to himself to justify the extra two annas. There was no mud that morning, but he had decided to play it safe.

Cursing under his breath, he struggled with the heavy padlock on his office door. There'd been a theft recently, and all the offices and waiting rooms were kept under lock and key until he arrived. Jiggling and jerking, he got the thing to open but saw that a button had popped off his coat. 'Can't be helped,' he muttered. 'He's only a bloody collector, not the Viceroy, for God's sake.'

He felt better when he sat down, checked the day's timetable and stored his tiffin box in a desk drawer. The smell of the brinjal curry was tempting, but he'd have to wait. Pulling the watch out from his coat pocket, he saw that it was 8:17. More than two hours before the uptrain from Tinnevelly. A peon entered and placed a tray with tea and biscuits on his desk. He shuffled a few papers and found the telegram. Where the devil was that useless assistant stationmaster?

Reading the telegram, he frowned. It had arrived only yesterday at noon and he wasn't sure that everything was ready. Collector Ashe and his wife were scheduled to arrive from Tinnevelly at 10:35. Once there, they would wait for the Boat Mail from Tuticorin to come in at 10:48. During that interval, he had to ensure that they were given tiffin and their trunks were carried across the tracks to the other platform. He would greet them, of course, but should he accompany them over the footbridge and see them into their compartment in the Boat Mail? Would they want to use the waiting room?

'Good morning, sir.' The assistant stationmaster greeted him with his usual smug smile.

'Ah, there you are. Everything ready for the collector?'

'Yes, sir. I've detailed two porters to handle their luggage.'

'Tiffin?'

'Brought it from home myself, sir. Boiled eggs, chapatis and potato masala.'

Wouldn't mind a bit of that for lunch, the stationmaster thought.

'Right,' he said. 'Check the first-class waiting room. Have it swept again. Not a speck, mind. Do you think he'll have anyone else with him? Besides his wife, I mean.'

'Sir?'

'CID people, for example?'

'The telegram didn't say, sir. I shouldn't think so.'

'Right. Now go away and don't bother me with any more unnecessary questions.'

*

At Tinnevelly station, Robert and Mary Ashe arranged themselves in their compartment. Das and the bearer supervised the storing of their luggage in a separate carriage. The bearer climbed into that same carriage, and Das returned to the first-class carriage.

'All stored away, sir,' Das said, standing on the platform. 'Have a restful holiday, ma'am.'

'Thank you, Das,' said Robert.

'I wish your mother well,' Mary added.

The whistle blew, Das executed a tiny bow and watched the train pull out of the station. Inside their compartment, Robert and Mary were laughing with nervous energy.

'We almost missed it!' he said. 'After all the trains and boats you've been on in the past few weeks. And we nearly missed this clunky thing.'

'The Orient Express comes to Tinnevelly!' Mary declared, though her words were cancelled out by blasts of steam from the engine.

Sitting opposite each other on upholstered, high-backed benches, their knees almost touched in the gap between them. The compartment was a private space that could be entered only by the side doors, which opened directly onto the platforms. No corridor connected their compartment to the other first-class compartments.

Mary took off her hat, Robert loosened his jacket and they settled back with sighs of satisfaction. They had made it. Another year and another trip to the mountains, just as he had promised her on their first night together.

'I hope we can get some decent tea at Kodai Road,' he said, referring to the station where they would leave the train and take a carriage up the mountain.

'Yes,' Mary said, 'it was dreadful last year. But at least we have our lunch.'

Mary had given strict instructions to the cook—nothing but fish cutlets, hard-boiled eggs, chapatis and bananas. Anything else would spoil in the heat. The food was carefully packed and in the care of the bearer, travelling in the luggage carriage.

'That's good. We'll need something to sustain us,' Robert said and fished out his pipe.

He didn't expect to enjoy the long journey after lunch. A two-horse carriage would crawl up a rough road and around hairpin turns, with the bearer and trunks following in a second carriage. They might see the children before dark, but only if the horses and the carriages sustained no damage.

Mary took out her knitting, while Robert tamped down and lit his pipe. He looked out the window and thought how lucky they were. All four children healthy and happy—he'd just learned that one of his married friends in Dublin had lost a young child to pneumonia. Mary was cured, thank goodness, and he was on track for promotion.

Lulled by the clacking wheels and rocking carriage, his body slackened. He hadn't realized how tense he had been over the past few months. Mary's absence, Hartley's warnings, the threatening letter and the strange Mr Walker—it had all piled up on him. He wished again that he had someone to confide in. He told Mary most things, of course, but she needed to be shielded from danger, especially now with her delicate heart.

'A penny for them,' Mary said, not looking up from her needles.

'Oh, just thinking about the children,' he said.

'Me, too. You know, we should have brought something for the Wilkinsons. They are too kind.'

His thoughts returned to Palayamkottai. The bungalow would be all right. Mary had seen to that. Das would shut up the office and check on the watchman from time to time. And Hartley knew where to contact him.

'I know. I'll knit a jumper for Mrs Wilkinson.'

'What? Oh, good idea, dear.'

The train chugged through the barren countryside north of Tinnevelly. Having waited for a long time, Robert decided that the right moment had come.

'I haven't had time to tell you, Mary,' he said.

The needles stopped clacking. Her eyes narrowed.

'You see,' he began and broke into a wide smile, 'you better get used to these long train rides.'

Mary looked at him in bewilderment.

'Because we're going to Madras in December.'

'Madras!' She dropped her knitting and clapped her hands. Shopping at Spencer's and lunches in the Ladies' Room at the Adyar Club. 'You've been transferred?'

'No, no,' he said. 'There's going to be a big celebration in Madras to coincide with the King's coronation in Delhi. The actual ceremony takes place next week in London, but he and the Queen will come to India in December.'

'And?'

'And we've been invited to stay at the governor's house during the celebrations in Madras.'

'Oh, Robbie! But what about the children? I mean, they'll all be with us in December.'

'It's only be for a week or so. I think we could ask the Elphinstones to take the little rascals in.'

'Yes, I suppose so.'

'Anyway, we have lots of time to arrange it. Lots of time,' he said.

He relit his pipe as they neared Maniyachi Junction. The slow-moving train had gone barely twenty miles from Tinnevelly, but he was already far away. The holiday in Kodai would be followed in a few months by that week in Madras. It would be a grand affair, an affirmation of British rule. Maharajas and princes from every corner of India would bow before the King and pledge their allegiance to the crown.

Puffing away, he calculated that the coronation would help stem the spread of anti-British sentiment in the district. Let those deluded extremists in Pondicherry rant on in their leaflets. 'The end of the white man's empire?' Hah! We're here to stay and make India a modern, civilized society.

'What are you plotting, now, collector saab?' Mary asked, having watched his lips tighten and his eyes light up.

'Our future,' he said and reached out to squeeze her hand.

*

At Maniyachi Junction, the stationmaster picked up a recent notice from head office marked 'Urgent'. A new schedule of fares was laid out in neat columns detailing changes, including tickets for servants travelling in third-class carriages to accompany luggage. They would now cost one anna for the first twenty-five miles and two annas for the next twenty-five. He scribbled a note to the clerk in the booking office, instructing him to make three copies of the document and return the original to him without delay. Ringing his little desk bell, he summoned the peon lounging outside his door and told him to deliver his note along with the official notice.

Nothing for it now, he muttered and set about the task of finishing his overdue report entitled 'Operations at Maniyachi Junction, Administrative Year 1909/1910'. Having reached the section on 'Accidents', he put down his pen and looked at his watch. Some days, the morning uptrain from Tinnevelly was late, but he'd had a telegraph message that it had set off on time. Nothing to worry about, then, he said to himself. He hadn't yet met this collector, but he'd heard that he wasn't one of the arrogant ones. Anyway, it wasn't as if he had to sit down and take tea with the man.

Shortly after ten, he rose from his desk and took up his usual observation post just outside his office door. Standing between the black station clock, mounted on one side of the door, and the heavy metal bell, mounted on the other side, he hoped that he looked commanding in his white coat, white trousers and black tie. He hid the missing button by casually sliding a hand over his stomach.

His default grumpy mood improved when he saw signs of life on the station. The sweeper was working his way down the far platform. Squatting on his haunches, and waddling duck-like, he brushed debris into a gunny sack. Two or three dozen passengers were milling around on the main platform, where the Tinnevelly train would halt. Other travellers were arriving on foot and by cart. The tea stall and sweet-stall were busy, and a queue had formed at the booking office. Voices rose above the hum of activity, bringing a smile to the stationmaster's face.

He swept his gaze up and down the main platform one more time. Nothing unusual, but he wasn't sure what he was looking for. He glanced at his watch again. Twenty minutes to go. Time enough for his second morning tea. Sipping away inside, he stared at his last sentence, which reported an accident that occurred two months ago when a portly man rolled off the platform, fell on the track and broke his leg. He was about to strike out the phrase 'due to excess intake of alcohol', when a man barged into his office. Well-dressed and irate, he demanded 'to talk to whoever was in charge'.

'That's me,' the stationmaster said and pulled himself up in his chair. 'What seems to be the problem?'

'Problem? One of your so-called porters refused to carry my luggage, that's what.'

The offended man explained that the 'cheeky bastard' demanded more money for carrying his three outsized trunks.

'It's one anna per trunk,' the stationmaster said. 'Paragraph 14.3 of the current regulations.'

'Damn the regulations,' the man shouted. 'I'm going to write to your superior and—'

As always, sound preceded sight at the station. Hearing a whistle shriek, the stationmaster excused himself and hurried outside. When he heard a second whistle, he pulled hard on the bell rope, twice in quick succession to announce the arrival of an uptrain. Half a minute later, he saw the sooty plume of the advancing engine.

Its furiously churning wheels screeched to a stop, and passengers poured out onto the platform. Most made their way to the footbridge and crossed over to wait for the Boat Mail, while others went to the tea stall, the waiting rooms or the toilet at the far end of the platform.

When the crowd had thinned, it exposed two young men standing together beside the train. One of them held a small box, the other a cloth bundle. They appeared confused, not knowing where to go. The stationmaster thought they looked familiar and was wondering why when his attention was drawn to the collector's luggage being offloaded from the separate baggage carriage. At that moment, the two men drew closer together, and the box changed hands.

*

'Just ten minutes or so,' Robert said, sitting in their compartment. 'We'll stay here, rather than the waiting room. More convenient. Then we'll cross over to the Boat Mail.'

Mary nodded and continued to knit. Robert looked out the open window and saw a group of children under the veranda roof of the second-class waiting room. They seemed to be looking at him and laughing. He smiled back and mentioned to Mary that Indian children were delightful.

The stationmaster kept his eye on the progress of the collector's luggage. Overseen by the bearer and the assistant stationmaster, it was carried over the footbridge to the other platform. He pulled out his pocket watch and saw that the Boat Mail was due in eight minutes.

Straightening his coat and cap, he approached the train. His English was good, he'd been told, but he rarely used it and had no idea what he should say to the collector or his wife.

When he reached the collector's compartment, he stood until he was noticed through the open window.

'Yes?' Ashe enquired, noting the man's neat uniform.

'I'm the stationmaster here,' he said with a slight bow. 'I want to welcome you to Maniyachi. And ma'am, also.'

'Thank you,' Ashe replied. 'Everything all right?'

'Yes, sir. The Boat Mail will arrive on time. Just six minutes now.'

'Excellent.'

'We have some refreshment for you. Please.'

The stationmaster again inclined his head, signalled to his assistant and withdrew.

At that moment, the two young men further down the platform separated. Madasami walked away with the box, while Vanchi came forward, gripping the pistol in his pocket. He clicked off the safety on the handle.

The assistant stationmaster was just emerging from his office with a tiffin tray when Vanchi reached the first-class carriage and jerked open the door of the second compartment.

'What the devil!' Ashe cried as Vanchi leapt inside and pointed the gun at him.

Seeing Mary, he hesitated. She screamed, and Ashe flung his pith helmet at the intruder, but it sailed through the window and rolled along the platform. Vanchi fired once, hitting him in the chest, and jumped out of the compartment. Ashe tried to follow, but Mary grabbed his coat and held him back. Halted, he fell to the floor.

Vanchi ran down the platform, while Madasami, who had been watching from the far end, jumped off and raced across the open fields. One of the porters chased Vanchi and tackled him, but Vanchi managed to throw him off and kept others at bay by waving his pistol in the air. The stationmaster rushed to his office and sent telegraph messages to Tinnevelly and Tuticorin. Still waving his pistol, Vanchi ran to the end of the platform and locked himself inside the toilet.

The Boat Mail arrived on the other platform, and a British official onboard was led to the compartment where Robert lay bleeding. After a quick word with the stationmaster, he arranged for the train to return to Tinnevelly with the wounded man and his wife.

A few passengers and porters now surrounded the locked toilet and began to pelt it with rocks taken from the railway tracks. More people joined in, throwing stones and shouting abuse at the man inside. The barrage continued until an armed policeman arrived and knocked down the door.

Vanchi lay on the floor, his face and neck covered in blood, the pistol still in his hand. No one had heard the gunshot. Carried off by a gusting wind, it had been swallowed by the countryside.

*

Three hours later, the sub-collector and superintendent of police from Tuticorin reached Maniyachi Junction and were taken to the toilet. They confirmed that Vanchi was dead. Examining the pistol, they saw that it had been fired twice and that the magazine was empty.

In Vanchi's pocket, they found a letter handwritten in Tamil:

> Having captured our country, our English enemies are trampling over our eternal dharma with their feet and destroying it. Every Indian is now attempting to drive out our enemies and restore our tradition and freedom. Our country has been ruled by Rama, Shivaji, Krishna, Guru Govindan and Arjuna, who protected dharma. But now it is George the Fifth, an impure man who eats the flesh of cows, who will soon be crowned king of our country. However, as soon as he sets foot in this country, three thousand of us in Madras Presidency have pledged to kill him. I, who am the least among them, have done this action today so that others will know about our plan. It is what every Indian should consider their duty.
>
> R. Vanchi Aiyar of Shenkottai

In his coat pocket, they also found a few coins and buttons, a train ticket and a cotton purse made in France displaying an image of Queen Victoria and the British royal coat of arms.

22

Palayamkottai and Shenkottai, 17 & 18 June 1911

Mary Ashe tried to comfort her husband during the train ride back to Tinnevelly. His chest wound had been staunched by a makeshift bandage, but her dress was splattered with blood. Cradling his head against her shoulder, she stifled her tears.

'You'll be all right, my dear,' she said through clenched teeth. 'We'll be there soon. We'll be there soon.'

Just fifteen minutes into the journey, she felt his body jerk and slump down. The doctor, who met her at the station, examined the corpse and informed her that her husband had died of an internal haemorrhage.

'He died instantly, Mrs Ashe,' the doctor said, though he knew otherwise. The single bullet, he later said at the inquest, had entered the right side of his chest, pierced his right lung and lodged in his liver.

From the station, Mary was put in a carriage and driven over the bridge to their bungalow in Palayamkottai. She spoke to no one and closed herself inside the bedroom. Again and again, she saw the man shoot Robert at point-blank range. So close that she saw the fear in the man's eyes.

Robert's body was taken from the station to the hospital for an autopsy before it was brought to the bungalow in a coffin. The large sitting room had already filled up with friends, officials and church members, both British and Indian. Mary continued to shut herself in the bedroom and refused to see anyone. The cook and servants, supervised by the bearer, did their best to prepare and serve tea to the unexpected visitors.

A little after five o'clock that afternoon, Mary heard a soft knock on her door. 'It's me, Felicity.'

Felicity Elphinstone, wife of the district medical officer, was Mary's best friend. Mary opened the door a crack.

'It's about to start, Mary. Come, I'll go with you. Look, I've brought this.'

Mary covered her head with a long, dark shawl and wrapped it around her shoulders. Leaning on her friend's arm, she watched as Robert, cleaned and lying in a wooden box, was lifted into the back of a four-horse carriage. The coach was draped in black and driven by a liveried man sitting high up in front. Mary rode behind in a smaller carriage, accompanied by Felicity and her husband. Dozens of well-wishers followed on foot.

The day's heat had drained away by the time the procession completed the short journey to the church. The smaller coach drew up under a neem tree, and the Elphinstones got down and waited, while Mary sat inside. This was the church where she prayed on Sundays and where she had attended weddings, baptisms and funerals.

Minutes passed before she stepped down with the shawl pulled tightly around her. Guided by her friend, she entered the church and tried to hold back the tears as she listened to the eulogy. The diligent student at Trinity College, the distinguished civil servant, the devoted father and the loving husband. After the short ceremony, she followed the pallbearers, who included Superintendent Hartley, Dr Elphinstone, the zamindar of Singampatti and an Indian lawyer, who was a friend of Chidambaram Pillai. They carried the coffin through a low metal gate and into the graveyard, where Mary liked to walk among the headstones, slabs, crosses and crypts, reading the names and dates.

With bowed head, she stood at the edge of the open grave

and smelled the freshly turned earth. Too exhausted to cry, she held on to her friend and raised her head only when the priest spoke. She heard the familiar words of the funeral prayer, 'ashes to ashes', but did not register them.

Nor did she notice a familiar face at the back of the graveside gathering. Das stood with his hands clasped at his waist. His eyes grew moist watching the priest throw the first handful of dirt on the coffin. Later, as the other mourners filed past the widow and spoke words of comfort, he mouthed his own appeal for forgiveness.

At nightfall, the other corpse reached Palayamkottai. It had lain in the latrine at Maniyachi Junction for several hours before a post-mortem was carried out by the assistant medical officer. The cause of death was confirmed when a single bullet was extracted from Vanchi's head. He was then wrapped in a white cloth and placed in a separate carriage attached to a train going to Tinnevelly.

*

The following day, a CID inspector and a sub-magistrate arrived in Shenkottai. The suicide note had enabled them to identify the assassin, and, although his accomplice had escaped, the police were determined to locate and arrest others involved in the murder plot.

A jutka brought the two men to the top of the Brahmin street, from where they walked down between the two rows of houses. It was late afternoon on a muggy day. The sub-magistrate held a file folder.

They reached Vanchi's house accompanied by a small crowd, who knew that this was not another telegram. The men's uniforms were different and so were their stern faces. Besides, Vanchi's long absences, sudden reappearances and more than usual detached attitude had stimulated gossip. Something shameful, such as infidelity or theft, was the most popular suggestion.

Seeing the officials approach, Thatha rose from his sitting

position on the veranda and steadied himself against one of the wooden pillars. Although he had ignored the rumours circulating among the neighbours, he sensed that the men had come about Vanchi. The furtive movements, the hush-hush conversations with Shankara and, most of all, the look in his grandson's eyes had alerted him.

He took his hand away the pillar and greeted the men with folded palms.

'Are you the father of Vanchi Aiyar?' the CID man asked.

Thatha relaxed a little. The inspector spoke with an accent that identified him as belonging to the same Tamil Brahmin caste.

'No, I'm his grandfather. His father is away. For work.'

Ponammal and Vanchi's mother huddled near the doorway. The crowd outside had swollen to include half the street.

'Come and sit down,' Thatha said to the visitors, and gestured to Ponammal to bring mats.

"That's not necessary. But I have some important news.'

The inspector came closer, and Thatha stepped down from the veranda. The grey-haired police official pinched his lips and drew in a breath.

'I have come to tell you that your grandson is dead.'

Thatha buckled at the knees and let out a soft moan.

'He shot and killed the collector of Tinnevelly, Mr Ashe. Then he shot himself.'

Vanchi's mother wailed, 'Ayyo, ayyo, kadavule!' Oh, God!

'It happened yesterday morning about 10:40, at Maniyachi Junction,' the inspector said.

Thatha wanted to say that he couldn't believe it, but he knew it was true. He now understood what he had seen one afternoon a week ago. He had been on his way back from the hills when he came upon Vanchi in the forest. His grandson had been standing stock still in front of the stone image of the warrior.

When he broke cover and stepped into the clearing, Vanchi whirled around.

'Oh, it's you, Grandpa.'

The old man came closer and saw streaks of vermilion on the stone and flowers scattered at the base.

'It's only a stone, my boy. It's all in the past.'

As Vanchi looked at his grandfather, Aiyar's words came quickly to his lips.

'No, Thatha. Our past is what makes us. We must defend it as we would our lives.'

At the time, Thatha had dismissed those words as something picked up from a pamphlet. Now, drawing himself up to face the inspector, he was filled with regret and shame.

The inspector waited for a minute before speaking again. 'He left a letter in his pocket. Perhaps you could tell us if it is his handwriting.'

The sub-magistrate came forward and took the letter from his folder. The crowd pushed forward into a tight circle around the men, hoping for a glimpse of the document.

Thatha looked at the letter, which he couldn't read, and confirmed that Vanchi had written it.

'Right,' the sub-magistrate said, replacing the letter in his folder. 'Now, you need to make a decision. We can return his body to you here—it's now in the hospital in Palayamkottai—or we—'

'No.'

'No what?'

'Do not bring the body here,' Thatha said. 'We will not perform a cremation for him.'

'Are you sure?' the inspector asked. 'Please think about this, sir.'

'I am sure. He is no longer my grandson.'

Thatha turned to look for Vanchi's mother, but Ponammal had already taken her inside the house.

'I see,' the sub-magistrate said. 'In that case, we will have the body cremated. The ashes will be scattered in the river.'

'No. Do not scatter his ashes. No ashes, nothing.'

After the men left, Ponammal announced that she would not shave her head.

Aftermath

That same afternoon in Pondicherry, Aiyar read the headlines with grim satisfaction. 'British Officer Assassinated', 'Terror Strikes South Indian Rail Station' and, in his own paper, 'Revenge Attack for Injustice to Chidambaram Pillai'. On the inside pages, he also read about a Mr Walker, who had been detained at Bombay while trying to board a steamer bound for Trieste.

Over the next few months, newspapers all over India reported in detail on the Ashe murder trial, or the 'Tinnevelly Conspiracy Case', as it was called. On the basis of information gathered through interviews and corroborated by leaflets found in Vanchi's house and Shankara's house, fourteen people were charged with conspiracy to commit murder and to 'wage war against the King'. Two more suspects avoided trial by committing suicide; one poisoned himself and the other cut his throat.

The fourteen who went to trial included Shankara and Nilakanta, but not Madasami and Aiyar. Although a reward of a thousand rupees had been offered for anyone who might capture Madasami and turn him over to the police, he was never found. As for Aiyar, the authorities suspected that he was the mastermind behind the plot and sent dozens of police into French territory, but he, too, was never arrested.

The six-month trial in the Madras High Court ended in February 1912. After hearing from more than a hundred witnesses, the three-judge panel acquitted all fourteen men on the charge of conspiracy, but nine were convicted of treason.

Nilakanta was imprisoned for seven years, Shankara for four and the others for shorter periods.

*

Mary Ashe waited for two weeks to resume her interrupted journey to Kodaikanal. Her children had been told by Mrs Wilkinson, in whose house they lived, that their father had died in a train accident. When their mother arrived, they wanted to know more and she eventually told them the full story.

The family returned to Ireland in early 1912 and subsequently moved to Exeter in England, where they lived with Mary's aunt and uncle. Mary's two daughters never married. Her elder son, Arthur, joined the army, serving in World War II and later in India. He married in 1948, had a son and a daughter, and died in 1986 aged eighty-four. The younger son, Herbert, married in 1941 and died three years later on a battlefield in Italy, having barely known his two-year-old daughter. Until her own death in 1954, Mary Ashe lived with her memory of the point-blank horror at Maniyachi Junction.

*

Robert Ashe was commemorated by two brass tablets put up in 1912, one in his old school in Dublin and another in St George's Cathedral, Madras. In the same year, a Celtic cross was erected at the head of his grave in Palayamkottai. Sculpted in Dublin from white Sicilian marble and paid for by his fellow colonial officers, it stands twelve feet high. At its base is an inscription that reads: 'Sacred to the memory of Robert William D'Escourt Ashe'. In the following year, a memorial pavilion was built in Tuticorin, funded by thirty-seven Indians and one British man. An elegant structure, topped by ornate iron railings and a cupola, it has since fallen into disrepair. For some Tamils, however, it remains a monument to a man who championed caste equality.

Memorials to his assassin appeared much later, decades after Indian Independence. Today, and since the 1980s, passengers travelling through the railway station where the murder took place will see that its name has been changed to 'Vanchi Maniyachi Junction'. Far fewer people view the life-size statue of Vanchi standing on a plinth near the bus station in Shenkottai. A more impressive image, again in the town of his birth, is a gold-painted bust in a temple-like memorial dedicated to him in 2013.

Predating all those commemorations, and surpassing them in scale and splendour, was an event that took place in December 1911. While the Ashe murder trial was entering its final weeks, the coronation of King George V, which the assassination was intended to undermine, was celebrated in grand fashion outside Delhi. The man whom Vanchi had threatened with death in his suicide note was feted by princes and cheered by large crowds.

Less spectacular celebrations were held all across the subcontinent. In Tenkasi, where a Coronation Arch was erected in 1912, the fictional Dr Raghavan might have given a speech extolling the glories of the British Empire. And if he had been asked by a reporter about his old student, he might have said, 'Vanchi Aiyar was a bright and capable student, who took pride in his culture but then came under the influence of wicked men.'

The boy from Shenkottai was disowned by his family and convicted in absentia of crimes against the British Crown. Decades later, though, Vanchi would be celebrated by many as a national hero, a man who sacrificed his life in order to achieve freedom for his country.

Author's Note and Acknowledgements

While this novel is based on real-life events and people, it is a work of fiction. I have followed the (limited) historical record but also compressed the time-line, and invented a few minor characters and events. For some place names, I have used spellings current at the time of the story ('Tinnevelly', for example, rather than 'Tirunelveli'). For others (such as Palayamkottai and Shenkottai), more recent spellings have been retained. To avoid confusion, it should be noted that the office of the collector of Tinnevelly District was not in Tinnevelly town, but in Palayamkottai, the older and larger town across the river.

I would like to acknowledge the vital contribution of Siva Subramanian for both his informative book *Ash Kolaiyum Intiya Puratci Iyakkamum* (The Ashe Murder and the Indian Revolutionary Movement) and his helpful comments while writing this novel. Thanks are also due to A.R. Venkatachalapathy for his published research on the Ashe murder, as well as for his personal support. A different sort of gratitude is owed to Neil Gower for his excellent map. I should like also to thank Kannan Sundaram for kindly providing the photograph on which the front cover image is based.

For a revisionist interpretation of the Ashe murder, one may consult *Ash Patukolai Punaivum Varalarum* (Fact and Fiction of the Ashe Murder) by Na. Jeyaraman. Brief fictional accounts of the murder and its surrounding historical context are found in *The Tigerclaw Treei* by P.A. Krishnan and *The House of Blue Mangoes* by David Davidar.